FATED CROWN

EVA CHASE

BOUND TO THE FAE

BOOK

Fated Crown

Book 6 in the Bound to the Fae series

First Digital Edition, 2021

Cover design: Yocla Book Cover Design

Ebook ISBN: 978-1-990338-07-6

Paperback ISBN: 978-1-990338-12-0

CHAPTER ONE

Talia

I stop at the edge of the park in the shade of an oak, several feet from the busy city street. The sight of the cars whizzing by and the roar of their engines sets my nerves jangling. My chest tightens up, only loosening as I take a few slow, deep breaths.

This place is technically my real home. I was born into it and lived in it for the first twelve years of my life. But it's been nearly a decade since I last set foot in the human world. My memories and Sylas's collection of Hollywood comedies haven't prepared me for the vivid reality of returning.

Does every part of the human world *smell* this bad? I've gotten used to the ever-fresh air of the fae world, warm and sweetly floral on the summer side and crisply cool on the winter side. Here, each breath brings a tang of burned gasoline and other chemical scents I can't identify prickling into my lungs.

Beside me, Corwin rests his hand on my shoulder and squeezes. He can read my uneasiness through our soul-twined bond—and I can pick up on his own distaste for certain elements of our current surroundings. His nose wrinkles as he inhales the same odors, and the rush of traffic makes his eyes skitter trying to follow it.

"There are other parts of your world that are much more pleasant than this," he says. "Humans have left some wilderness relatively untouched, and even the smaller villages can be reasonably peaceful."

The other member of our party, a broad-shouldered woman from Arch-Lord Uzziah's coterie, snorts and raises her pointed chin toward the road. "You couldn't give me enough treasure to convince me to live this far from the Heart and among these creatures, that's for sure."

Her gaze flicks to me, but she shows no obvious concern about the insulting way she just referred to people like me. She motions for us to follow her. "From my observations, he should be in that building across the way. Around this time we may catch them rambling around in the courtyard."

"Okay." I rub my arms, catching a tingle of the magic that's wrapped around us. Before we emerged from the Mists into the human world, Corwin cast a spell around us to make us invisible to human eyes. A Golden Retriever we passed in the park sniffed in our direction and offered a few brisk barks, but the man holding his leash looked straight through us, so the illusion appears to be working on its intended targets.

Of course, I'm pretty sure one of those cars could still splatter me all over the road, invisible or not.

We walk to the nearest corner, where the streetlights gleam red and then green. The act of crossing on the walk signal feels so mundane and yet so foreign at the same time that my chest starts to clench up all over again. When one of the cars honks at the vehicle in front of it, I jump half a foot in the air and wobble on my warped foot.

Corwin grasps my elbow to steady me. He keeps his fingers curled loosely around my arm the rest of the way across. Apprehension is coiled in his stomach, much like the tension wound through me beneath my more visible jitters.

We haven't even gotten to the reason for our visit yet. I'm not sure what I *want* to happen, only that no matter what does, it's going to be hard.

Uzziah's woman leads us across a grassy field lined with some kind of sports markings toward a two-story brick building that stretches the length of the block. Teenagers lounge on the front steps outside the double doors of the main entrance. We slip past them unseen and around to the other side of the building, where two wings jut out around a large cobblestone courtyard that holds several metal picnic-style tables. More teens are sitting around the tables or in clusters on the cobblestones, eating their lunches and chattering with each other.

"There he is," Uzziah's coterie woman says, pointing to the edge of the courtyard by the end of the wing opposite us. My stance tensing, I follow her gesture with my gaze.

The boy she pointed out is sitting at a table with his back to us, nothing showing but burnished brown hair that curls around his ears and a lean frame in a black long-sleeved tee and baggy jeans. I can't tell anything for sure from that. My heart thumps harder as we circle the courtyard to consider him from a better angle.

With each detail of his face that comes into view—the angle of his jaw, the slope of his nose, the glint in his wide-set eyes—an ache swells around my heart. It *is* him, isn't it? My little brother, Jamie, who'll be seventeen now if he survived the attack by the monstrous wolf-shifting fae who attacked my family, which I've always believed he didn't.

Then he turns his head, revealing the other side of his face, and my heart just about stops. Any remaining doubts flee.

He must have had reconstructive surgery to deal with the worst of the scarring, but it didn't remove the effects of the attack completely. Pale pink marks across his left cheek and jaw, running down to his neck and probably across his chest as well, show where the wolf's vicious fangs carved open his skin.

Oh, Jamie. My pulse lurches, propelling me toward him, but my legs lock at the same time.

He has no idea *I'm* alive. He definitely can't have imagined I've spent the better part of the last decade among faerie beings he'd never have believed existed. I can't just march up to him and launch a sudden family reunion. Even if a pang is ringing through me to wrap my arms around him, to tell him how sorry I am for... for everything.

For teasing him into chasing me into the woods so long ago. For not knowing he'd survived until just now. For leaving him alone all this time.

A burn of tears forms in my eyes. I blink hard, grasping for Corwin's hand.

It wasn't your fault, he says gently through our bond. *You couldn't have known what you were leading him toward, and you had no opportunity to find out what had become of him while you were caged all those years.*

I know, I reply. *But even after I got out, it never occurred to me to confirm what happened to him and my parents. I just assumed that I'd seen right, even though it was dark and I was terrified.*

I rub my face, the ache inside me expanding even farther. Wouldn't it be wonderful if Mom and Dad had survived too, if they'd had each other to get through the trauma and my disappearance? But this is the only direct blood relative the winter fae turned up with their extensive search, at least among those that interest them.

The fae sage indicated that my connection to their kind came from my mother. It seems my maternal grandparents passed on in the last nine years—losing their only child in such a horrible way can't have helped. Jamie has been living with my aunt and uncle on my father's side and our two young cousins here in this city, a few hundred miles distant from the town where we lived before.

It was far enough distant that we didn't see them very often back then. At eight years old, recovering from a savage mauling, my brother had to move in with people who were only one step above strangers, even if they were family on paper. I don't wish the fae that stole me away had taken him too, because what I went through was more than I'd wish on anyone, but he hasn't had it easy by any means.

As if to illustrate that thought, a trio of guys saunters by the table where Jamie is eating alone. One of them does an exaggerated double-take at Jamie's face and clutches at his chest in mock-horror. "Oh my God! It's the creature from the Black Lagoon."

The other two guys burst into laughter. Jamie's shoulders tense, but he keeps his gaze fixed on his sandwich. My hands ball into fists at my sides.

The bullies aren't done yet. The guy who made the first remark sits down on the table next to Jamie's tray and swats at his container of fries, sending half of them skittering onto the cobblestones. "I don't think the Swamp Thing should be getting food from our cafeteria. This isn't a school for monsters."

At the sneer in his voice and his cruel smile, I can't hold myself back. I march over, fury flaring up through my throat onto my tongue. "The only monsters are the ones who did that to him—and *you*, as far as I can tell."

But none of them react, because of course they can't see or hear me.

Talia, Corwin says softly, coming up beside me. I turn to him, debating asking him to take the magic off me right now so I can give these jerks a piece of my mind for real, but Jamie is getting up.

He gives the guys a bored look, picking up the rest of his fries so they're out of reach. "If they serve you, I guess anything goes."

The first guy's expression goes from amused to pissed off in an instant. He springs off the table. "What the hell did you say, McCarty?"

He steps forward as if to grab my brother, but just then a teacher ambles by. She gives the guys a questioning look. "Is everything all right here, boys?"

The main guy puts on an ingratiating smile. "Completely fine, Mrs. Green. Right, Jamie?"

Jamie shrugs and walks off before the teacher leaves.

With a heavy heart, I watch him head into the school. He not only got torn from our family and horribly wounded, but the scars the fae left on him are making him a target for the villains of the human world.

If he could know he's not really alone—if he could have me to turn to again…

Corwin's arms come around me in a careful embrace. A hint of discomfort travels into me—he isn't totally at ease showing even this much affection in front of our unfriendly spectator from Uzziah's flock—but he offers that affection all the same, because it matters more to him how I feel. I rest my arms over his and hug them to me, abruptly aware of the deeper inner turmoil he's trying to suppress.

If I returned to the human world on even a semi-permanent basis, it'd mean leaving my soul-twined mate behind—and my other lovers too. Corwin doesn't want to interfere with my decision, but the thought of having me so far away for any length of time wrenches at him.

I don't know what to say to him. I don't know what I want to do. I owe so much to so many people… But how can I abandon my brother all over again when he's been on his own for so many years already?

I managed to find a balance between my loyalties to the summer and winter fae. Is there some way I can bridge this gap as well, even though it's so much wider?

Uzziah's coterie woman must be thinking along similar lines, although with very different motivations. She clears her throat and turns away from the courtyard to face me. "That was him, wasn't it?"

"Yes." The magic they used to trace my genetic line will have already confirmed it, but I guess she wanted to hear it from my own mouth too.

"Excellent." She rolls back her shoulders. "If he's as useful as you are, this will solve all our problems and simplify the cure completely."

I blink at her, dread trickling through my stomach. Corwin's body tenses against me at the same time. The other winter arch-lords didn't say anything about Jamie "solving problems" before we set off on our journey here. It was supposed to be just a chance for me to check that their story was true and see how Jamie is doing now. But I'm familiar enough with the fae way of thinking to guess what she's getting at.

"What do you mean?" I ask.

A satisfied smile curves the woman's lips. "Two cures for two realms. You can stick with the winter realm alongside your mate, and the Seelie can make use of your brother. We couldn't have asked for an easier solution."

CHAPTER TWO

Talia

The new castle that my summer and winter lovers have collaborated on, which straddles the border between their realms, contains just a few rooms right in the center. On the second floor, there are a string of chambers dedicated to my personal use. Below them lies a large ballroom we might host parties in if the two realms ever become that friendly, and a smaller meeting room beside it. The outer areas of the castle aren't finished yet, but the middle portion is complete enough for us to make use of it.

Both the table there and the floor, walls, and ceiling show the merging of the two materials that form the castle. Sylas's polished wood twines with Corwin's glittering diamond right down the center of the space. The mix of warmth and coolness usually appeals to me, a sense of harmony amplified by the soft pulse of the Heart's energy that flows through the space, but the company we have in this room today has left me uncomfortably chilled.

All eight of the arch-lords from both sides of the border are sitting around the table, the three from summer on one side and four of those from winter on the other. Assorted members of their cadres and coteries stand along the walls behind them, including my other two lovers: Sylas's half-brothers, August and Whitt.

Corwin had me sit at the head of the table while he took the foot. I appreciate having him across from me whenever I need the reassurance of catching his eyes, but my position feels like a lot of pressure. But then, we are here to talk about a situation that concerns me more than anyone else.

None of the arch-lords look particularly happy about that—or the building they're in. The six of them who didn't have a hand in designing this space are glancing around with expressions that range from wariness to outright revulsion. Laoni, the winter arch-lord who's been most hostile toward me and Corwin, has even wrinkled her nose.

But even though the outer rooms aren't finished yet, this central space seemed like the best setting for a joint meeting. To enter the structure immersed in the border so close to the Heart, everyone had to take the vow to do no harm.

I wish I could take a little more comfort from that fact. The real problem is the harm they want to do to someone who isn't even here, who doesn't even know they exist yet. And I'm increasingly convinced I'd like it to stay that way.

"The situation with the curse is too urgent for personal feelings to come into it," Laoni is saying now. "We must bring the boy here and determine whether he has a similar connection to the curse."

The edge of distaste in her voice suggests that the personal feelings of a human like me matter even less than if I were fae. There's a new glimmer of hostility in her gaze along with the usual disdain. I'm not sure how much of it's because I'm now officially Corwin's mate or because of the minor but unexpected magical power I displayed during our confirmation ceremony.

If I thought wielding a little of the same powers the fae have might bring me more respect, I was wrong. If anything, I've gotten the impression the other winter arch-lords object to my presence even more now that I've shown I'm less helpless than they'd assumed.

Celia, the strictest of the summer arch-lords, gives her counterpart a narrow glance. But she agrees, if grudgingly. "If the powers Talia possesses come from their family line, it stands to reason that her brother would have them as well."

"You can't just tear him away from his life like that," I protest, my hands clenched in my lap beneath the table where they can't see them. "The fae have already destroyed his family and left him scarred. He's had a chance to recover from that, and now you want to rip him away from everything he knows—to use him against his will?"

Terisse, a winter arch-lord who often sides with Laoni, frowns at me. "I thought you were dedicated to healing us of this ailment. Didn't you give your loyalty to the fae when you swore to stand with Arch-Lord Corwin as his mate?"

"*Talia* dedicated herself," Corwin puts in. "That doesn't mean she's required to approve of her brother being forced to make a similar sacrifice unknowing."

Sylas shifts in his seat where he's poised close by at my right. "I believe Talia's generosity of herself should earn her some consideration on this matter. She *has* sacrificed a lot for us. If we're going to ask more of her and hers, we should allow it to be on her terms."

"And what terms would those be?" Laoni sneers. "As far as I can tell, she wants us to forget the idea and what we've discovered—she'd rather we'd never found out her brother was living at all. Perhaps she's already imagining leaving us herself to join him in the world she belongs to."

Her words hit close enough to the truth that my stomach twists. I will my voice to stay steady. "No matter what happens, I swear I'll continue helping you hold back the curse however I can. But you can't reasonably ask me not to care about anything else. You all have more than one responsibility you have to balance in your lives. Why can't I look out for the fae *and* my family?"

"Corwin and his flock should be your family now," Uzziah says coldly.

Sylas makes a disbelieving sound. "Come on now. Do you expect us to believe that all of you required *your* mates never concern themselves with the packs or flocks they came from after they confirmed their bond to you?"

Laoni glowers at him. "If a member of my mate's former flock turned out to be instrumental in fighting this curse, I'd absolutely expect him to prioritize that over a little discomfort."

I can't stop the protest from bursting out of me. "A little discomfort?" But when all the gazes around the table turn toward me, I'm not sure how to follow that up without insulting all the fae here.

August takes a step toward me and then catches himself. The arch-lords are aware of his and Whitt's relationship with me now, but the news is very fresh in their minds, and I know they all have qualms about that unusual arrangement too. It probably wouldn't look good for him to offer any gestures of affection in front of them, especially when the winter fae look down on any displays of emotion at all.

To my surprise, it's Donovan who speaks up next. The youngest arch-lord often lets his colleagues guide his judgment, but he's the only one other than Sylas and Corwin who's ever supported my right to make my own decisions.

He keeps his tone mild. "What exactly are your concerns about bringing your brother here, Talia? If we can understand where you see the harm, we may be able to offset it."

I drag in a breath and resist the urge to drop my gaze.

It's all right, Corwin says through our bond, his gaze intent on me. He knows what I've been through at the hands of the fae better than anyone else, even the three men who rescued me from captivity, because he's been able to experience the memories directly from my mind. *You're simply stating facts. If they question any, I can vouch for the truth of them, as can Sylas in many cases.*

That's true. I do have people on my side here.

I look around at the other arch-lords' faces, trying to show confidence on my own. "I've made a home for myself here, but I didn't come because I wanted to. I suffered for nine years at the hands of the Seelie lord who took me and his cadre. And even since Sylas took me in and I've been able to help with the curse with much more freedom, I've been insulted and treated like a tool rather than a person more times than I can count. I've been attacked and had some of the highest fae scheming to take my freedom away."

"We did settle that matter," Celia says, her stance tensing.

"One of them," I say, meeting her gaze straight on. "The fae who killed my parents, stole me from my home, and tormented me for years haven't been punished at all. A lot of you don't see doing that to a human as a crime at all. Right here at this table, talking about my own brother, I'm being treated as if I'm less than the rest of you."

The fae around the table stir uncomfortably, but none of them attempt to deny that accusation before I go on. "Jamie has already suffered so much because of the fae. Why would I want him brought somewhere he'll have no one he knows except me—if you even let us see each other more than occasionally—and where nearly everyone around him won't care how he thinks or feels about anything that's happening to him?"

There's a momentary silence. Corwin extends a tendril of his love to wrap around me like a gentle embrace.

Terisse speaks first, sounding slightly chagrinned. "You can't blame us for putting our own needs first when it's a matter of the survival of all our people. It isn't simply about fae compared to humans, but thousands of fae lives compared to that of one human."

"You already have one human," I retort. "Me. And you're not listening to me. Have you even thought this through properly? You're so quick to assume that Jamie could help you, that it's worth dragging him into the fae world and upending everything he believes in to see how he might benefit you—but obviously he didn't have any effect on the curse back when I was taken, or Aerik and his cadre would have noticed and brought him too."

"Of course we've taken that into account," Laoni snaps. "We've also taken into account that your ages were rather different, and powers can take time to emerge— often triggered by factors such as puberty. Given what the Seelie have reported of their sage's words about your family line, it's a logical assumption that whatever connection to the fae exists in you, it'll exist in him as well."

Celia leans forward, her gaze fixed on me. "We could certainly make sure he's comfortable and treated well. And what if it wouldn't need to be a permanent relocation? We have two curses or a curse with two aspects... Couldn't it be that if the two of you offer your unusual healing abilities together, you might eliminate the problem completely?"

Oh. I have to admit that in my worries about what would happen to Jamie and my struggle about what I owe him, that possibility hadn't occurred to me.

I don't trust most of the fae around me to know what treating a human "well" actually looks like, but—if that were possible—if it would only be a short while and then Jamie could go home—how selfish would I be to stand in the way of it?

Every part of my body still balks at the idea. I swallow thickly. "*Would* you let him simply go back to his old life after he's seen your world?"

"I don't see why not," Uzziah says. "We can wipe his memory of the experience with magic so he won't remember we exist."

Of course they can. I rub my forehead. It still feels wrong to put my brother through whatever he'd face here even for a short time, even if he won't remember it. And it's easy for them to say now that they'd send him back. Somehow I suspect they'll be more hesitant if it turns out he can cure them like I can. They'll want to keep him here in case they need him again. No matter what, most of them see him—and me—as only a resource they want to keep control over.

We don't even know yet if your brother will provide any sort of cure at all, Corwin reminds me. *It may be as simple as a few tests and then dismissing him as unnecessary.*

Coming here even for a day would still mess with his head, I reply, but then a spark of inspiration lights in my head, bringing so much relief my breath catches.

Sylas has started to speak. "We've dealt with our curse for decades now. I'm sure we can wait at least a few more days to give Talia time to—"

"No," I break in. "I have an idea right now. It'll be the full moon in less than a week. That's the perfect test right there—and my brother doesn't even need to be in the fae realm to carry it out. The day of the full moon, send someone to the human world to collect a little of his blood without him realizing it. I know you have enough magic to manage that. Then test it on a few of the Seelie to see whether it stops them from going wild. If it doesn't, then we already have our answer."

If it does cure them… I don't want to think about that. I'll have until the full moon to decide what I'd do then.

Donovan skims his hands across the table as if clearing the problem from it. "There you go. A simple, unobtrusive solution, at least to the initial question. I don't see why we couldn't begin that way."

Laoni scowls at him, but she obviously doesn't have any good argument against my proposal. "The Seelie won't handle it alone," she says. "One of us will need to oversee the process as well. This woman has had quite the effect on more than one of you, and I don't want personal biases skewing the results you report."

Celia bristles but keeps her voice flat. "Having one of you present to observe would not be a problem, though I assure you we wouldn't resort to deception, especially on such a vital matter."

"It's settled, then," Corwin says, shooting a quick smile down the table toward me.

I smile back, but my stomach is still churning with uneasiness. Have I just saved Jamie from a bunch of misery—or set him up for even more?

CHAPTER THREE

Whitt

I was the obvious choice for this particular mission. As Sylas's spymaster, my skills are naturally inclined toward stealth and subtlety. And while others might have the same qualifications, I wouldn't trust anyone outside our inner circle to treat Talia's brother with the necessary care.

Like, for example, the lug of a winter fae arch-lord who has insisted on coming along to "supervise" my methods.

Arch-Lord Uzziah, whose dour-sounding name fits his appearance and his personality to a T, hasn't stopped frowning since he met me near the border to travel to the fringelands. He seems to be taking his part in this venture as a personal affront, even though he and his colleagues were the ones who insisted on him joining me. About half a dozen times already, I've bitten my tongue against reminding him that if it were up to *me*, I'd be here alone.

As we come up on the house we've determined Jamie lives in, cloaked in both our magic and the shadows of very early morning, Uzziah's frown pulls into a deeper grimace. He draws in a snort of a breath and shakes his head. "How these creatures can live with all this filth around them, I'll never know. Dulled minds, the lot of them."

And this man works alongside Talia's soul-twined mate. I restrain a shudder provoked much more by him than our surroundings and manage to speak politically if not totally politely. "And yet the Heart deigned to bless at least one of these 'creatures' with the power to heal all our kind. It's almost as if *it* thinks they're owed some respect."

Uzziah shuts up, but his glower holds plenty of words he simply isn't saying out loud, none of them particularly polite either. When we come to a stop in front of the bungalow, rather charming as human structures go with its blue-trimmed white walls and darker roof, he sighs. "So then, what's your plan from here?"

"Your people identified the specific bedroom the boy uses." I amble across the lawn to the side of the house, dodging a coiled hose, and stop by a window near the back. It's closed, a hum in the air suggesting some sort of mechanical cooling system is running inside to take the edge off the late spring heat, but that isn't a problem. "I can manipulate the glass and go in that way. Then it'll be a simple matter of drawing a bit of blood. I'll only need a few minutes."

The winter arch-lord's bushy eyebrows draw together. "I'll be coming in with you."

I barely stop myself from rolling my eyes. "You'll be

able to see just fine through the window. The room itself is rather small."

He studies me as if he assumes I'm making excuses to hide some nefarious plot rather than pointing out a simple practicality. "I'd prefer to have as clear a view as possible of the proceedings."

"Fine. Just stay well back and give me plenty of space to work."

I roll the true name for glass off my tongue, focusing on the pane in front of me. At my urging, the material melts away, leaving an empty frame large enough for me to clamber through. Uzziah follows, huffing a bit as if it's a strain. Thank the Heart our spells cover all the sounds we make as well as hiding us from sight.

The boy's room *is* small, just a narrow bed in one corner, a tiny side table next to its headboard and a compact desk tucked up against its foot. There isn't enough space to place any furniture against the opposite wall, which has pictures and posters tacked all over it. The closet door next to the window hangs ajar, a few rumpled shirts poking out from a heap on the floor inside. The artificially cool air trickles past us toward the now-open window.

The boy himself is lying on the bed, the sheet tangled around his slim frame. His face is buried in the crook of his arm against his pillow, but I can make out enough of it to note bits of family resemblance between him and Talia. I'm familiar enough with her to taste a hint of their connection in the human scent lacing the room too.

Ignoring my instructions, Uzziah stays right next to me. I motion him back toward the closet, but instead he steps around me to stand by the side table. Well, at least he's a little more out of the way there.

I slide a vial—bronze rather than glass, to avoid concerns of breakage—from my pocket and crouch next to the bed. Jamie's nearest arm sprawls across the mattress almost to the edge of the bed. I whisper a few words to encourage his mind into a deeper sleep and ease his hand just a little farther so it extends out into the air.

Holding the vial beneath his wrist, I compel my magic to open a tiny cut to the vein closest to the surface. A trickle of blood spills into the vial. When I've gathered a couple of teaspoons' worth, enough to cure an entire pack of the full moon curse, I direct the flesh and skin to close again.

My efforts will leave a faint mark, but one so slight he's unlikely to notice it. If he does, he shouldn't think it anything more than a small blemish of the sort humans seem to produce at random.

I nudge his hand back onto the mattress and straighten up. Once I've stoppered the vial, I tuck it away. Uzziah stays where he is with his arms crossed, scrutinizing my every move. I raise my eyebrows at him. "Any concerns?"

He waves his hand dismissively, but he only takes one step toward me before he pauses, looking at the boy again. "It's a pity our own cure can't be harvested so easily."

"You have Talia at your beck and call whenever your curse strikes another victim," I point out. "We Seelie all face ours at the exact same time."

He doesn't respond to that. His gaze hasn't shifted

from Jamie. Something in his expression has changed, a calculating glint breaking through the dour gloom.

Apprehension ripples through me. I've already tensed before he even speaks.

He gestures to the boy and then finally meets my gaze. "We're here now. It's hardly a full test unless we can try it on both sides of the border. We may as well just take him and be done with it."

Somehow I had enough faith, however slim, in the bird-brained Unseelie to be surprised by his proposal. "We gave our word to Talia that we'd make this first attempt without disturbing her brother," I say, not bothering to smooth out the sharpness that's crept into my voice.

"What of it? It wasn't an official vow—there'll be no harm done in changing our minds now that we've seen how simple the prospect would be."

No harm done? After all the mite's done for his people and the way the Heart bound her to one of his closest colleagues, that's how much respect he has for Talia? The casualness of his tone sets my teeth on edge.

But before I can come up with a suitable retort, he's already stepping closer to the bed, ready to scoop the boy right up over his shoulder from the looks of things. With a jolt through my nerves, I push in front of him, blocking his way. "We follow the plan agreed to on between all the arch-lords. If you want to argue for a change of course, do it in front of them."

Uzziah glares at me. His tone turns biting. "I think you're forgetting the difference between our stations, mongrel. You don't give orders to an arch-lord."

I glare right back at him. "No, but I follow the orders

I got from my own. And Arch-Lord Sylas expects me to return with only this sample of blood, not the whole boy."

"I'm not sure his colleagues would have the same issue. You all are too wrapped up in that dust-destined woman's apparent charms to think clearly." His lip curls with a sneer, and he motions for me to move aside. "Get out of my way. I have the authority here, and I say we bring him before there's any more need for debate."

I stand my ground, my legs locking. "I say *no*. We got what we came for. The day is on the verge of breaking. Let's leave as we were meant to, and I'll see no need to mention to anyone that you attempted to deviate from our agreement."

It isn't a lie. I might not deem it strictly necessary, but naturally that doesn't mean I won't tell Sylas anyway.

Whether Uzziah detects the subterfuge in my statement or simply doesn't care, he attempts to shove me aside. Uneasiness twangs through me at the thought of scuffling with an arch-lord we've so recently negotiated a hard-won peace with, but I will not let down both my lord and my love in one swoop for this mangy raven's self-interest. He needs to see this attempt is getting him nowhere.

Without hesitation, I shove him back, as hard as I can. His shoulders thump into the wall, the sound muffled by the spell on us but not totally muted. On the bed, Jamie stirs.

The winter arch-lord's hostile gaze shoots daggers at me, as if it's *my* fault we might have woken him.

"Attempt to touch him again," I warn in a low,

menacing voice, "and I won't hesitate to throw you right through the wall. Just try me."

Fury twists the other man's features, but I'm taller and stronger than he is, and he doesn't want this coming to a full fight besides. The temptation was all in making an easy theft of the boy. He doesn't want to leave traces of our presence here any more than I do, though I'm willing to risk it to ensure Talia's brother stays where he belongs.

Never before have I been so glad of the castle we're constructing with Corwin. Imagine if Talia had to keep living fully on the winter side for weeks at a time, subjected to pricks like this.

"I'm going to remember your insolence," Uzziah hisses at me.

I curl back my lips, letting my wolfish fangs emerge. "I'm counting on that." It's only because he's an arch-lord that I don't add "you feather-headed asshole" on the end.

I stay between him and the bed as we head to the window. The dawn light is just touching the sky, turning it from deep blue to hazy gray. Outside, Uzziah mutters to himself as I seal the glass. His words are inaudible, but his tone is deeply peeved.

He's lucky I care enough about him and his colleagues keeping a somewhat favorable opinion of my lord that I don't show him just how peeved *I* am.

We make our way back to the spot in the nearby park that connects to the Mists. Uzziah doesn't speak the entire journey back in the swift carriage. I'm content to listen to the warble of the passing wind, but my stomach rests heavy in my abdomen.

I can't think of any better way I could have handled

that situation, but I'm not convinced the way I did was actually *good* either.

When we reach Hearth-by-the-Heart, it's mid-afternoon by our time, though only a few hours have passed since we left the human world. Our days rarely match up with the world beyond the Mists. One of Uzziah's coterie members along with a couple sent by the other Unseelie arch-lords are waiting outside the castle to oversee the actual administration of Jamie's blood. Uzziah himself marches off across the border without more than a brusque nod toward Sylas, who came out to meet us.

I hand the vial over to August, and he hurries off to the kitchen where he's been preparing the usual tonic from Talia's blood for the many summer fae we won't be experimenting on tonight. Astrid goes with him, keeping a wary eye on the winter fae who are following too. I want nothing more than to flop onto a comfortable sofa or perhaps throw back a gulp of good absinthe, but I know Sylas deserves a full reporting first.

He takes in my expression and motions for us to go inside as well—up to his study. Once the door is closed and he's taken his chair behind his desk, he fixes his impervious gaze on me. It used to sometimes irritate me how unshakeable he always seems, but lately I've found myself increasingly appreciating that quality of his.

"What happened?" he asks.

I pace the length of the room, my claws itching in my fingertips at the memory. "The blasted raven arch-lord tried to steal the entire boy away after all. He wasn't satisfied with taking a little blood. Figured his people should get to make their own experiment."

Sylas's eyes flash. A growl comes into his voice. "But clearly you prevented him."

"Yes. I had to get rather… forceful about it. He wasn't pleased." I turn to face my brother, grimacing. "I may have created more trouble for our relations with the winter realm."

"I'll deal with that trouble if it comes up," Sylas replies. "I wouldn't have had you do anything else. They'd better not interfere with our test tonight."

A small smile crosses my lips. "I suspect between August and Astrid, the feathered fae down there don't stand a chance."

"Indeed. But we'll want to remain on guard." Sylas rubs his jaw, his expression going momentarily pensive, and then focuses on me again. "In all other respects, the task went smoothly?"

I nod. "We didn't disturb Jamie or anyone else around. He should have no idea he was ever visited or that any part of him was taken." As long as we don't have to go back and retrieve the entire young man after all. My mouth sours at the thought.

But if it turns out Talia's brother could be the final piece in the puzzle of solving the curse, how could we refuse to protect our people?

I can see the same inner struggle playing out in Sylas. Before he can say anything else, Talia bursts into the room, her expression pinched. I avert my eyes from the marks on her arm, as gentle as I know August is in his blood-taking.

"Did it go all right?" she asked. "Is Jamie okay?"

"Everything's fine, mighty one," I say, moving to her

and ruffling the waves of her hair with its new mix of purple and pink. "Your brother slept through the entire thing."

I slip my arm around her slim shoulders, wishing I could sweep her up in an embrace so complete it'd shield her from all the horrible decisions that might lie ahead of us. "We've got hours left before nightfall. Why don't we get in a few rounds of that driving video game August is so fond of to see if one or the other of us can't get good enough to beat him next time."

I'll do whatever I can to distract both of us from the looming question about to be answered—and all the others that'll arise afterward, regardless of the result.

CHAPTER FOUR

Talia

The drinking of the blood tonic has never been such a spectacle, at least not at any of the times I was around to watch. Pack-kin from domains all across the Seelie realm have already come by to pick up their vials. Now a bunch of us are gathered in the clearing in front of the Heart to see what will happen with Jamie's.

Ten fae from the three arch-lords' packs volunteered to take the untested tonic. The arch-lords wanted enough test subjects to be sure no effects we see are a fluke but few enough that it won't be too difficult for the rest of their pack-kin to contain them if they succumb to the curse. The ten are standing in the center of our ring, speaking to each other in uneasy conversation as we wait for night to fully descend.

At least a hundred other fae watch and wait around them, including Laoni, Uzziah, and several winter fae folk they've brought with them. A couple I recognize from their coteries, but others appear to be simply guards, there to protect them from the "savagery" of the wolf shifters, I guess.

Corwin has come as well, of course. He and Sylas have insisted on staying close to me and keeping me at the back of the ring, near where the Unseelie are standing. Sylas summoned a tree trunk he shaped into a sort of pedestal-slash-stool for me to sit on, both to keep me even farther out of reach from slashing claws and teeth and to give me a clear view over the heads of the much taller fae.

The wooden seat is smooth and warm against my skin, but I'm finding it hard not to squirm. What happens tonight could protect Jamie from the fae or confirm him as a target. But it's hard not to feel guilty about hoping his blood *won't* help when I know how many of the people around me must be wishing for a fuller cure than I've been able to offer.

I want that too… just not at the expense of my little brother.

I sink deeper into the seat, which is wide enough for me to sit cross-legged, and lean against the arched back, taking a few deep breaths. If the tonic doesn't work and the ten fae who volunteered transform into raging wolves, I need to be ready. I've conquered a lot of the fears that've gripped me ever since that fatal night when Aerik and his cadre attacked my family, but I haven't had to face a Seelie in the grips of the curse in months. I don't want to lose myself to the panic even for a minute while Laoni can see my reaction.

I'll be right here with you no matter what happens, Corwin assures me, picking up on my anxiety. He reaches up to brush his fingers over my arm, which is currently level with his shoulder. *Sylas won't leave your side either. The summer fae know exactly what they're dealing with, and they have your version of the tonic ready to dose these ten if necessary.*

I know, I reply, but that doesn't stop my nerves from jittering. Even knowing I only lost two members of my family all those years ago, not three, hasn't dulled the horror of my memories of the attack as much as I'd like. I'm not sure I'll ever escape the terror they provoke completely.

The sky has deepened from blue to indigo. Stars are starting to twinkle into view. The moment of transformation can't be more than a few minutes away. I can't feel it myself, but the Seelie will know as soon as the possibility has passed us by.

My gaze strays to the other Unseelie arch-lords. Laoni is stirring restlessly on her feet. Maybe she shouldn't have insisted on coming an hour early if she didn't have the patience for the wait.

One of the Unseelie guards standing by her glances her way. He must have quite a bit of human heritage, because his ears are rounded like August's and no hint of unusual color shows in his dark brown hair, which is tied back in a short ponytail. The only way I know for sure he's fae— other than the fact that I can't imagine Laoni bringing an actual human to protect her—is the dark wings he's keeping folded close to his back for now.

"Is there anything that would make you more comfortable, my lady?" he asks Laoni, seeming both careful and hopeful with the question.

Laoni's attention snaps to him, and her chin rises haughtily. Her voice comes out flatly cutting. "Certainly nothing *you* could provide. Mind your duties."

His head jerks back toward the clearing, his mouth tightening, and I wince inwardly on his behalf. She's always been sneering toward me, but I've never seen her treat any of her flock-folk with that much hostility.

I haven't seen her around her flock all that much, though, so maybe her response isn't that unusual.

How does Laoni keep the respect of her flock if she speaks to them like that? I ask Corwin.

He frowns, following my gaze to the guard with the dark brown ponytail. *She isn't normally so severe with them, from my observations. I believe I've seen her speak harshly to that specific one before. Perhaps he's overstepped sometime in the past, and she feels the need to keep him particularly in his place.*

Odd that she'd keep him on her staff at all if that's the case, but what do I know about how that woman's mind works?

The other fae around us adjust their weight on their feet, the sense of their restlessness creeping over my skin. Then the full moon gleams a little brighter—and all ten of the Seelie in the center of the ring flinch and shudder.

The full moon transformation is nowhere near as seamless and graceful as the purposeful one I've seen many Seelie enact by now. The fae who took Jamie's tonic lurch onto their hands and knees, their shoulders hunching, their limbs spasming. Fur sprouts from their skin in bursts. My fingers tighten around the edge of my chair, the ridged bark there digging into my palms.

The prepared pack-kin, August among them, rush forward before any have shifted very far—a jaw jutting into a muzzle here, a tail unfurling there. They already have the vials with my tonic in their hands.

The cursed fae snarl and gnash their teeth even in their only partly transformed state, but with two kin to each of them, it isn't long before the proper tonic has been splashed into their mouths. One manages to wrench away from the helpers and lunges toward the rest of the crowd, but two more fae leap in to restrain him. In less than a minute since the transformation began, they're all standing on wobbly but fully human-like legs, their faces flushed with a mix of exertion and embarrassment.

I release my grip on the chair, dragging in a breath that's only a little shaky. The sight of their initial wildness sent a jolt through my pulse, but not much more than that. Part of me is relieved. Jamie's blood didn't cure them at all.

But another part dreads whatever's going to come next, now that the arch-lords who put so much stake in this possibility will be disappointed.

The expression on Laoni's face looks like total disgust. For all she's criticized the Seelie for their violent nature, she's never actually seen a cursed transformation before. Even Corwin feels a little shaken.

I didn't realize it took them quite so… brutally, he says through our bond. *It's certainly clear the curse is gripping them, bending them to its will, rather than letting loose something they enjoy freeing. Even if my colleagues might want to think otherwise.*

Maybe this demonstration will set them a little straight

then, and they won't complain about the Seelie wildness so much, I say, but my stomach stays knotted. What now?

Sylas, Celia, and Donovan have stepped into the ring from their positions among their own packs. "Thank you for your service tonight," Celia says to the ten volunteers. "Even if the experiment was a failure, it was important that we determine as much. Please, make your way home and get some rest now that you're well again."

"And if you experience any ill-effects that you haven't encountered before, let us know immediately," Sylas adds, though I don't think any of us believes there's much chance that Jamie's blood will turn out to harm the fae if it doesn't help them.

"Well," Laoni says in a disgruntled tone as Corwin helps me off the seat, "we're back to just the one cure, then."

Her guard turns away from the scattering crowd of Seelie. "I suppose that does keep things simple, at least."

Laoni glares at him. "If I want your opinion, I'll ask for it. Not that it's ever likely to come to that." She swivels away from him with an imperious air and fixes her gaze on Sylas, who's striding back to rejoin me and Corwin. "You'll be returning the human woman to her soul-twined mate on our side of the border while that misshapen castle of yours is still under construction?"

Despite the words, she almost sounds as if she wishes he'd say no. She really can't decide whether to welcome me for what I can offer her people or shun me as the weak but unpredictable mortal I know she still sees me as, can she?

"Talia will return tomorrow," Sylas says evenly, setting a protective hand on my shoulder. "We'd like to keep her close by for the night in case anything unusual arises from this experiment."

"Yes, yes, of course." Laoni spins on her heel, the other Unseelie following her as if they can't get across the border fast enough. Corwin lingers long enough to give us an apologetic grimace and bends to press a quick kiss to my lips. The flare of heat that comes with his touch sears even hotter with Sylas looking on, reminding me of the day not that long ago when my two arch-lords showed me how much pleasure they could bring me together.

A hint of heated amusement passes to me from Corwin even as he draws back. *I might have been uncertain of proceeding with that collaboration at first, but I can say I'm now looking forward to bringing you to such heights again.*

I can't hold back a mischievous smile. *Well, once the border castle is finished, we'll definitely need to celebrate.*

The look he gives me then is hot enough to make me spontaneously combust, but he pulls himself away with a wordless promise of delights to come.

Whitt and August have joined us during that silent conversation. Whitt watches Corwin slip into the border haze and then raises his eyebrows at me. "Somehow I get the impression you two were having a *very* interesting conversation, mite."

My cheeks flush. They can all probably smell my arousal. But it's already fading, tempered by the uncertainties still twisting through me.

I take in the emptying clearing, feeling weirdly adrift. I spent so much time carving out a real place for myself among the fae, and now everything about my situation has turned precarious all over again.

August nuzzles my hair. I can tell he's sensed my mood, the gesture more soothing than provocative. "It's been a long night already. Should we go home?"

I nod. "But first we should talk about what happens next, right?"

"We'll have time in the morning if you're tired now," Sylas begins, but I touch his arm to stop him.

"I don't think I'll be able to sleep until I have a better idea where we go from here. But we'd better talk back at Hearth-by-the-Heart."

"I can help with that," August announces, and scoops me up against his broad chest as he's become very fond of doing. I give him a mock-glower, but the truth is, there's nothing quite like being nestled in his brawny arms.

"Fine." I lean against him and let him carry me back to Sylas's main castle. I've been on my feet a lot today anyway, and my warped one is starting to ache even with the brace.

My men hold their own councils until we make it to Sylas's office. As August drops into an armchair with me on his lap, Whitt leans against the edge of Sylas's desk and studies my face.

"I'd think the immediate matter is pretty much settled," he says. "Your brother's blood had no effect on our curse, so he clearly doesn't hold the same powers you do. We have no cause to interfere any further in his life. But there's clearly something else on your mind."

I hesitate. I don't often wall off my bond with Corwin these days, but if I'm going to talk about this subject with him, I'd rather it's later, face to face like I am with my Seelie men right now.

I summon an impression of a seal of light over our connection before I speak. Then I look down at my hands, feeling abruptly awkward in August's arms. "I *hope* we can leave him alone now. I don't know if the Unseelie will try to insist on testing specifically their curse, even though it's so much more complicated. But, even if we can… *I* can't forget about Jamie just like that now that I know he's alive."

"Of course you can't, Sweetness," August says, kissing the back of my head.

I swallow hard. "I just don't know how to be there for him and not mess up the balance we've finally managed to find between here and the winter realm… It was hard enough figuring out a compromise that didn't mean constantly traveling back and forth, and the human world is a lot farther away."

The men are silent for a moment. Then Sylas speaks, low and firm. "If you feel you need to reconnect with your brother and be part of his life again, I'll do whatever I can to ensure you get the opportunity. Even if it means less time by our sides. From what I've seen of your soul-twined mate, he'll understand too. You never should have been stolen from your world to begin with, Talia, and we'd be little better than Aerik if we tried to deny you your family after all this time."

"I doubt the other arch-lords will feel the same way," I mutter, remembering Laoni's comment about only having one cure. "Now it's even more obvious how dependent both realms are on me to hold back the curse. I don't think everyone's happy about that."

"We shouldn't be. I've always said it shouldn't be your responsibility." Sylas frowns. "We still need to determine a larger cure to end it completely."

"Has there been any news from the Unseelie's summer settlement?" August asks.

Sylas shakes his head. "No one there has been struck by the curse, but it's only been a short time. Having that group of them living among us won't prove whether they can escape their curse that way for several months, perhaps years. I'd like to seek a faster solution if I can."

"But in the meantime, whatever you need, we'll figure out a way to make it work," Whitt says to me. "Strategy is my speciality, after all."

They're being so supportive that my stomach clenches up. I swipe my hand over my face and admit the thing that's been gnawing at me most of all. "I want to see Jamie again, talk to him, make up for all the time I've been gone. But I also don't want to leave all of you for however long that takes. It's not about responsibilities, just… I hate being apart from you. I've been looking forward to the border castle being done so I don't have to leave any of you behind even a little, and now…"

Is it awful that I feel that way? My brother's had no one for years, and I'm selfishly worrying about losing a little time with my lovers. But the human world isn't mine anymore, and I barely know Jamie after missing more than half of his life. It's all such a muddle.

Whitt pushes off the desk and comes to stand next to August, wrapping his hand around mine. "You've had to make so many difficult decisions since we found you, mighty one. If I could take this one on for you I would. But I'm sure there's no rush on how long we spend coming up with the best course of action. You have time to sort out your feelings—and we can all put our minds to brainstorming solutions."

I give him and then Sylas a tight but genuine smile. "You're right. I don't have to decide anything yet."

But how long can I really leave Jamie the way I saw him a few days ago, alone and harassed by his classmates, before *I'm* the villain here?

CHAPTER FIVE

Talia

The breeze that streams around the crystalline windshield of Corwin's flying carriage is nippy enough to keep me focused on the present. The snowy landscape around us whips by. We're soaring over the terrain as quickly as Corwin feels is safe.

A woman in a flock a few hours from his domain came down with the freezing curse in the middle of the night, and the messenger who summoned us reported that she appears to be deteriorating quickly. Corwin asked me to come back from the summer realm early this morning and had the carriage already waiting.

This woman will be the first winter fae I've healed since the man during our bond confirmation ceremony— and *he* was only the second Unseelie I've ever healed. My nerves are prickling with the worry that I haven't figured the process out as well as I think, that I'll stumble again and fail.

So many lives are depending on me. No matter what I choose when it comes to Jamie, I'll feel like I'm being selfish, either in abandoning him or abandoning all these fae.

Corwin sinks down on the bench next to me and slips his arm around me. I lean into the warmth of his body, breathing in his wintry forest scent.

I'm sure it'll be fine, he says through our bond so as not to have to compete with the warbling of the wind. *I saw how you looked when you cured that man. You had the answer, and you put it into action. Once we've reached the village and you're fulfilling that purpose again, you'll feel how right it is.*

I inhale deeply and nod. *I hope so.* The shame of remembering the fae I couldn't cure before who've now died lingers in the back of my mind. *We still don't know how long even the cures that worked will last.*

What is it humans like to say? We'll cross that bridge when we come to it? I think that applies here.

That's fair. Unfortunately I seem to be faced with multiple other bridges already, and I'm not even sure which to cross.

I shove those thoughts away and gaze over the side of the carriage at the looming mountains we're approaching. These jut twice as high into the sky as the tall plateau that holds the domains around the Heart. Their peaks gleam like spears of icy snow.

From a distance, I thought they were made of a mottled rock with patches of pink and yellow amid the gray. Now that we're closer, I can see that those are actually patches of vegetation: delicate golden trees clinging to the lower crags, stretches of pale peachy flowers dappling the steep slopes higher up. And just coming into view around the side of the nearest mountain are a series of Unseelie dwellings.

The outer parts of the homes built into the mountainside appear to be made out of the same golden wood as the local trees. They all have terraces to land on for entry into the rooms carved right into the mountain, as with Corwin's folk village. The lord's palace shimmers in the sunlight, rising several narrow stories from a jutting ledge, with curved branches fanning out along its rooftop.

I wonder what Sylas would make of this kind of tree-built castle, so different and yet oddly similar to his.

"That's our destination," Corwin says out loud, rising to direct the carriage's final course.

As we glide closer, I realize many of the terraces I noticed are occupied. Anywhere from one to a whole family of fae stand on them, their faces turned toward us, apparently tracking our arrival.

A nervous shiver runs through me, and I hug myself, rubbing my arms. The woman who's sick must be a major figure in the flock to draw this much interest in her hopeful recovery. Which means so much potential anguish if I can't make that recovery happen.

Corwin brings the carriage to a stop at a nook for that purpose in the larger terrace outside the palace. As he helps me out, a true-blooded fae man with a lilac tint to his silvery hair hustles out to meet us, two staff—maybe members of his coterie—hurrying behind him.

"I'm incredibly grateful you could make it here so quickly, Arch-Lord Corwin—and Lady Talia," he says, with a bob of his head that appears to encompass both of us. I blink, a little startled by the formality he's offered me. But I guess that's how any lord's official mate would be referred to. I've just spent too much time among the other arch-lords who probably cringe at the thought of calling me a lady like one of their own.

"Of course," Corwin says.

I dip my head in return, unsure of the proper formalities. "I'll do whatever I can for your flock member."

The lord's gaze lingers on me for a moment, but not with any doubt or hostility, more simple curiosity. "It's a wonderful gift the Heart has given you. Come. We've brought the afflicted one to the village common so there'll be plenty of room."

Corwin pauses, his eyebrows drawing together. "We don't need a particularly large space."

"Oh, yes, it's not that." The lord laughs, a hint of embarrassment flushing his cheeks. "A few of my flock-folk were able to travel to your confirmation ceremony—I wish I could have come myself. They've been talking about how amazing it was to watch Lady Talia heal the curse. Several have already told me they'd like to see the process for themselves. If that would be all right?"

He wants me to perform for an audience? Is *that* why all those fae were watching our carriage arrive?

My back tenses instinctively at the thought, but... I healed that man on a stage in front of over a thousand gathered fae. It isn't as if I haven't faced this kind of situation before. It only makes the possibility of failure even more uncomfortable.

Corwin glances at me. *It's up to you. Whatever you're*

comfortable with. If we say you'll have more chance of success without any distractions, I'm sure they'll understand and comply.

I waver on my feet, debating. I don't want all those eyes fixed on me while I'm trying to work the magic I'm still not fully confident in, but will refusing stir up doubt and suspicion? We're already facing enough of that from the arch-lords—we can use all the supporters we can get.

It's actually kind of nice, when I let my anxiety settle, to know the fae here have been talking about me so effusively, even if it's mostly because of what I can do for them.

"We can try that," I say to the lord, hedging my bets. "But it might turn out I need more privacy to totally concentrate."

He offers another small bow, this one just for me. "Naturally, we wouldn't want to interfere with the cure. Just say the word. I'll have a room ready in case it comes to that. Here, I'll escort you down myself."

He makes a quick gesture to the two fae with him, who leap into the air with their wings whipping out and soar down to the buildings below, presumably to prepare that room... and maybe to spread the word that the show is starting? Apprehension raises the hairs on the back of my neck, but I will myself to stay as calm as possible as the lord leads the way into his palace.

Somehow in this wintry realm even the golden shade of the wood has a cool feel to it. The sharp smell of sap hangs in the air inside. The lord strides to a spiral staircase deeper inside the building, which winds down into the rock.

The wooden steps give way to stone after the first couple dozen. The air turns cooler but lies still against my skin. Veins of glowing quartz run through the pale gray rock, lighting our passage. I grip the banister tightly and set my warped foot down as steadily as I can.

Finally, we reach a short hall that opens into the village common. Other than the different shade of the stone, the space looks a lot like the common for Corwin's flock, if a bit smaller. Patches of winter crops and projects in the middle of construction stand around the edges of the space, but they're quickly becoming hidden by the fae streaming in to gather around the center with its high, domed ceiling.

A padded chair has been set up under that dome, with two fae standing by the chair and a woman seated in it. The balls of magical fire hovering around her only emphasize her cursed state. Streaks of frost ripple through her dark hair, and her skin has already paled to a deep grayish blue color like a lake viewed through thin ice.

Her shoulders have hunched, her head jutting stiffly forward at an awkward angle. The curse's grip has altered her so much I can't tell whether she was young or old before it caught her.

My chest constricts. I walk over to where she's sitting, Corwin and the flock's lord following only part of the way. For the last few steps, I'm on my own. Even the fae who were watching over the woman back up a short distance. But while they're giving me plenty of room here in the middle of the common, dozens of gazes are fixed on me from the crowd all around. The whole flock must have turned up.

Silence falls throughout the huge room. I drag in a breath and focus on the cursed woman. She peers back at me with frost-hazed eyes, her mouth twisted into an even more pained shape than it formed before.

"I'm going to do my best to bring you out of the cold," I tell her. Someone in the crowd gasps, and someone else shushes them. I do my best to tune out my awareness of the spectators as I add, "I'm so sorry this happened to you. No one deserves it."

Now that I've done it purposefully before, it's easier to summon the thoughts that'll bring tears to my eyes. This woman might have children she'll be torn from like my mother was from me and Jamie. Those children might be watching right now, just as August had to witness his mother's death. The cold is turning her as helpless as I felt when I was locked up in Aerik's cage with no idea if I'd ever see sunlight again.

One moment she was living and laughing, and the next she had death staring her in the face. Barely any time to do whatever things she might have left undone. Not even a chance to get in a few last days of happiness before it's all taken away from her.

The burn starts to form behind my eyes. I turn away from her, covering my face with my hands so my tears aren't obvious to the watching crowd either.

I imagine how my mother would have felt if she'd known she'd never be with her children again, never get to see them grow up—that they'd face so many torments without her. I think of all the hopes and dreams this woman might have had that the curse is wrenching from her.

I know what it's like to lose everything.

When the tears trickle out, I wipe them from my cheeks, the dampness cooling my fingers. Then I turn back toward the woman with an apologetic smile. She's staring at me, but I can't tell how much the tension in her expression is from the curse's rigidity and how much she's actually startled by the emotion I'm showing. By now, everyone here must have heard what my cure involves.

I reach out to her and stroke my tear-damp fingers over her cheek.

In that first instant when the cold of her skin seeps into my fingertips, my pulse lurches with the thought that the chill might not shift. But it never happens immediately.

"I want you to have all the life you were meant to," I say, just as a spot of warmth forms beneath my hand.

The warmth spreads over her face and through the rest of her body, the bluish cast and the frost fading away in its wake. Tentatively, she pushes her posture straighter. She inhales with a faint rattling sound and then again more clearly.

A joyful chuckle tumbles from her lips. She grins at me. "The cold is gone. It was in me right to my bones, and now everything is warm again."

My own joy sweeps through me. I find myself grinning back at her, barely aware of anyone else in the room. "I'm so glad I could help you."

To my surprise, her hand shoots out to grasp mine. None of the other fae I've tried to cure have offered any physical gesture of gratitude. She squeezes my fingers and gazes up at me with a softer smile. "It is an honor to have been blessed by the one the Heart blessed for us."

I'm not sure how to answer that remark. The words send a weird quiver through my chest. Then the fae who were standing by the chair before move forward to make sure the woman can get to her feet, and I ease back.

Corwin approaches me from behind and rests his hands on my shoulders. *There you go. You've mastered it now. The curse won't claim another while you're with us.*

Despite the pressure that comes with that statement, in that moment I'm only relieved that it worked. I haven't let anyone down today—not as far as I know, at least.

Then a voice rings out, echoing off the high ceiling. "All gratitude and grace to the Heart-blessed human!"

As my head jerks toward the speaker, several other voices rise up in a chorus of eager agreement. The crowd surges toward us, the nearest figures still keeping a respectful distance I'm sure is at least as much for Corwin's benefit as it is for mine, but approaching much closer than before. They stop just a few feet from me, wide-eyed as they take me in.

Under their scrutiny, my face flushes. But their gazes feel more awed than anything else. "The Heart-blessed human," a few of them murmur, using the same phrase the earlier voice did.

One young woman eases a little closer, her stance bashful. "Lady Talia, would you—would you touch my cheek as you did for Vinma? If I could receive your blessing, perhaps…" She glances down at her hands, shy about whatever it is she thinks my power can do for her.

Corwin speaks up as I grope for words in my

confusion. "Talia's touch doesn't have any magic in itself. It won't stave off a curse that hasn't set in or accomplish anything else."

"But—the Heart shines so brightly on her—I'd just like to have been that close to the one it chose to conquer the curse." She peers at me again, her eyes shining with hope.

I don't have it in me to say no, as bewildered as the situation has made me. "All right."

I extend my hand, and she tips forward to meet me. My fingers barely graze her skin. She draws back, beaming as if I've given her some great gift. Immediately, several others start pushing forward, asking for me to "bless" them too.

Did you have any idea this would happen? I ask Corwin as I offer up my hand to each fae who wants it.

No. It never occurred to me… I suppose the healing at the ceremony was quite a spectacle, even though we didn't intend it to be. And my people have suffered from the curse for a long time—nearly everyone has lost at least an acquaintance to it if not a friend or family. I feel his smile even though I'm not looking at him. *If they're starting to see you as a savior, I can't say I blame them. As long as we make sure they understand the limits of your powers, I don't see the harm.*

Neither do I, but it doesn't exactly sit easy with me either.

I must touch the cheek of at least two dozen fae before they stop approaching me. When I wave goodbye, even more voices call out their thanks and other benedictions to me. By the time we reach the carriage, the whole flock appears to be out on their terraces again to see us off. I wave again, my heart somehow buoyant yet heavy at the same time.

This is the first time any fae beyond my lovers have seen me as just as worthy as their own kind. It's both exhilarating and reassuring.

The problem is, I can't help wondering how many expectations will follow on the heels of this new adoration.

CHAPTER SIX

Sylas

With a heaved breath and a low intonation of the true name, I urge the wood I'm shaping to expand out, filling out the walls of the room. It's slow, focused work, and after a few hours adding to the construction of the border castle without a break, a headache is starting to form at my temples. We're so close to completing the plans Corwin and I laid out that I haven't wanted to waste any moments I can spare on the project.

I step back, studying the outside of the building and rolling my shoulders. Whitt nods to me from across the field where he's been adding details to a room on the other side of our end of the castle.

At least we're no longer having to work immersed in the border haze. The farthest reaches of the structure now spill out into the grassy field on the summer side.

At the rustle of footsteps and the clearing of a throat, I

turn to find one of our sentries striding across the grass toward me. He dips into a bow. "My lord, Lord Tristan has arrived and wishes to speak to you."

Wonderful. I can look forward to even more of a headache.

I manage not to grimace in front of the sentry, but it's a near thing. "You can escort him to the front drawing room of Hearth-by-the-Heart's castle and tell him I'll be with him shortly."

Whitt is watching me, having followed the conversation with his sharp ears. When I catch his eyes, he gives me a questioning look.

I shake my head. I'd rather not have Tristan think I feel the need for backup when speaking to him. After all his conspiring with his cousin, the former arch-lord of this domain, I don't want him seeing anything in me but total confidence in my ability to defend myself and my people.

I take a moment to shake off the exertion of my conjuring, breathing in the warm fresh air, and then I stride toward the castle of my own domain to see what this mangy miscreant wants with me today.

Tristan hasn't bothered to take a seat despite the many chairs in the room. He's standing by one of the side tables, his pale, mint-green hair falling forward to shade his eyes, examining a vase that was a gift from a lady from one of the neighboring domains. Possibly a lady whose hopes for me have been dashed now that I've declared my devotion to Talia, but I haven't encouraged any interest beyond the professional, so she can't fault my behavior.

At my entrance, the younger lord turns. It'd be easy to underestimate him—to assume he's less of a threat than

Ambrose was. His frame is trimmer, his features more delicate. But rancor emanates from his pose, and I've heard enough of his thoughts on various subjects in the past to be wary of him. Physical power is far from the worst threat a man can present.

His tone comes out tart. "I apologize if I interrupted you in the middle of important work, my lord. Thank you for attending to me."

I hold back a glower. Without saying the words, he's clearly indicated how *un*important he thinks the construction of our border castle is, and that he isn't sorry about it at all. But it's simpler to take the comment at face value.

"I'm here to serve all my people," I reply. Even wretched pissants like the man before me. I fold my arms over my chest. "What can I do for you, Lord Tristan?"

He purses his lips before going on. "Arch-Lord Ambrose had a great deal of possessions. I realize that due to his questionable actions, those were confiscated by the current arch-lords. But I was hoping that, as his kin, I might be able to request a couple of items that have been in our family for some time and would have greater value to me than you."

I raise an eyebrow. "We finished taking down Ambrose's castle weeks ago. Why are you only mentioning this now?"

Tristan spreads his hands. "Given the circumstances of his death, I felt it was more respectful to give you and the other arch-lords time to make your own assessment of his belongings first."

The circumstances which involved attempting to frame

and then murder Arch-Lord Donovan—and nearly doing the same to me in the end. I smile tightly. Many of Ambrose's possessions were part of an illicit collection of artifacts and tools forbidden by fae law, which he'd amassed in preparation for the war he wanted to wage against the Unseelie. I don't know how much his cousin is aware of that, but I'm not about to inform him of the details he might not know.

"Many of the lesser items we dispersed among his pack-kin," I say. "I do still have some things stored that I hadn't decided what to do with yet. If you describe the items you hoped to collect, I'll check whether they're still here."

"I'd prefer to look for myself," Tristan says, pulling his spine straighter, though it still only brings him to half a head shorter than me.

I keep my tone even. "And given the nature of many of the items we discovered Ambrose had been gathering, I'd prefer to handle it myself." I wouldn't put it past this man to slip something we hadn't realized the malicious significance of into his pocket to secret it away. Anything he asks for, I intend to make a thorough inspection of first.

Tristan's lips twitch with a restrained frown, and a brief vision swims before my deadened eye—him lunging at me with fangs bared and claws free. He looks exactly as he does right now, down to every article of clothing, so even through the jolt of defensive adrenaline, I know it isn't a glimpse of some future attack. I'm seeing what he *wishes* he could do to me right now.

I offer him another thin smile and let a hint of wryness

creep into my tone. "Such violent thoughts don't become a lord of your standing, especially when they're directed at one of your arch-lords."

Tristan stiffens, his eyes widening just slightly. I've told no one other than Talia about the unearthly glimpses my magic-struck eye offer, but Tristan doesn't need to know how I discerned his thoughts. Better he assumes I'm simply that perceptive with my regular senses.

"I'm not sure what you mean," he says.

"Ill intent has a way of showing through." When he doesn't remark on that, I lift my chin toward him. "Are you going to tell me what these heirlooms you're looking for are or not? I can see to them right now." And hopefully get him out of my domain for the rest of our long lives.

He hesitates for a few seconds longer but must realize I'm not budging on this matter. "There's a necklace, gold with several emeralds set in it, that was fashioned by my great-grandfather for my great-grandmother. The framing around the emeralds looks like shearvine leaves. And a cherry-wood puzzle box inlaid with pearls, about the size of my hand—he made that too."

The second description triggers a memory. "I believe Ambrose's mate took the box with her. We gave her the chance to gather the belongings that mattered most to her from the palace." Under careful supervision, of course. "You'll have to take that up with her. I can check for the necklace now. Please wait here. I'll have one of my staff bring you something to drink, as I'd imagine you'd appreciate after your journey."

As I leave the room, I make a discreet motion to the woman who was poised outside, listening in case she was needed. She bobs her head and hurries to the kitchen. Two guards have moved within view of the room to keep an eye on Tristan while I'm gone, not that I've set him up in a place containing anything significant he could interfere with.

Stepping into the storeroom where I set aside all of Ambrose's things that showed no offensive purpose and were too fine for me to feel comfortable simply discarding, my nose wrinkles. A hint of his scent, the acrid undertone that permeated his entire palace, still wafts off them.

It only takes a few minutes of pawing through the assortment to find the necklace in question. It is a lovely piece of craftsmanship. Everything in here has already been inspected, but I murmur words of magic over it anyway, testing it one more time for any enchantments or other hidden features.

There's nothing. Either it really is that meaningful to Tristan to have this family memento, or he was hoping that I'd give him a chance to search for it himself and that he'd be able to pocket some other item he wouldn't want me scrutinizing so carefully while he was at it.

I tuck the necklace into a silk bag and bring it back to where Tristan is now sipping the duskapple wine my packkin brought him. He opens the bag and checks the necklace as if he thinks I'd try to pass off some other trinket for the one he wanted.

"Well," he says, fixing the bag to his belt, "I'm glad to at least have that. After all the stories I've been hearing, I was a little concerned you might have gifted it to that human you're apparently so besotted with."

My hackles rise automatically, but I keep my voice

mild. He's provoking me deliberately now, and I won't let him gain any higher ground by giving in to my frustration. "I would hardly have presented her with a token tied to the man who wished to wrench her from her home and treat her no better than an animal."

Tristan shrugs, a cruel glint coming into his eyes. "Fair enough. With her brother proving to be a dud, I give you my best wishes toward getting her with child in all haste, my lord. The more cures we have on hand, the better, as I'm sure all our people would agree. I'll take my leave."

He swivels without giving me a chance to respond, no doubt to add insult to injury. I grit my teeth, my fangs emerging despite my best attempt at reining my temper in. I'd love nothing more than to bite his head off quite literally for his insinuations, but he's framed them as a polite wish for the general well-being of the Seelie rather than the assault on Talia's honor we both know it is.

Back when Ambrose was still alive, Tristan pushed for us to use my soon-to-be mate as nothing more than a broodmare. That's the only value he sees in her.

The trouble is, he may be right that a significant number of the summer fae would believe the chances of Talia's children carrying the same power in their blood matter more than her choice about whether she has children or not and when. They wouldn't see the insult because they barely see her as more of a person than Ambrose did.

My headache has returned. Not even the thought of returning to the border castle to speed the time until my love will have a real home settles my spirits.

Talia's position among us has remained precarious for

far too long. There must be *something* else I can do to free her from the weight of all our expectations. It'd be in the service of my people too, finding them a true cure that ends the curse for good rather than only for one moon.

I've already exhausted all the avenues I've been able to come up with on my own, but perhaps that means I need to push those with greater insight for more answers.

The idea that's sparked in my mind catches fire quickly. I only debate for a few minutes, considering the implications, before deciding there's no point in waiting.

In the hall, I catch the attention of one of the staff. "Tell Whitt and any other of my cadre who ask that I've taken up an expedition for the rest of the day. I should return by nightfall." They all know how to reach me should an emergency arise.

The carriage I conjure from a juniper is slim and small for maximum swiftness. As it rushes toward my destination, I sit back and contemplate the exact appeal I'm going to make.

Normally when approaching the great sage Nuldar, one is expected to request his consideration with a message and wait for his approval. But as old and respected as he may be, I'm an arch-lord now, and this is a matter of grave urgency. What does he have to pass the time with other than making vague proclamations for those who ask for them anyway?

Well, I'll leave out that last point when I'm actually speaking to him. But perhaps I'll get a straighter answer when he has less time to dwell on it and get his thoughts muddled up.

The field that lies at the edge of Nuldar's forest is

vacant, much different from my last journey here with an entourage of arch-lords and their underlings. The drooping leaves of the starfall willows glitter beneath the sun, murmuring as the light breeze ripples through them. As soon as I've brought my carriage to a halt, I spring out of it and set off through the trees.

When I come up on the tree Nuldar has become one with, I slow down, still wanting to show my respect. The aged fae, his skin melded into the pale, silvery gray of the trunk's bark, appears to be sleeping. The wizened face embedded in the tree doesn't stir as I kneel a few paces from the roots.

Then the eyelids twitch and open. The ancient sage peers down at me, his expression inscrutable.

I bow my head. "Great Nuldar, I apologize for arriving unannounced. I wish to speak to you about the gravest matter affecting our people, and I couldn't stand to delay my appeal. Would you be kind enough to hear me now?"

The aged fae is silent for a long stretch. Then he clears his throat with a rattling sound more wooden than fleshy. "You may speak, Arch-Lord Sylas," he rasps. "What I may answer remains to be heard."

I inhale deeply, steadying myself. "The human woman I brought before you last time, Talia, has proven to offer a temporary cure to both the Seelie curse and that of the Unseelie. But no action we've taken has revealed any way to make the cure permanent, nor have we uncovered any connection between Talia and any other party that has led us to other answers."

When I pause to be sure of my words, Nuldar lets out a rough sound. "What is your question, arch-lord?"

I'll only get one. I'm lucky he's been willing to speak with me at all. I doubt it would do any good asking him what the solution is outright—others have tried that before me and have gotten only riddles.

Sometimes asking for a method of finding an answer accomplishes more than requesting the answer itself. And now, with Talia, I have to assume we have more pieces of that method to help us interpret the sage's answer.

"What steps must we take, with what we currently have, to determine how to fully end the curse?" I ask.

Another long silence. Nuldar's eyes close. Has he decided to ignore me after all?

Then he blinks and fixes his deep blue eyes on me again. "You need do nothing at all," he says. "The answer is already on its way to you, soon to arrive if unimpeded. Giving it room to come will bring it faster than chasing after it—better a snare than a hunt. You must only be sure that your snare *is* a snare and not yet another caught in a trap. If it can capture a single heart, it will bring all you need to know back to you. Prepare well."

With that, he goes completely still. I wait, still kneeling, until I'm sure that's all he'll say. Then I straighten up with another dip of my head. "Thank you for your words of wisdom, honored sage."

I hurry back to my carriage, repeating his declaration in my head, my spirit unsettled. I'll have to see what Whitt makes of this talk of snares, but the first part was clear enough—I simply don't like it.

The fastest way to end the curse is to do nothing at all and wait for a solution to fall from the sky? Nuldar said we'd have the answer soon, but for a fae that old, the word is relative. He could mean decades more.

But if what Nuldar says is true, then anything we do to search for answers on our own could push them farther away from us rather than getting us closer to healing our people.

CHAPTER SEVEN

Talia

This is only my second time this deep in the fog-drenched territory at the fringes of the fae realm, and I find it just as eerie as the first. The cool haze drifts between the trees, which loom with their branches spread so broadly that only muted sunlight penetrates their leaves overhead. It gives the forest the feel of twilight even though it's actually midday. Here and there, distant rustling sounds reach my ears.

My fingers itch to curl around August's arm, to hold onto him as we venture through this haunted terrain, but I don't want to be in his way if he needs to quickly leap to our defense. Ferocious beasts prowl the edges of the summer realm just as they do in the winter lands. I have my dagger in its sheath at my hip, but I'm not exactly an expert with it.

I walk along between him and the Unseelie representative the arch-lords sent along for my second trip to the human world: the guard with human-like ears I saw Laoni sniping at on the night of the full moon. Now that we have a clearer idea of what to expect, both sides agreed that it was better to send fae who could pass for human. If we need to shed the magic keeping us unseen for some reason, they won't have to be as careful about how they appear.

The guard, who introduced himself to us as Kesral, peers into the depths of the fringe forest, the damp breeze stirring the short ponytail he's tied his dark brown hair into like before. Here, his stance is confident, his expression cautious but not particularly tense. He seemed a little wary of August on our journey by carriage out here, but by the end he'd relaxed enough to make a little small talk on August's favorite subjects: food and combat strategies.

I haven't seen anything that would explain Laoni's hostility toward him. Is it just because he has less fae blood than many of her other staff? She trusted him enough to give him this duty. Or is it a punishment in her mind to send him off as a sort of chaperone for my trip to the human world?

None of those questions seem right to ask, but curiosity itches at me.

August stops at a thicker patch of darkness between two tree trunks. It gleams with an almost liquid texture, just as Whitt described the portals between the worlds to me months ago.

August leans close and takes a sniff, then shakes his head. We know the one that'll lead us to the park not far from Jamie's house is in this general area, but apparently the portals sometimes shift around a little. He's already checked a few before without finding it.

"It shouldn't take too much longer," he assures us. "That one was almost right."

Kesral lets out a grunt that sounds dryly amused. "Never much of an exact science, is it, making the trip?"

That remark gives me an opening I can't resist. I glance at him, watching his reaction cautiously. "Have you traveled to the human world frequently?"

He shrugs, his gaze still scanning the forest around us for threats. "On the winter side, of course. When Arch-Lord Laoni requires something from those lands, it's often me she asks."

"Because you can blend in." I pause and then venture, "Was one of your parents human? August's mother was. And obviously both of mine." I bite my tongue, my cheeks flushing at my fumbling attempt to make the question less awkward. I don't think I succeeded.

Kesral just chuckles though, the warmth of the sound putting me back at ease. "It isn't so hard to tell, I suppose." He runs his fingers over the curve of one of his ears. "My blood father. My mother very much wanted a child, and when she and her mate hadn't been able to in a long time, they decided she would seek out a human to her liking at an opportune time. And here I am. I don't think of him as a father in any way other than that, though. My real father is the one who helped raise me."

He speaks about it easily enough—and I guess it is easier when his story isn't anywhere near as tragic as August's.

"It's pretty common in both realms," August says,

leading the way to the next portal. "If fae never slipped out of the Mists to romance a human here and there, there'd be a lot fewer of us."

Kesral hums to himself. His voice drops as if he's not totally sure he wants his next words to be heard. "Unfortunate that more of our kin don't recognize that fact."

My gaze darts to him again. I grapple with my next words for a moment before spitting them out. "Do the other fae treat you badly because of it—because of your heritage?"

His expression stiffens, maybe with the fear he's said too much. "I wouldn't say badly. Only sometimes a little differently. I'm sure you've experienced some of the varied opinions on humankind during your time with us, though Arch-Lord Corwin is known for being sof—permissive with them."

He was going to say soft-hearted. I won't let myself be offended by that when I'd bet Kesral has overheard Laoni complaining about Corwin in much more insulting terms.

"That's different," I say. "I'm totally human, even if I have a few unexpected powers—powers that are nothing compared to what any fae can do, including you. And, I mean, your heritage obviously doesn't make that big a difference. August can serve on an arch-lord's cadre no problem."

My lover shoots a crooked smile over his shoulder at me. "Oh, there are a few who'd mutter about that, I promise you. And I do get some recognition from having a father who's not just fae but a true-blooded lord. I'd imagine Kesral has had a harder time of it than

I have, if the winter realm is much like summer in that respect."

From the twist of Kesral's mouth, August must be right. The other man is silent for a stretch. Then he says, "I'm certain I'd never aspire to being part of my lord's coterie. She is clear on my place within her flock. I'm honored to support her rule in the ways assigned to me."

I want to ask about Laoni's harsh attitude toward him, but I'm not sure how without overstepping the tentative friendliness he's offered. And maybe it does just come down to how much human blood runs through his veins.

If she's like that with a fae man who's still very much fae despite his birth father, how does she treat whatever human servants she's brought to her domain? What about the other winter lords?

I haven't really had a chance to see how anyone other than Corwin interacts with humans besides me, and he's definitely considerate of his servants in a way I can tell is unusual. Sylas hasn't kept human servants at all in the time I've been with him... because of what he feared his former brother-in-law would do to them while Kellan was still around.

I've been so focused on saving the fae from their curse, I never considered all the other people here who might need my help. If I leave more permanently, who'll be left who would even think of speaking up for all the other humans kidnapped by the fae?

The question feels like a shackle tugging me in yet another direction. I shove aside those worries as well as I can, pushing on through the fog.

Then August lets out a triumphant exclamation by the

portal he's stopped at. I hurry over, everything falling away except my need to see my brother again.

The whole reason I wanted to make this trip was to get a better idea of how he's living now. I only had a glimpse last time. How can I decide where I'm needed most, how much I owe who, when I know so little about his current situation? If I'm going to have to choose between all the responsibilities tugging at me, it'd better be an informed one.

August extends his hand to me, and I wrap my fingers around his. As we step through the portal together, Kesral follows close behind us.

The closest experience I can compare the trip to is walking through a hall in a mirror maze. The landscape around me shimmers and wavers as if undulating through water, although the air is perfectly still. I can't help closing my eyes for a moment like I did last time, dizziness scattering my thoughts.

When I open them again, we're just stepping onto the grass in the park. There's a tiny clearing amid several saplings where the undulating impression remains. We won't be perceivable to humans until we walk beyond that boundary.

August intones the words to wrap concealing magic around us. He was practicing with Whitt earlier today, and he motions to the air with more assurance now. A brief tingling washes over my skin and then fades away.

"All right," he says, looking pleased with the result, and nods to Kesral. "You were with one of the scouting parties that first located Talia's brother—I assume you remember the way?"

"Yes, the house that appears to be his main residence is north of here." Kesral sets off, and we fall into step behind him, letting him take the lead now.

We couldn't predict exactly what time of day we'd come out into, but the growing warmth in the air and the position of the sun suggest it's late morning. If it's a weekday, Jamie and our cousins will be at school and our aunt and uncle at work, so hopefully we'll be able to explore his current home without interruption or discovery.

Kesral picks up his pace as we reach the streets beyond the park, and I propel myself after him, my limp becoming more pronounced. An ache is starting to spread up from the warped arch into my ankle. August gives me a concerned glance, and I can tell he's struggling with the urge to offer to carry me. He doesn't want to embarrass me in front of company.

I reach for his hand again and squeeze, a silent reassurance that if I need him, I'll say so.

The house Kesral brings us to strikes a tiny chord of memory somewhere deep in my mind. A lifetime—or more than a dozen years—ago, my parents drove us out here to visit Aunt Becca and Uncle Walter. I think they'd just moved into the house then? My memory is pretty fuzzy. We were only here for the weekend. Dad and Aunt Becca had a falling out several years before that and hadn't been talking much; I remember the atmosphere was still kind of tense.

How did she feel about suddenly taking in his grieving, savaged son?

We go around to the back door where we're mostly out

of view of the neighboring houses. August casts a quick spell to confirm no one is in the house, and then Kesral steps in to magic the lock open. We slip quickly inside.

Sunlight streams from the window on the back door and through another bright pane in the kitchen we find ourselves in. It's a little messy, breakfast dishes piled in the sink and a box of cereal left out on the counter, but homey enough to bring a smile to August's lips.

I note a few photos attached to the fridge with magnets—two of my aunt and uncle with their own kids, but another with Jamie there too, on a dock at the edge of a lake. They all went on a cottage trip together?

He's grinning in the photograph, but I can't shake the sense that he looks a bit sad all the same.

August prowls through the room, opening and closing cupboards with eager interest. I guess he hasn't had a whole lot of chance to study the culinary habits of the average urban family.

"They appear to have plenty of ingredients on hand," he says. "And I can smell that they served a well-cooked roast chicken last night." He licks his lips so avidly I have to giggle.

We sneak down the hall to check out the other rooms. A few toys belonging to the younger kids dot the living room floor, and a game system that looks newer than the one August likes to play on is tucked away in the TV cabinet. My cousins appear to share the largest of the three bedrooms, with a set of bunkbeds and even more toys lying around. Nothing too fancy—I wouldn't say they're spoiled. But what about Jamie?

His bedroom turns out to be on the opposite side of

the main hall. Whitt had told me it was small, but I'm still a little startled by the lack of space, only a few feet between the bed and desk and the wall opposite.

A crisp, citrusy smell laces the air that I don't associate with my brother at all. Has he started wearing cologne? I guess that wouldn't be so surprising at his age. He must be thinking about impressing girls.

It looks like he has a girlfriend right now. Between the band posters tacked to the wall, I spot several printed photos of him with his arm around a pretty teen with blue streaks in her fawn-brown hair and freckles across her cheeks. His smile in those looks relaxed and genuine, like he couldn't be happier. Some of the clenching sensation inside me releases.

He isn't an outcast or anything. Those guys at school might have harassed him, but he's found other people who care about him.

Mixed in with the girlfriend pics are a couple with a larger group, Jamie and the freckled girl and a couple other guys and girls. He's even got one from a Christmas that must have been a few years back, with him laughing and raising his arms defensively as the cousins shower him with torn wrapping paper.

Is he actually okay? Has he found a place where he can belong, just like I'm starting to among the fae?

August and Kesral have hung back by the door to give me space to make my investigation. "It all seems pretty good, actually," I tell August as I sit down at the desk. The room might be small, but Jamie has given it a sense of home. "He's doing well in school too." There are a couple of assignments off to the side of the desk, one with a B+ and the other with an A.

I open the drawers expecting to find more of the same, and instead stumble on a stack of charcoal sketches. The one on top is Jamie's girlfriend, a little rough but recognizable. He did love to doodle when he was a kid—I had no idea he'd gotten this good. He must be a little shy about them since he hasn't tacked them up.

Lifting the papers onto my lap, I start to sort through them. I've only gotten a few deep when my hands jerk to a halt.

I'm staring into a pair of glowering eyes in a darkly furred wolfish face with fangs bared. It sends a jolt of memory through me so strong that my heart is thumping twice as fast in an instant.

And loud enough that August can hear it. He leans into the room. "Is everything all right, Sweetness?"

"Y—yes. It's just a picture." But what a picture. And the next, and the next—black beasts slashing their claws across the pages, violently jagged lines, shaded puddles that make me think of blood. I swallow hard, my fingers shaking.

No, Jamie hasn't left the past completely behind. If these drawings are anything to go by, it's still stalking him even more determinedly than mine does me. But he's hiding it away like he has no idea how to shake it.

How *could* he know how to deal with it? How could he understand what actually happened, let alone explain it to anyone else?

There's no one in the world who has any idea what he's going through… except me.

CHAPTER EIGHT

Talia

I know my fate matters a lot to the fae and their rulers, but I wasn't expecting such a huge welcoming party waiting for us on our return. Not just the summer arch-lords and some of their staff but all five of the winter arch-lords are standing around outside the castle of Hearth-by-the-Heart, waiting for August's carriage to draw to a halt.

I seek out Sylas's and Corwin's faces first. Both have schooled their expressions to a lordly calm, but I know Sylas well enough to read the tension in his jaw, and Corwin's uneasiness travels to me through our bond.

We tried to hold them off until you'd had a chance to catch your breath after your journey, he says. *But the others on both sides insisted. I suppose we should be a tiny bit grateful they've finally agreed on something so easily?*

No humor warms those words. I scramble out of the

carriage to find out what's going on, wobbling when my feet hit the ground.

"Has something happened?" I ask as August joins me. "What's the matter?"

The arch-lords exchange a glance, and Celia speaks up. "Let us take the discussion to the Bastion. If the Heart objects to our proposal, it can do so there." The look she aims at Sylas suggests *he's* been objecting to whatever this is.

But he doesn't argue now, just inclines his head. His dark eye holds my gaze, his mouth twitching with just a trace of a grimace.

The whole gathering tramps across the fields and smatterings of forest to the building where the summer arch-lords conduct their business. *If there's been some new catastrophe, I'd like to know now,* I say to Corwin silently, my stomach knotting.

Nothing new, he says with a whiff of reassurance tempered by… sadness? *Only that our colleagues have come to some new conclusions after determining that your brother isn't a solution to our problems. They claim to have your best interests at heart, but I can't help suspecting they're actually tackling something else they see as a problem.*

Which is?

His inner voice takes on a bit of strain. *The fact that a human is bound to any of us in the first place, and that we've embraced that bond. And a human with unpredictable talents on top of that.*

This has something to do with separating me from my lovers? I bristle inwardly, but I try to keep my face as impassive as they have as we reach the tall stone palace with its gleaming veins of gold.

In the huge central room, cadre, coterie, and guards fall back to the rounded walls, leaving only me and the eight arch-lords in the center. Celia's lips are pursed, Donovan's forehead knit as if he's still working out where he stands on this subject. Of the winter arch-lords other than Corwin, only elderly Neve looks at all at ease with her vague smile. Laoni, Terisse, and Uzziah gaze down at me with an aura of authority.

"You've returned from visiting your brother," Laoni says without preamble.

I shift my weight from one foot to the other. "I didn't exactly visit with him. He still doesn't know I'm alive. I was just checking on his home, making sure he's been comfortable there." Discovering he hasn't really been. The memory of Jamie's violent sketches flashes behind my eyes.

Celia picks up the thread. "We understand that you've been somewhat torn. You've committed yourself to living among us here in the Mists, assuming there was nothing left for you in your own world. But now it turns out that's not true."

Are they going to question my loyalty to the fae like Laoni has tried to in the past? I fold my arms over my chest. "You don't have to worry about me taking off on you. I'm not sure yet how much I need to do for my brother, but I'll keep helping with the curse in every way I can."

Terisse dips her head. "But what if we could make it easier for you to accomplish both?"

I wasn't expecting them to offer to help *me*. I glance

from one face to another warily. Corwin stays silent, only giving off a whiff of impatience that they're taking so long getting on with their point. He wants me to have room to make my own decision—about *what?*

"In what way?" I ask.

"Clearly, the Heart has seen fit to give you gifts that benefit us," Laoni says. "But you were born in the human world and would have remained there if not for your cruel kidnapping at the hands of that summer fae lord. It is your true home. We believe we could allow you to return there and make a life for yourself there while still drawing on your aid."

Return there… permanently? My gaze darts to my lovers—Sylas and Corwin around me, August and Whitt back by the wall. Corwin can't hide the pang of pain that shot through him at her suggestion.

It's your choice, he says, keeping his tone steady. *You can make it freely. You know how much you mean to me, my soul, but I wouldn't keep you from your world and your family if that's where you feel you should be.*

Neither would my Seelie men. They showed that much when we found out I was linked to Corwin, when we thought I might have to move to the winter realm permanently. But now—after all the ways we've struggled to find a compromise that lets us all stay together—

But I've considered it, haven't I? Not just about visiting the human world now and then but really going back, at least for a few months or even years, until I'm sure Jamie's okay. I just hadn't let myself think about it too deeply because I couldn't see how I'd be able to balance that with my duties to the fae.

"What about the curse?" I say tentatively. They can't mean to tackle it on their own again now that they have a cure in me. "How could I still heal people if I'm not here?"

Uzziah motions to the summer arch-lords. "The Seelie only need your blood one night a month. They could send someone to collect it from you—stealthily, so no one in your family would be aware. In the same way, we assume we could bring any new victims of our curse to you for you to offer your tears. The actual process only appears to take a few minutes."

"It would require a fair bit of effort on our part," Laoni says, as if they're making this proposal out of selfless generosity, "but we're willing to put in that effort to see you restored to your proper place."

Something in me hardens. That's what this is really about, isn't it? My "proper place." She and her two sycophants have never liked how devoted Corwin has become to me, and no doubt they like the fact that I'm staying so closely tied to three of my Seelie lovers at the same time even less. And I'd bet Celia would be happy to have me and all the complications I've brought into her life out of the way, so I only affect her when it's time to take my blood or tears.

They don't give a damn what my brother means to me. They're just seeing yet another opportunity to use him to serve their purposes.

But the worst part is, I'm not totally sure I shouldn't take them up on this offer anyway. After what I saw in Jamie's room today, maybe I should go back and reconnect with him for as long as it takes to heal *him*, regardless of the arch-lords' intentions.

I swallow thickly. "Thank you for making this offer. I'll need some time to think about it. I'm not sure yet what would really be best for everyone involved. There isn't any rush, is there?"

Laoni's lips flatten, but before she can say anything, Celia speaks up. "Of course not. We simply wanted you to know the opportunity is there so you can take one concern off your plate."

It hasn't really worked that way at all. Now I'm even more unsettled about the decision I have to make, knowing the arch-lords have their own agenda. In this moment, the weight of all the factors I need to consider feels almost suffocating.

Sylas steps in, setting his hand on my back with a little more familiarity than he might have before the rest of our audience was aware of our relationship. "Talia has had a long trip today, and she'll need her rest. You've made your proposal—now let's give her some peace to consider it."

"We're trying to do what's best for all parties involved too," Terisse says before the winter arch-lords step away, and I think she actually means that. I just don't agree with her assessment of what's "best."

Corwin hangs back as his colleagues leave. "Are you all right?" he asks, and flicks his gaze briefly toward Sylas. "I know it's your time in the summer realm now—I wish the border castle were already complete—but if you need me to stay to talk things over, or just to be here…"

And give the other arch-lords even more reason to think you're prioritizing me over your other responsibilities? I say through our bond, and sigh out loud. His affection wraps around me like an embrace, but I don't want to keep him from his people and his realm. I have three men here who can comfort me, after all. "I think I really do just need some rest. But if I need you after all, I know I can reach you in a moment."

"And I'll be with you immediately." He smiles and leans in to kiss me tenderly. The heat of his mouth, his own pleasure at the kiss, and the sense of my other men watching us with full approval all send a thrill through me despite my worries.

I clutch his shirt for just a second before letting him go. *I love you.*

And I love you. We'll see this through like we have so much else.

As he heads toward the border, Sylas guides me to one of the other exits, August and Whitt falling into step on either side of us. "What did you make of your trip, mite?" Whitt asks, his tone gentle. He can't be happy about the idea of me leaving the fae realm permanently any more than the others are, but he's kind enough not to push the subject.

I exhale raggedly. "I don't know. Jamie has obviously settled in with my aunt and uncle pretty well. It looks like they've accepted him into the family, and he's made at least a few friends… But I found some drawings of monsters and other dark things that I think must be from his memories of the attack. He hasn't totally gotten past it."

"The effects haven't completely left you either," August points out. "It isn't surprising—something that traumatic has a way of sticking in the brain."

"I just—I want to help him. But what if revealing myself brings up even more trauma or whatever? It's impossible to know. And I don't want to leave all of you." I rub my forehead. "Right now I think I just want to sleep. Maybe things will seem clearer after that."

"Let's get you right to bed then," August says, managing a teasing tone, and scoops me off my aching feet like he's probably been wanting to for hours now.

I let out a noise of protest that I don't mean all that much and then settle against his brawny chest. He carries me the rest of the way to the castle with swifter strides than I could have managed, his brothers matching his pace. But once we've stepped into the grand entrance hall and he sets me down, Sylas motions to me.

"If you can spare a few minutes before getting your rest, there's something I'd like to speak to you about first. It shouldn't take long."

I nod. "Of course."

He must make some gesture to the other men, because they don't follow us to Sylas's study. Inside, he motions for me to take what's become my favorite armchair in there and goes to his desk. But rather than taking a seat behind it, he retrieves something from one of the drawers and then sinks into the chair beside mine, tugging it around so he's facing me.

"A few days ago I went to see Nuldar again," he says.

I blink at him. "You didn't mention it."

"You were with Corwin then, and I hadn't decided what I was going to make of what he said yet. I'm still puzzling over it somewhat." He sighs, some of the tension he must be carrying just as I am leeching into his expression. "The main things he indicated were that the solution to the curse should become apparent to us without us needing to do anything but wait—in fact, attempting to speed it along might impede it instead—but we also must be prepared."

My mouth twists into a crooked smile, thinking of the first answer we got from Nuldar. "I don't suppose he bothered to mention *how* we should prepare?"

Sylas smiles back with a matching wryness. "He didn't. But I feel that there are some steps we can take that are general preparation against any harm—and that, as tied as you've been to the curse so far, it's particularly important that we equip you properly. Which is why I made this for you."

He holds out a loop of bronze like a wide, flat bracelet, a decorative pattern of flowers etched in its polished surface. "I tried to form it to interfere with your typical activities as little as possible. You could wear it on your wrist or your ankle. I'd have one on each if I wasn't concerned that having more than one would draw attention to their importance."

I take the bracelet from him, running my fingers over the smooth metal. It's too narrow for me to fit over my hand—but I could widen it with magic and then tell it to contract again once it's on so it hugs my wrist closely.

Oh. I glance up at him and find him studying me. "It's a hidden weapon," I say, checking that I've understood properly. "I can use the true name for bronze to change it into a blade or whatever else I might need to defend myself in an emergency."

"That was my thought. My fellow fae have only seen you make use of the true name for light—they won't immediately associate the bracelet with your potential powers, especially with it being so odd to think of a human using true names at all." Sylas runs his hand along his jaw. "I probably should have given you something like this when I first found out about your abilities in that area, but it's not the sort of strategy we'd generally use ourselves, so it didn't occur to me right away."

"Better now than never." I've mostly stopped carrying my pouch of salt—at first because we were worried it'd offend the Unseelie while I was finding my place there and now because I don't want to distress those who come to me for help—and my dagger could be snatched from me if I'm taken by surprise. But no enemy would think they had to remove a bracelet to fully disarm me.

With the images from Jamie's drawings lurking in the back of my mind, it's easy to summon the sense of terror that gives power to the true name. "*Fee-doom-ace-own*," I murmur, willing the metal band to expand and then shrink against my skin. When it's resting around my wrist, it looks like nothing more than a pretty bangle. I doubt most of the fae would give it a second glance.

My sense of Corwin, nearly always with me, doesn't intrude, but a faint impression of gratitude toward Sylas trickles through our connection to me. I send a tendril of fondness back and gaze up at the man who offered this gift.

After all he's done for me, it's hard to doubt the summer arch-lord's feelings for me. Still, I can't help being filled with awe that a man with so much power and strength cares so deeply what happens to me. I might not agree with the fae dismissing or mistreating humans, but I know there are many ways I can't really match him.

But none of that matters to him. He loves me for what I *can* offer, and to him it's enough that he sees me as a better mate than any of the fine fae ladies who've vied for his attention. He's sheltered and protected me but also trusted and believed in me enough to let me stand up for myself when I've been able to. This bracelet is the perfect symbol of that love.

I slip off my chair. Sylas leans into my hug, pulling me right onto his lap and nestling my head against the crook of his neck. His earthy, smoky smell has never felt so welcoming.

"I love you," I say. "I really don't want to leave you. Any of you. If it wasn't for Jamie, I'd never even consider it. You know that, right?"

Sylas tightens his embrace, nuzzling my hair. His deep baritone comes out husky. "I do. And I hope you know how much I love you, Talia. You've healed so much more than just our curse. But part of loving you is letting you go if you believe you have to. Make your decision based on what feels right to *you*, not how the rest of us will feel about it."

Tears prick at the backs of my eyes. "There's just so much... So many things to consider that clash with each other. So many people counting on me, so many people I want to be there for."

"I know. I don't have to make the exact same choice you do, but I've had plenty of hard ones in my time as a lord. Balancing my loyalties to my pack, my brothers, the rest of the realm, and my mate—both past and current." He presses a kiss to my forehead. "I don't envy you your position."

"Does it get easier?" I have to ask. "Figuring out what to do when you're pulled in different directions?"

He considers his answer for a long moment. "Maybe a little. You learn through trial and error which factors will matter most in which situations, which sacrifices will tear at you the least. And perhaps you get better at finding a way to compromise so that you don't end up torn at all. I think you've already proven quite adept at that."

"I've been trying to think of an option that means losing nothing," I mutter. "No luck so far. If you think of anything, let me know."

Sylas chuckles and ducks his head to seek out my lips. As our mouths meld together, the pressure on me doesn't exactly lighten, but it is a little easier to set it aside just for now, in the hopes that a better answer will come to me in the meantime.

If I don't find one soon enough, will the other arch-lords force the issue of me leaving? No bracelet will defend me against all of them if they set their minds to seeing me gone.

Corwin

With the sun lighting her pale face and beaming off her pink-and-violet hair, my mate is nothing short of gorgeous. She leans over the edge of the carriage, peering at the icy forest we're passing over, and then glances back at me with a sly glint in her eyes. "You said this is one of your favorite places in the realm. Why's it taken so long for you to show it to me, then?"

I make a vague motion with my hand, maintaining the casual atmosphere I've tried to set for this expedition. "It's a farther trek than places like the frostfire forest. And perhaps I wanted to save a few things to discover together once you were fully my mate."

The smile that crosses Talia's lips at that remark, both shy and sly, sends a bolt of desire straight to my groin. What a mate she is. My heart swells so much just looking at her that a tiny edge of fear creeps around the edges of my affection—the thought that it might be too much, that I might be too immersed in her to keep my head straight.

Especially when I might have to say goodbye to her sooner than I ever imagined.

But that's a fear driven by decades of sneers and judging glances, not by anything I truly believe. I simply have to keep reminding myself of that. What could be wrong with appreciating seeing the woman whose soul is twined with mine happy and relaxed for the first time in days, if not weeks? I can't remember the last time she showed this sort of playfulness, we've spent so much of our time together rushing from meeting to curse victim and back again.

Sylas sent a brief message to me before I came to meet Talia at the border that she could use any break I can provide from the responsibilities we fae have heaped on her. I can already tell his instincts were right.

Every part of me initially resisted the idea of sharing Talia's affections, but it's turned out that having other men who care so much for her in our lives benefits our own relationship as well. Now, I'd hate to lose their contributions to her happiness.

But today can be just about us. I took care of all my pressing responsibilities ahead of time, and my coterie can manage any new concerns that come up until my return. Even if another of my people falls victim to the curse, it doesn't take them so quickly that we need to be immediately available.

Talia has given so much of herself to my people, but she should be allowed a life that belongs just to her as well.

With a sweep of my hand, I direct the carriage toward

a tall slope of rock so polished by natural forces that it gleams like marble. Around the other side, the top of the hill plunges into a sheer cliff. I bring the carriage to a stop some twenty feet above the ground where a crevice only a little wider than I am offers passage inside.

Curiosity hums through Talia and into our connection as I help her out of the carriage, which afterward I let sink to the ground where it won't require magic holding it up. She doesn't ask any questions though, knowing I wanted to show her rather than try to explain what we're about to experience with words and memories. Her fingers curl between mine, her gaze roving avidly over the glossy walls of the passage we step into.

"Not many venture out here since it isn't equipped to admit many visitors at once and it's rather distant from any village or other area of interest," I say. "But my father used to like to come out here to compose his thoughts, and as I got older he'd bring me as well. I find it has a way of both settling and lifting the spirits."

A faint melody is already seeping through the passage to our ears. Talia's gait begins to sway in time with it, perhaps without her even being aware of it. Her smile grows—she knows how fond I am of music. But this is more than a collection of lovely sounds.

We step out into a small cavern—about the size of my study in my palace but with a conical ceiling that rises many times higher to a pinprick of sunlight up above. Pointed stalactites of all sizes dangle from the slanted surface around the peak. A breeze winds through them, summoning the lilting notes and casting ripples of bright color across the rock. The hues seem to match the music, fiery reds and yellows when it skips along briskly, cool blues and purples when it smooths into more of a lull.

Talia steps carefully into the center of the space, inhaling with a gasp. "It's beautiful. And I see what you mean about it being calming but also uplifting at the same time. I think I could watch it for hours."

I beam at her. "We can stay here for hours if you'd like. I had Charles and Beth pack us some food, so we won't want for anything."

I spread a cloth over the stone floor that's thin but soft enough to provide a comfortable resting spot, and Talia sits down, still staring up at the dancing hues. A faint sheen of color touches her skin, making her look even more ethereal. After a bit, she lies right down on her back so she can watch the spectacle without straining her neck. I seat myself next to her and let my fingers drift idly over her fanned hair.

A sense of peace descends over me, as if this space is all that exists in the world, no troubles lurking in wait outside. Talia exhales with a shaky sound that stills my hand. With a pinch of concern, I rest my fingers against her temple. "Are you all right?"

"Yes," she said. "I mean, there's still a lot that's not exactly okay, but nothing I need to think about right now. This is a perfect escape."

She says that, but I can tell it isn't perfect because it isn't complete. Awe and delight emanate from her, but threads of tension still wind through them. She hasn't entirely relaxed. Which I suppose isn't unexpected, but I can't help feeling it means I've failed.

But there's more I can offer her, more that could wash those worries from her mind for a short time, isn't there?

I stroke my fingers down her cheek and drink in the giddy tingle that resonates through her body at my touch, skin-to-skin. We're even more attuned to each other's physical and emotional states now that we've confirmed our bond.

As I trail my hand farther down to the curve of her neck and shoulder, desire flickers between us, as much mine as hers. Her gaze slides from the ceiling to me, a hungry gleam shining in her eyes.

And yet something in me balks with a twinge of that earlier fear. We aren't in the privacy of my palace. This place isn't often frequented, but there is a chance that another party could stumble on us here. I've never done more than kiss her where we weren't safely behind a locked door.

Talia peers up at me, taking in my reaction, waiting patiently while I grapple with it. The heat of her longing courses into me, but she won't make any demands of me. If there's anything I know about my mate, it's that she'd never do anything she thought might harm or disturb me —well, unless there were worse consequences for *not* doing it.

I wet my lips, thinking of our interlude with Sylas just a couple of weeks ago. There is something to be said for the passions stirred by taking an unconventional route. What better way could there be to sweep her away from the troubles she hasn't been able to shake?

If someone *should* stumble on us, they'll simply see an

arch-lord honoring his soul-twined mate in every way she deserves. I have nothing to be ashamed of in that.

I dip my hand lower to caress the swell of one of her breasts. Pleasure quivers from her into me, bringing my cock to half-mast before she's so much as touched me. With a murmur that's almost a purr, she arches into my palm as I swivel it over the tip. Her nipple hardens beneath the fabric, her breath already quickening.

It's an intoxicating sequence, generating bliss in her body that travels into me to inflame my own, and then my enjoyment spurring hers onward even more. The blessing of the soul-twined connection is that when we're so in sync, so devoted to each other, every bit of joy and desire the other feels sparks the same in us. It flows between us in a delicious cycle that in moments like these I never want to end.

Talia reaches up to tug on my jacket, and I lean in to claim her waiting lips. Her kiss is hard with longing, and I'm pleased to note that I can no longer sense any stress laced through her emotions. She's totally absorbed in the escape I'm creating for her.

I want to lose myself in her just as much. As I deepen our kiss, I loosen the ties down the front of yet another elegant dress her Seelie friend designed for her, that makes my mate look every bit the arch-lord's lady. Each inch of skin I uncover sends a heady thrill through me.

My fingers brush over the ridges of scar on her shoulder, and I give them the same gentle attention as the rest of her lovely body. She should know the only thing about them I regret is the pain that came with them. As far as I'm concerned, *she's* perfect.

I tug the dress farther down and can't resist lowering my head to kiss my way across her collarbone to her breasts. When I suck the pert peak of one into my mouth, the noise she makes shoots straight to my groin.

My erection is straining against my trousers now, but I'm not going to rush this. We came together so quickly at first with the urgency of our uncertain bond driving us. My beloved is meant to be savored.

Talia's fingers tangle in my hair, twining with the thick curls. The graze of her fingernails over my scalp sends an exquisite quiver through me. I work over one breast and then the other, lingering whenever her breath catches and her chest arches toward me again, until she yanks my lips back to hers.

As our mouths collide, she pulls at my jacket. Before I can finish stripping it off, she's already fumbling with the buttons on my shirt. I toss that aside as well, humming encouragingly as her slender hands trace over the planes of my chest and the true names marked there.

She charts me like a map, her fingers drawing heated lines in contrast with the cave's cool air. I delve my tongue into the sweetness of her mouth, cupping her breast at the same time, and swallow her moan. But as she squirms the rest of the way out of her dress with the help of my urging hands, a shiver travels through her that's not all pleasure.

Her human skin isn't as tolerant of the wintry chill as mine is. Without the warming spell on her clothes, goosebumps are rising over her skin.

Concern flashes through me before I latch onto an easy solution. With a smile, I sit us both up, guiding her onto my lap so she's straddling me in just her panties.

Talia tips toward me, tucking herself close to my body's warmth, but I have more to offer.

The muscles on my back twitch with the release of my wings. I fold them forward around us, forming a sort of cocoon from the thickly-feathered appendages: a bubble of warmth that's all ours. Talia looks around at them and then grins at me with such genuine delight it sends a flutter through my pulse.

I draw her into another kiss, adjusting her against me. Her sex pushes against my rigid cock, and I have to swallow a groan. Not that holding it back can stop my mate from noticing. She kisses me back just as eagerly, rocking her hips at the same time in just the right way to increase that torturous pressure.

Tucking my fingers between her thighs from behind, I stroke them over her slit. The thin layer of cloth that separates us is already damp enough to drive me wild. I bring my hand around in front and delve it right beneath the fabric to tease her skin to skin. At Talia's whimper, I curl my forefinger right inside her.

I love being with you like this, she says in our private way, her inner voice as ragged as her breaths. *I love how you make me feel and tasting how good* you *feel too.*

Her words only stoke the flames of my passion higher. I add a second finger, pulsing them in and out of her, my own breath stuttering at the bliss I can feel coursing through her at my touch. *And what would you like from me next, my soul?* I ask, though the urgent need to be filled is already radiating from her body so strongly I might recognize it even without our bond.

Take me. Make me yours all over again. Show me all that fire you keep inside.

How can I deny a request like that? I wrench down my trousers and then divest her of her panties. Before I can make good on my intention, she reaches between us to grip my shaft. There's no restraining the groan that tumbles out of me as she works her hand up and down my length. She rubs herself against me, spreading her liquid to mingle with mine, and it's all I can do not to ram into her in one swift thrust.

Instead, I position her over me and ease her down inch by wonderful inch. I've been this close with lovers before, but there's nothing like her slickness closing around me in tandem with the heady sensation of fullness that emanates from her. It takes all my self-control not to give over to my most feral urges and drive us both to our peaks as quickly as I can.

Talia leans into me, rocking her hips up and down as I gradually increase my thrusts, welcoming me deeper and deeper. I wrap my wings tighter around her, and she strokes her fingers down the feathers. Her touch sends an electric current through the flesh beneath. A choked sound escapes me, and I pull her mouth to mine.

As our kisses become shakier and our pace more frantic, one of my hands slides around her ass to adjust her angle. Her head tips back with a moan when my cock hits that giddying spot within her channel, but a flash of memory reaches me at the same time: the ecstasy of her caught between two of her Seelie lovers, both inside her at the same time.

I tease my fingers over her other opening, and she

gasps, clutching me harder. *Shall I satisfy that desire too, my mate?* I ask.

Her inner voice comes to me in fragments. *Yes. Oh. That's— so good.*

She starts to clench around my cock. I barely manage to hold the ache in my balls in check until the full tremor races through her body. Her sex clamps around me, and my own release races through me in a surge of molten bliss.

Talia sags against me, still enveloped in my wings, still impaled on my now-softening cock. I hold her there, unwilling to let her go just yet. As I loop my arms around her and tuck my chin against her temple, the thought passes through my mind that I wish I never had to let her go at all.

But I might have to in a nearly permanent way.

I've tried not to dwell on the decision I know my mate is struggling with. I try to shove it away now, but a glimmer of awareness passes from Talia into me. Awareness—and a nervousness that it might not be her choice after all.

I hug her even closer. *You will do what's right for you. And if what's right for you is staying here in the fae realm with us, then I'll fight to the death to defend that choice, even if it's against my own colleagues.*

Her response is a wordless mix of love, gratitude, and sadness that I have to say that at all. Then she dismisses those thoughts for the moment as I did, letting the joy of our intimacy wash the worries away. She nestles closer to me with a sigh that's all satisfaction.

We linger like that for quite a while, until hunger

seeps into Talia's reverie. I bring out the snacks my kitchen staff packed for us, and we enjoy them under the warbling lights above.

It seems we've recovered the peace I hoped to bring Talia here. The whole journey back to Heart's Cadence under the sky darkening toward evening, a gentle smile plays on her lips like the breeze plays with her hair.

I knew we couldn't keep that peace forever, but my stomach knots when I see a messenger step out to meet us as soon as we've drawn up at my palace. I suppose it was too much to ask that we hold onto it for even a few minutes once we're back in the thick of our problems.

As we disembark, the man hustles over. He bobs into a bow. "I'm sorry to call on you so soon after your arrival, Arch-Lord Corwin. It's about Fina—the woman in Stonehaven your lady cured of the curse some weeks ago. The chill has come over her again."

CHAPTER TEN

Talia

"It's been about a month," I say, trying to count back through the weeks in my head as I peer over the side of the carriage, watching for the lights of the flock village to come into view through the night. Focusing on the practical details pushes back a little of the dread that keeps trying to strangle me. "A similar timeline to how often the summer fae need my cure."

Corwin nods, his normally impassive expression grim. "I'd hoped it might last longer for us, but I suppose we're lucky it isn't a shorter time span. Returning to one person is a lot less of an imposition than curing the entire Seelie population."

Of course, the real question is how easily I'll be able to cure Fina a second time.

Zelpha, the member of Corwin's coterie who's warmed up to me the most, gives me a gentle nudge with her muscular shoulder. "You're an old hat at this now. We zip over there, bring her out of the chill, and we'll be back not too long after bedtime."

I guess my worries aren't hard to pick up on even without a soul-twined bond. Her mention of bed makes my jaw twitch with the urge to yawn. Even though Corwin and I spent most of the day away from the bustle of his domain and the pressures of fae politics, I'm already feeling like curling up under a nice warm blanket and not coming out for a day or two.

But this woman needs me. Fina's the first winter fae I ever cured. I wonder how close she is to giving birth. It was her pregnancy that hit me with so much emotion I was brought to tears when I first met her—the thought of failing to save not just her but her unborn and obviously treasured child…

Zelpha's right, though. I know what I'm doing now. There's no reason it shouldn't work exactly the same way the second time.

I pull away from the biting wind and tuck myself against the crystalline windshield, still watching for the lights. The carriage bottom casts a pale glow over the snowy landscape below and just ahead of us. When I make out the edge of the valley that holds Fina's village, relief rushes through me even as my gut twists tighter.

I won't let anyone down. I can do this.

My sense of Corwin through our bond echoes those thoughts with additional reassurance. He directs the carriage down into the valley, and not just a few but many lights gleam into view up ahead. Several beam along a broad terrace at the foot of the lord's castle. The messenger said we're supposed to go there, even though last time I looked after Fina in her own home. Maybe because it was her second affliction, the lord wanted to keep a closer eye on her.

The terrace is wide enough for Corwin to land the carriage right on it. He takes my hand to help me out, and a slim man with hair a mix of mauve and dun brown comes hurrying out to meet us. I catch a murmur of voices trickling from the bright doorway behind him before it swings shut in his wake.

"Good, good, I'm glad you could make it here so quickly, my lord. And my lady." He dips into a bow for both of us, a sign of respect I'm not sure I'll ever be totally used to. With a sweep of his arm, he gestures us toward the castle, which is made out of jagged pinkish-gray stone like a more subdued version of the man's hair.

We walk through a small entry room into a vast space that must be intended for balls and other celebrations. Glowing gems dot the ceiling, filling the room with a hazy light, and beneath it a few dozen fae are gathered. Their conversations fall silent as we enter—they all turn to watch us.

To watch me. Their gazes prickle over my skin, and my chest constricts. It's like when I healed the man in the village common the other day, with most of his flock come to witness it—except that at least was the middle of the day when they might have been out and about anyway.

The lord confirms my suspicion. "Many of my flock wished to wait up to witness your curing. We are honored to have the first Unseelie to have received your blessing among us, Lady Talia, and look forward to seeing Fina twice blessed tonight."

I swallow hard, and Corwin squeezes my hand. *It's all right,* he says. *They're celebrating you and what you can do for us. I'm glad to see them recognizing how special you are.*

I guess that's one way of looking at it. I draw in a deep breath and let the lord usher me across the room to where Fina sits hunched on a large velvet cushion by the room's large hearth. As always with the curse victims, the heat of the flames doesn't appear to be reaching her at all. Her skin has grayed, her lips turned outright blue. Her arms have locked around her belly, which is even more rounded now than before.

It seems her neck has already frozen stiff, because she doesn't turn her head toward me, only managing to cast her gaze in my direction at an awkward angle. Her lips part, but the words she tries to form come out as a mumble.

An ache runs through me from throat to gut. It's worse than last time. Did the curse creep up on her that much longer ago, or has it taken hold so much faster?

The only good thing about her obvious distress is that I don't even need to work to summon tears. They're already welling up behind my eyes. I have to remind myself to turn away from her, to go through the motions of hiding my grief. The burning fills my eyes and seeps down to the back of my mouth.

Why can't I be enough? Why couldn't the curse have left her for good?

I have no answer to those questions, and they don't change what I have to do now. As the first tears trickle down my cheeks, I swipe them away. Our audience stands silent and mostly still, only swaying on their feet a bit as those farther back crane their necks to see. When I raise my head and turn back to Fina, a small gasp reaches my ears.

The winter fae are so unused to overt displays of emotion that my tears on their own are startling.

I walk up to Fina and touch her icy cheek like I did before. "Be well," I say, saying the first words that come to mind. "Both you and your baby."

There's a raspy intake of breath somewhere behind me, and then the warmth I'm waiting for blooms beneath my fingers.

Fina inhales with a shudder. Tentatively, she stretches out her arms and legs as the chill and the stiffness recede.

I move to step back, but she catches my hand. She peers up at me with eyes glistening with what might be a few tears of her own. *I've* never seen a winter fae cry before. I stop, lost for words.

"Thank you," she whispers, her voice still rough from her ordeal. "You've given me four blessings now, two for me and two for my baby. I don't know how to repay that generosity."

"You don't need to repay me," I say quickly. "I'm helping you—and everyone else the curse takes—because I want to. Because I can. I wish I could stop it completely."

Murmurs ripple through the crowd. "Heart bless Lady Talia as she blesses us!" one man calls out. I hear a woman remark in a hushed voice that this is a magic beyond any she's seen before. They all shuffle around, seemingly unwilling to be the first to leave my presence.

It's not so different from the last time, but their reverence doesn't feel any less strange. I'm still just... me, with powers I have no real control over. But I know Corwin is right, that it's better for them to appreciate me like this than for me to keep facing the same suspicion and disrespect they might have shown before.

The kind any other human in this world would face.

Corwin ends the spectacle by placing his hands on my shoulders and raising his voice to carry through the room. "It's late, and my lady needs her rest. We thank you all for paying your respects!"

The lord shoos his flock-folk off and ushers us back to our carriage. Even he stares at me a little wide-eyed as I clamber back into the vehicle. "It is a wonder to witness what you offer, but I hope we won't have need to call on you again," he says.

I bob my head in acknowledgment. "If you do need me, don't hesitate to send a message. I'll want to come."

But as I sink into the bench at the bow of the carriage with Corwin and Zelpha on either side of me, his statement starts to weigh on me. Corwin glances at me here and there as he focuses on navigating out the valley, but he doesn't push for me to open up.

Zelpha doesn't have the same qualms. She twists the tip of her loose braid around her forefinger and studies me. "What's eating at you, Talia?"

The fact that *she's* not overtly awed by me somehow makes it easier to open up. I rub my mouth. "I was just thinking—if the curse comes back every few weeks, and it keeps striking new people as well... This isn't like the Seelie curse where I just need to give my blood once a month and the fae can distribute it among themselves. I have to be with each Unseelie victim. Within a few months, I might need to be visiting someone every day. And after that…"

In a year, will all my time be taken up with traveling from one flock to another to heal those either newly cursed or succumbing for a second time—or a third, fourth, fifth time for that matter? How could the arch-lords really think that it'd work for them to bring all those fae to me in the human world? They'd be making the trip constantly.

My colleagues weren't aware of the exact timelines when they made that suggestion, Corwin says, sensing my thoughts. *But if you wished to remain with your brother for that long, we'd find a way to work around it.*

Out loud, he adds, "Now that we know how the cure works, and that the curse will return and the requests on your presence will multiply, we can start asking that the victims be brought to the border castle for you to work your cure on them there rather than us going to them."

That will make it easier. But it still means I'll essentially be on call every day at every hour someone might turn up. Especially if the curse continues to take hold faster and faster.

I press the heel of my hand to my temple and risk saying the words I know will cast a shadow over all the good we've done. "It won't be sustainable. Maybe for a few years, but eventually—" Eventually it'll be dozens a day. Will I even be able to summon that many tears over and over again?

Corwin and Zelpha exchange a look. Zelpha's mouth slants into a wry smile. "Well, we always knew your cure couldn't sustain us forever, right? This is a stopgap measure until we can find a more permanent solution."

"And hopefully we'll strike on that before the situation becomes overwhelming," Corwin says.

I touch the bronze bracelet Sylas gave me, thinking of the prediction Nuldar the sage gave him. The solution might be coming soon... whatever that means in fae terms. Nothing about this situation has been simple so far, though, so I'm not going to count on the next developments being any different.

What can I do about the problem now anyway? Fretting doesn't help anyone, least of all me.

When Corwin sits down on the bench next to me, I tuck myself under his arm and try to think about nothing but how lucky I am in so many other ways.

I doze for a bit during the trip back, and Corwin leaves me at my bedroom with a lingering kiss good night. But after I've washed up, I find I'm keyed up all over again. And hungry. We grabbed something to eat on the journey to Fina, but I didn't have a proper dinner.

I slip through the halls and limp into the kitchen, planning to put together a quick midnight snack. To my surprise, Beth is still there, eyeing several spice containers she's set in a row on the counter in front of her.

She startles at my entrance and then giggles, a blush coloring her cheeks. She hasn't seemed to know exactly how to relate to me after finding out I'm both human like her and not like her at all with the powers I can wield.

Seeing her reminds me of my earlier thoughts about how the fae treat most of their human and somewhat human companions. "What are you doing?" I ask as I grab a loaf of bread to cut off a slice.

Beth lets out another giggle and tugs an errant curl back from her face. "I want to come up with better flavoring for the moss-shoots. I feel like they're missing just a little something the way we prepare them now. I've been trying different combinations, just tasting them, to see if I can figure out the right one, but it hasn't really worked so far." She frowns at the spice containers.

I consider her as I spread a little butter and some preserved fruit on my bread. I carry the snack over to the island and perch on the stool across from her. "You really like doing this, don't you?" I ask. "Working in the kitchen for Corwin and everything?"

Beth shrugs, looking self-conscious all over again. "Yeah. It's kind of fun. Dad says they never had ingredients anything like we've got to work with back where he came from. And it's not like it's all work-work-work. I've gotten to see some pretty spectacular things."

I hesitate, not sure the question will come out right, and then push myself onward. "Corwin's very… kind with his human servants. I've gotten the impression that's not really the case with a lot of the fae lords. I'm not sure if you talk much with the staff in other domains or anything. Have you heard about anything—like people being mistreated or overworked?"

Beth freezes in place and drops her gaze. "I mean, Dad does say we're lucky to be in Heart's Cadence. I have heard a few things. But I don't know for sure—I mean, people might exaggerate or whatever. I wouldn't want to accuse any lords of anything."

Of course not. "I wouldn't want you to either," I assure her quickly. "I just… I've been thinking that because of what I can do, I've been able to get more recognition than humans normally do in this world. Maybe I can use that to help out other people who've ended up here. I think we all deserve some happiness."

Beth shivers. "There are definitely some people around the Heart who don't get a chance to be happy much at all." Then her gaze darts to me. "You won't tell any of the arch-lords I said that?"

"You don't have to worry," I say. But my hunger has been swallowed by a heavy lump in my stomach.

I told myself I needed to find out more about how Jamie's coping before I decided how much he needs me. How can I even think about abandoning this world without figuring out exactly what my fellow humans here are facing too?

CHAPTER ELEVEN

August

Seeing the border castle almost complete fills me with exhilaration. I can't keep the smile off my face as I move around the new kitchen—fully wood and on our side, as I requested—adding the last touches to the equipment. Talia watches me from a stool she's already made her own, perched there with her malformed foot dangling. She seems content just to watch me in silence.

But when I lean back against the counter to take in my work with a satisfied air, she straightens up on her seat. "August… Could I ask you about something it might be hard for you to talk about?"

Something catches in my chest that she even feels she needs to check first. I turn toward her. "Of course, Sweetness. Anything." We're in this together—all five of us now—and that means no secrets, no shying away from difficult conversations. And I know Talia would never bring up a potentially painful subject unless she believed it was important.

She looks down at her hands before meeting my eyes again. "It's just—I've started wondering about the other humans who are stuck here in the fae world. I know a few of them are here at least sort of by choice… Corwin would let any of his human servants go back to the human world if they asked… but from what I've heard, that's pretty rare. Obviously a lot of the fae I've had to deal with haven't seen me as anywhere near an equal."

"They're getting there," I say, sidling closer to take her hand. "As they see just how much you can do—"

She shakes her head. "It shouldn't matter how much I can *do*. Or any of the others. Just because they don't have magic, that doesn't mean they shouldn't get any say in what happens in their lives."

The anguish in her voice makes my heart ache. "Is this about your brother? I can tell you that the summer arch-lords have accepted that he can't help with the curse, and they won't push to bring him here anymore. If the Unseelie are still making demands, we'll deal with them."

"It's not really that either. Though I guess it's part of the same problem." Talia lowers her head, a few strands of her hair falling across her face. "I've barely been around other humans since I came to the fae realm, after being so isolated with Aerik and then Sylas not having any on his staff. But lots of the other packs have human servants, don't they? Their lives matter too."

She pauses, and I wait for her to decide where she's going with this topic. Her fingers tighten around mine. "You told me about how easily your father killed your mother when you were a kid. Was that how he treated all the humans in his domain? Like their lives didn't mean anything at *all*, and the only thing that mattered was what he felt like doing with them? Do *most* of the fae see us as that worthless?"

Now I understand why she hesitated to get into this subject. The memory of my mother's murder makes my stomach turn even now, hundreds of years later. But it's a reasonable question, one I might even have prompted with the things I've told Talia in the past. My early hesitations about taking Talia as a mate seem incredibly distant now that she's become so entwined in my life, but there was a time when I was wary of even how *I* might end up treating her.

I release her hand to stroke my fingers down her back. "Honestly, I don't completely know. As you can obviously tell, there are other fae like Aerik and Kellan who see humans as not much more than easy prey. But even when we did have human servants at Hearthshire, Sylas made sure that they were well cared for. I remember there was one woman who became pretty miserable, and he had her taken back. Donovan seems considerate in his treatment of his own servants."

I stop, frowning as I try to come up with a better answer. Finally, I have to admit, "I'm not sure which is more common. Even in Thundervale under my father, I didn't pay all that much attention to how any of the staff were treated other than my mother. And he's harsh to the fae who serve him too. I'd like to say he's one of the worst, that most are kinder..."

"But it could be that's how it goes in a lot of other packs too," Talia fills in.

I grimace. "Yes." Guilt twists through my gut, loosening only when a flicker of inspiration hits me. "Do you want to get a better idea with your own eyes? We could visit some of the nearby domains and ask to speak with the human servants... I wouldn't bother the arch-lords unnecessarily, but any of the lesser lords will kind of have to welcome an arch-lord's cadre-chosen." I smile a little slyly.

To my relief Talia smiles back. "I'd like that. I feel like I kind of owe it to the other humans here to speak up for them while *I'm* here, since some of the fae are starting to respect me more."

What a perfectly Talia thing to say. I press a kiss to her temple before she hops off the stool. "You're already doing so much, Sweetness. You don't need to take on more crusades."

Her expression turns serious. "But how can I spend all this time trying to heal the fae without doing anything for all the people like me who've ended up trapped here, maybe not much better off than I was in Aerik's cage? At least the fae are looking out for each other. The humans in this world... if I don't do anything, they have no one."

I can't argue that point. The fact that I hadn't considered it before myself brings back a pang of my earlier guilt.

I motion for her to follow me out of the kitchen. "Sylas hasn't given me any duties for the morning. We could pay a call on the domain that borders ours just beyond the Heart's hill right now if you'd like."

Talia heads for the door with a bit of a skip in her uneven steps. "Yes, please."

I don't have the carriage-summoning magic myself, so I direct her to the stable to pick out the steadiest horse we have. If I were traveling alone, I might simply shift, but arriving to request a favor with a woman riding on my wolfish back doesn't seem like the most dignified approach, as much fun as it might be otherwise.

Fae horses aren't exactly calm in temperament most of the time, but I pick out one I trust not to test the reins too much and scoop Talia up so she's perched between my legs on the saddle. Thankfully, the skirt of her dress is loose enough that it only rides up to her knees. I wrap one arm around her waist to secure her. "Comfortable?"

She laughs, settling closer against me in a way that sends a pulse of heat through my groin. "I'm not sure I'd want to try this for a long trip, but for a short one it should be just fine."

I can't resist nipping the crook of her neck. Then I guide the horse toward the path that leads from our domain down the broad hill around the Heart.

For the first several minutes, cantering along with my love nestled against me and the sun beaming down on us through the trees, it's a pretty enjoyable excursion. But as we reach the bottom of the slope and head on toward the border of the nearest neighboring domain, thoughts of the grim purpose of our visit rise back to the surface.

I don't actually know what we'll find here. Will it make Talia trust the fae even less? Make returning to the human world seem like a better option, no matter how much she cares for the few of us who've treated her well?

I swallow down those worries and focus on presenting an authoritative front for addressing the lady who rules this pack.

The sparse but vibrant forest we've been riding through falls away completely, and the castle comes into view up ahead. The lady must have a particular affinity for plant-life, because the tall, rippling structure looks as if it's been created out of a mass of intertwined vines. The houses of the pack village look similarly woven, nearly blending into the grassy plain they've sprouted from.

Several members of the pack are out and about, tending to gardens or working their various crafts. At our arrival, a man polishing a bronze platter looks up and then stands. "Hey, there. What brings you to Petalrise?" His gaze moves to Talia, and he pauses. "You've come from Hearth-by-the-Heart?"

"We have," I say, helping Talia to the ground and then dismounting. "I'm from Arch-Lord Sylas's cadre. Our companion wished to speak with your lady about some of the workings of her domain, if she's present."

Won't it be sweet when I can call Talia my mate as Corwin does? Although if some of our brethren have their way, that day will never come.

Two attendants have already headed our way from the castle. One reaches for the horse's reins. "I'll see your steed to the stable. Lady Gullven will attend to you shortly."

The other attendant leads us into the castle. The rooms inside are filled with a greenish-gold light and a scent like newly grown leaves.

I've only had a few minutes to worry that the lady of the pack might find our visit a big imposition after all when she sweeps into the room and dips into a slight bow. I have to catch myself on the verge to bowing to *her*, still not totally used to the respects now paid to me as part of an arch-lord's cadre. Despite only being cadre-chosen, I'm now on a slightly higher level of authority than any regular lord or lady.

"What can I do for you, honored guests?" she asks.

I don't like the way her attention lingers on Talia with a slight furrow in her brow. I set my hand on Talia's shoulder. I can give her a proper title with her connection to Corwin, at least. "Lady Talia would like to learn more about the other humans living among us fae. I was hoping you'd give us permission to speak with whatever human servants you currently employ."

Employ isn't really the right word for it, since as Talia rightly pointed out, the humans in question won't have had much choice about making the journey to our world. They aren't being compensated for their work either. But I don't think saying "enslave" would encourage Gullven to agree.

More skepticism shows in her expression, but she nods. "I don't think they're so busy that it should be a problem. You can stay here in the sitting room, and I'll have them brought to you. And one of my staff will see about refreshments as well. I have another matter to attend to, but if you should have need of me, just send word."

"We appreciate it," Talia speaks up, her voice soft but confident in a way that makes my chest swell with pride. She really is finding her footing as a lady in her own right, regardless of what any of my fellow fae might think of her heritage.

Gullven slips away, and a few minutes later a young fae woman arrives with a tray of duskapple wine and pastries I can tell just on sight are a little under-baked. Talia nibbles at one as we wait for the human servants to arrive. "Not as good as yours," she murmurs to me with a hint of mischief in her voice.

Finally, another fae staff member appears, ushering four other figures into the room. There are two men and two women, all dressed in fae clothes that look a little rougher than what any of the fae staff we've seen have.

They come to a stop in the middle of the room, and the fae man gestures to us. "These are our guests," he tells the servants. "They would like to speak with you. Please answer their questions."

He steps back to the far wall to watch. One of the men stands still with obvious wariness in his stance, but the other man and both of the women gaze around them with vague bemused expressions I recognize in an instant. I'm so used to that demeanor that it didn't even occur to me to mention it when I was talking with Talia about the humans here.

"Why do they look so out of it?" Talia asks. Any cheerfulness in her mood has snuffed out at the sight of them.

"Their meals will include a regular dose of some kind of faerie drug," I say, my spirits sinking. "There are a few that have a calming and mildly euphoric effect. It helps keep them happy."

Talia shivers. "Because otherwise they'd be upset about being stolen from their homes."

The fae man speaks up hastily. "We only bring over those who've joined in our revels in the human lands. They come to us of their own accord."

Talia fixes her eyes on him. "But they can't know when they join a revel that they're giving their whole lives away. And it isn't exactly their 'own accord' when there's fae magic involved."

The man's gaze darts from her to me and back again, as if he's not sure who he should be addressing or how much he should even say. "It's how we've always done things," he says haltingly. "We see that they have everything they need."

Food and clothing and an occasional bath, he means. Talia doesn't need to speak for me to know what she'd be thinking—they're tended to much like our pack-kin Elliot tends to his sheep.

Talia's mouth has tightened, but she walks up to the row of figures, starting with the one at the farthest right. The woman's glazed eyes settle on her without any change in her vague expression.

"What work do you do in the castle?" Talia asks, her voice heart-wrenchingly gentle.

"I keep the kitchen clean," the woman says in a flat voice. "All the surfaces shining. That's what they ask, and that's what I do."

"And when the kitchen's already clean?"

The woman blinks as if she doesn't understand the question. "There's always something else that needs to be wiped down or polished. So much cooking and baking. When it's done for the night, then I sleep."

Talia's hands clench at her sides. I don't know whether I want more to yank her away from this confrontation or rage at the fae who've taken these humans. Neither is really an option.

She moves down the line, talking to a man who spends his days cleaning and mending clothes for the other servants and staff—because I'd imagine Lady Gullven sees that job as a waste of the Heart's magic—and the other woman, who alternates between fishing in a nearby lake and looking after the castle's garden. Scars from the hooks and lures she uses mottle her fingers.

She also has a bruise on her cheek. When Talia asks her about that, she raises her hand to it and only says, without a hint of emotion, "I wasn't listening well enough."

I wince inwardly.

When Talia reaches the one man who appears to still have his wits, his posture tenses even more than before. She studies him for a moment. "They don't make you take the faerie drugs."

"No," he says. "It would interfere with the work Lady Gullven expects me to do."

"And what's that?"

His jaw flexes. He might not be in the grips of a drug-induced haze, but I'm sure he's discovered the consequences of saying anything critical of his "employers."

He draws in a rough breath. "I'm an artist. I paint for

her. Some of them she keeps; some I think she uses as gifts or similar purposes."

Talia seems to weigh her next words carefully. "You don't look all that happy about it. Did you *want* to come here? Why have you stayed?"

His mouth twists into a wry grimace. "I had a gallery, back home. Lady Gullven happened to wander into it one day—I'm not sure how she ended up there. She must have liked my style, because she invited me to come paint for her. She showed me how she could make the images I created come alive with magic, all the effects I could incorporate with the enchanted supplies she could give me... I made a deal with her. I don't think I totally understood—I can't go home until I've fulfilled it."

"What would fulfill it?" Talia asks.

"That's at Lady Gullven's discretion."

I'm familiar with those kinds of bargains. It's a common fae trick to stealthily make the terms dependent on their approval in a way that works in their favor, so they get to decide when the deal is over no matter what the other party does. Not a single one who extends an offer like that doesn't recognize that they're exploiting the person on the other end. They simply don't care.

Talia asks a few more questions of each of the servants and then tells the fae man that she doesn't want to bother them anymore. As we walk out to the stables, her face stays pensive. I long to reach for her, but I doubt there's any way to comfort her distress away.

And it's not just distress. I can see the determination forming behind her eyes at the same time. My chest tightens with unspoken thoughts.

I was afraid that seeing the way many of the fae treat her kind might drive her away. Maybe the real problem is the opposite. Now she has yet another cause she'll feel she has to champion, another duty weighing down on her… when she might be better off if we'd let *her* go home after all, away from the pressures and dangers of our world.

Am I showing my love by fighting to have her stay here, or would a truly loving mate be encouraging the opposite?

CHAPTER TWELVE

Talia

"There," Harper says, looking down at me with her hands on her hips. "You're not to move from that spot for at least an hour." She sets her slim frame down next to me on the grass with typical fae grace.

She led me out to this knoll overlooking the Shimmering Falls in Donovan's domain insisting that we needed a chance to talk after I've spent so much time running back and forth between the realms. I'm starting to think the walk was less a friendly excursion and more an intervention. Both my friends and my lovers seem to be dragging me away to some restful spot pretty often these days… I'm obviously not hiding the tension coiled inside me as well as I'd like to.

I lean back on my hands, letting myself take a moment to enjoy the soft grass beneath my palms and the faint, warm spray of the waterfall that reaches us even here. The rhythmic warble of the falling water soothes my nerves. And it occurs to me that I haven't just hung out and chatted with my closest fae friend since I found out about Jamie.

I make an apologetic face at Harper. "I'm sorry I haven't been around much lately. There've just been so many things going on…"

She waves off my apology. "I know. I'm not going to complain when you're running around taking care of so much and all I've got to do is keep making my dresses." She pauses and shoots a grin at me. "I got some ideas from the winter fae dresses you've brought back. I think I can combine elements of both styles to make some really striking designs."

Her enthusiasm is so infectious that it's easy to smile back. "I can't wait to see them."

"Oh, you'll probably be my first model for them after myself." She tucks her sleek blond hair behind her ears and peers out over the landscape ahead of us. Her next words come out more hesitant. "Is it true that you're thinking of going back to the human world? Like, to live there instead of here?"

I bite my lip, not sure what to say. Harper *is* my closest friend here, and I'm also hers. She's the only person who was born into Sylas's pack after they were banished a century ago. All her pack-kin are decades if not centuries older than her. I might be only twenty-one, but comparatively, from what I've gathered, that puts us at about the same point in our life-spans. And like her, I've spent most of my time in the fae world isolated and unsure of my place.

But now that the pack has risen to the most

prominent position possible, I'm sure she'll make more friends among the other packs. Friends who'll have more in common with her than I do. Friends who won't age so much faster than she will. She'll be fine no matter what I choose.

"I'm not sure what I'm going to do yet," I say. "My brother's still having a bit of a hard time of it. It's just tricky to know whether me turning up out of the blue will really make things better for him or just confuse him. I have no idea how I'd even explain where I've been all this time." I rub my forehead.

Harper nods. "I understand why you'd want to help him. You basically always want to help everyone, and he's family on top of that. I wish our worlds weren't so far apart. It's not like with the winter realm where you can step across the border and be home in just a few minutes."

"Soon I'm going to have a home that's right there on the border." Sylas's pack and Corwin's flock were just putting the final touches on the joint castle this morning.

Will my lovers continue their alliance even if I'm gone for… however long I'd feel I need to be gone for? Corwin would wait for me—I know that for sure. He isn't going to find another soul-twined mate, as unfair as that might be to him. Sylas, August, and Whitt would wait for me too if I asked them. Somehow that knowledge reassures me and gnaws at me at the same time.

No matter what I do, it's definitely going to be unfair to *someone*. Maybe including me.

But the point of this excursion is to relax, not worry about all that. I slip off my boots and wiggle my toes in the grass. "Have you gotten any new customers for your dresses? I thought I saw one of Donovan's cadre-chosen wearing something in your style when some of them joined Whitt's last revel."

Harper giggles, a blush I don't totally understand coloring her cheeks. Does she think I'll be offended that she's making clothes for people other than me? "Yes, I got a few requests from the other arch-lords' packs. My goal is to see a ball where more than half of the ladies are wearing dresses I designed. I hope there's another one soon! Perhaps Arch-Lord Sylas will host one to celebrate the border castle."

"I think that would be a great idea. I'll mention it to him, since he's probably more focused on logistics and making sure the summer and winter fae don't go for each other's throats."

Harper giggles again, more openly this time, but there's still an odd gleam in her eyes as she glances at me. "He's really going to make you officially his mate, isn't he? And Whitt and August too. Four mates! I can't even imagine."

I laugh, my own cheeks heating. "I hardly can either most of the time. I definitely didn't plan for it to happen that way. And it's been complicated with the soul-twined bond and everything. I just hope the other arch-lords come around to accepting it." It isn't as if I'll be in their lives all that long by fae standards anyway, even if I stay here.

"They'll just have to," Harper says matter-of-factly. "It's what the Heart and your hearts want." Then she pauses with an air as if she's deciding whether to say something else. She looks down at her hands, which are fidgeting with a flower she's plucked. "When you felt the soul-twined bond with Corwin… They always say you know right away, the first time you see each other. Was it like that for you even though you're not—I mean, even though you're human?"

The moment when the bond seared through me is burned into my memory. "Yeah. The winter arch-lords had come to see Sylas as the new summer arch-lord during his coronation celebration. I'd never seen them before then. The first moment my gaze locked with Corwin's, I felt it. You definitely couldn't miss it."

I glance at her, a suspicion tickling at the edges of my mind. Why would she be wondering about that? "Is there someone you'd want to spark a soul-twined bond with?"

The bashful way Harper ducks her head confirms my guess before she even speaks. "I know it's silly. You're obviously a special case. No fae who isn't true-blooded ever had a soul-twined mate that we know of. But I just—it's a nice hope, right? It's *possible* even if not very likely. Of course, if the whole eyes meeting thing has already happened and nothing was there, I guess there isn't any possibility at all." She tosses the flower away.

If she's that concerned about it, I have to think the man she's interested in is true-blooded, or it wouldn't make any sense to be worrying about being his soul-twined mate. They could just become regular mates.

The trouble for her would be that, from what I understand, every true-blooded fae ends up forming a soul-twined bond eventually. They might strike up other relationships in the meantime—or sometimes even at the same time—but that one deep connection is always going to come first. And not being true-blooded herself, Harper couldn't be that one.

"Do you want to talk about it?" I ask tentatively.

My friend shakes her head quickly. "No. It's silly, honestly. I shouldn't even be thinking about it."

"I'm sure you'll have lots of chances to meet other potential mates as Sylas gets more settled in as arch-lord and starts hosting more events," I say, even though I know that comment wouldn't comfort me in the same position. There are millions of unattached human men back in the world that used to be my home, but that fact won't stop me from missing my fae lovers terribly if I have to leave them.

Before that melancholy thought can take hold any further, Corwin's voice carries abruptly through our bond. *I'm sorry to interrupt you when you're taking some time for yourself, beloved, but one of the flocks has brought a new cursed victim to Heart's Cadence for you to "bless," as they put it now. You don't need to come over immediately, but as soon as you've finished your visit with your friend…*

No, I'll come right away, I reply, despite—or maybe because of—the heaviness that wraps around my heart. *I won't be able to enjoy just sitting here chatting if I know someone's suffering while they wait for me.*

I pull my boots on and stand up. "I'm sorry. It hasn't been even an hour yet, but Corwin's just told me there's another winter fae hit by the curse. They're waiting in his domain for me to heal them."

"Of course." Harper scrambles up. "We'll have lots more time to talk later."

Will we? I don't voice that question out loud.

We hurry back across the forested terrain as quickly as my warped foot will allow. By the time we've passed Donovan's castle and the Bastion has come into sight, my foot is throbbing, and I'm wishing we brought a carriage or a horse.

That thought must travel to Corwin, because a second later he's telling me, *Stay where you are and give your foot a chance to recover. I'll come the rest of the way to you.*

It's all right, I try to say, but I can tell he isn't going to listen. He's already grabbing one of the carriages he keeps waiting in case someone needs one quickly.

Harper waits with me until he arrives. It's a bizarre sight, watching the pale, narrow vehicle with its crystalline features gliding through the vibrant summer landscape. Several Seelie outside of Donovan's castle stop to stare.

I scramble in with Corwin's helping hand and turn back to Harper. "Will you tell Sylas or one of his cadre-chosen where I've gone?"

She bobs her head, but Corwin interjects. "I've already talked to Whitt myself. We just finished the last essential pieces of the border castle." A soft smile touches his lips. "It's ready to be inhabited now. Not quite so much rushing back and forth from here on, I hope."

Knowing that buoys my spirits until we come up on the haze of the border. "I'm glad that they brought the latest victim to us instead of us having to travel across the realm," Corwin says. "But... it's a little more than I expected."

I tear my eyes away from the spectacle of the wooden end of the joint castle protruding from the fog and look at him. "More how?"

He hesitates, with an impression of awkwardness he can't hide from me. "You'll see. It isn't anything *bad*, just... You know how it's been the last couple of times."

I do, but somehow I'm still not prepared for us to emerge from the haze to find not just the curse victim and a few helpers but maybe three dozen figures gathered by the glow of the Heart. Maybe they think my power will work even better if I'm closer to it? But all these people...

How far did they come? I ask Corwin as we clamber out of the carriage and go to meet them.

A few hours' journey, Corwin says in a bemused tone. *That's at least a third of the flock, including a couple of their lord's coterie members. They weren't able to make it to our confirmation ceremony. They say they wanted to support their flock-fellow, but it's clear they're just as eager to see you work your cure with their own eyes.*

My "blessing," as they're calling it now. An uneasy itch travels over my skin.

I have to remember that it's a good thing the winter fae are so impressed with me now. Ever since August and I left Lady Gullven's domain, I've been wondering what I can do for the other humans on both sides of the border— and also those associated with them through birth, like Kesral, if that's possible. If they care so much about what I can do for them, will they care at least a little about what I have to say as well?

As Corwin ushers me over to where a fae man hunches right in front of the Heart's pulsing glow, I see other figures drifting toward us from Laoni's and Uzziah's castles. Noticing the commotion and coming to discover what it's about, presumably. It'd be hard to miss this gathering.

Excited murmurs carry through the crowd. "There she is!"

"Lady Talia is with us!"

"She came so swiftly."

I drag in a breath and give them all the best smile I can summon. The awed faces gaze back at me, some beaming in return, others more cautious. A woman I'm guessing is the cursed man's mate squeezes his shoulder, watching me too.

"It only struck him this morning," she says. "Whatever you can do for him, my lady…"

The man coughs out a croaked voice. "I'm honored to accept your blessing, Lady Talia."

Seeing them together, a lump is already rising in my throat. Turning away, I think of both them and me—of that woman losing her mate to the curse when she should have had so many more years with him, of me possibly leaving behind the men I've come to love so much.

As tears prick at the backs of my eyes, I sense Corwin's urge to reach out to me, but he knows I have to draw on whatever sadness I can to perform the cure.

When I picture the woman clinging to the man's frozen form if the curse completely takes hold, the tears begin to trickle out. I wipe them away and turn to face him. The motions come to me more confidently now that I've seen them work several times.

I can do this. The Heart has given me this power. It *wants* me to push back the curse. And maybe to accomplish other things too, that I don't fully understand yet.

As I stroke my fingers across the man's cheek, the fae

gathered around us lean closer. There's a sense of a collective breath held. Then, as he shudders and starts to shake off the chill, that breath bursts into pleased gasps and sighs of relief.

"The blessed one!" someone calls out. "Thank the Heart for Lady Talia!"

At the voices echoing the same sentiment, I gather myself, gazing out over the small crowd. I can tell Corwin has picked up on my intention, but he doesn't dissuade me, offering a nudge of encouragement instead. His motion of support gives me the courage to speak up.

"I'm so glad that I can help all of the fae with the powers the Heart has given me, even though I'm a human," I say. "I hope that it helps you all see that the Heart can shine on humans just as well as the fae. It would make my own heart rest easier if I knew that you'll go back to your lives thinking better of the humans who've ended up in the fae realm—treating them with the same kindness and respect you'd offer me."

I get several nods from the gathered fae and some more called words of praise, but I have no idea how much they're just giving the appearance of being agreeable versus actually listening. It isn't as if I could change the entire culture around the fae treatment of humans in one day. Those words are a start though, even if it's a small one.

The fae from the curse victim's flock linger a while longer, many of them coming up to me to ask for a brief touch as its own sort of blessing, others just seeming to want a closer look. The cursed man bows in gratitude, and his mate bows even lower. "Thank you so much," she says, sounding a little choked up, which is startling from an Unseelie.

As they drift back toward the carriages they arrived on, Laoni and a couple of members of her coterie weave through the crowd to reach us. The dark expression on the arch-lord's face puts me immediately on guard, and Corwin tenses too.

"Meet us in the Hall of the Heart in one hour," she demands. "Both of you. It's time decisions were made."

Why is she upset? I ask Corwin as she strides off without waiting for an answer.

I'm not sure, he replies, but the realization is already rising up in me.

This is the first time any of the other arch-lords has seen how their people are responding to me now—how they're acting like I'm some kind of holy savior. And I don't think Laoni is happy about that development at all.

Talia

I've seen the Hall of the Heart many times through Corwin's eyes, but this is only my second time entering it. The high ceiling and the gleaming white marble all around take my breath away for a second. Seeing the stern expressions three of the arch-lords waiting for us are wearing, it's hard to catch it again.

I can't think of any valid reason they could have to complain about your behavior, Corwin reassures me as we walk together to his spot at the long marble table. *If you're uncertain of how to respond to anything they say, let me take the lead.*

I nod inwardly, although I hate letting anyone else fight my battles. Sometimes I need it—I know I can't face off with fae in every possible way on my own—but they're *never* going to respect me if they don't see me standing up for myself however I actually can.

Neve offers us a soft, dreamy smile. The others just eye us silently until we come to a stop at the table.

Laoni clears her throat, but Corwin jumps in before she can speak. "What is this about? What decisions were you talking about, Laoni?"

She glowers at him. "What do you think? Your mate has had quite a while to think on our proposal for her return to her own world. We would like to see that matter settled before it becomes any more fraught."

Fraught because the rest of the winter fae might protest me leaving their world now that they're becoming so impressed by me? Somehow I suspect Laoni is thinking more about ending whatever influence I might be gaining among her people than about how they'll feel about my absence.

"I didn't know there was a time limit on deciding," I say, keeping my voice as steady as possible. "There's more I want to understand about both worlds before I'm sure which would do the most good—not for me but for everyone involved."

Uzziah lets out a faint cough. "An honorable sentiment, but it does bring into question your motivations."

I sense Corwin bristling, though he doesn't show it other than in a slight terseness that creeps into his voice. "What exactly do you mean by that? Talia's 'motivations' have been nothing but pure. She's been selflessly helping us in a way none of us have been able to accomplish for weeks now."

"It may appear selfless, but who's to say the human isn't gaining something from it as well?" Laoni says archly.

"She *can* lie after all, unlike the rest of us. Why else would she be so hesitant to do what's right for her family and for the brother she should owe the most loyalty to?"

Terisse's mouth twitches with a hint of discomfort, but she speaks up too. "Yes, how can we be so sure of her loyalty to us or even you if she'd abandon one of her own blood so easily?"

Guilt jabs through my stomach. "I haven't *abandoned* my brother," I retort. "I don't even know if suddenly jumping back into his life would be better for him than staying out of it. The situation isn't that simple."

Laoni studies me. "Or are you saying that because you don't want us to question why you're so intent on staying among us?"

I grit my teeth, but I'm not sure how to answer. "If I stay, it'll be because I can't stand the thought that people might end up suffering more without me right here to help with the curse." And because of all the suffering I might be able to save the other humans here from, though I don't think she'll want to hear about that. "And because I'm trying not to upend Jamie's life all over again."

Laoni folds her arms over her chest. "Take another day, then. I want us to be able to come up with a definite plan of action for handling our curse victims by then. We've been living in uncertainty long enough."

I'm not usually a violent person, but right then I'd like nothing more than to punch her right in her smug face. My fingers curl into my palms, but I hold my hands still at my sides. "Fine," I say. Corwin sets his hand on my back, and we walk back out of the building.

You don't need to agree to their demands, he says as we

go. *We can insist on more time. We've been living in uncertainty for decades before now.*

I pause, but I can't ignore the constricting sensation in my chest that's been growing tighter since the first moment I found out Jamie was alive. *No. I think I do need to make a decision, not just for them but for me too. I'm not really getting any closer to an answer with all my fretting about it. I'd like to visit Jamie one more time before I'm sure, though.*

I'll make arrangements so that you can travel to the human world first thing in the morning. Corwin's hand moves to grasp my hand. *They were only trying to push their own agenda with their comments, you know. I have no doubts about your loyalty. I know how much you care about your brother.*

I squeeze his hand in return, but his reassurance doesn't erase the guilt still prickling through my gut. Laoni and the others might have been trying to shame me for their own reasons, but that doesn't mean their points were totally wrong. I *do* owe Jamie more than I owe anyone here in the fae realm, don't I? I should be able to find a way to help him when he's obviously struggling, even if it's hard at first.

Tomorrow I'll see him again, and hopefully it'll all become clearer.

"Sylas and the others should be waiting for us in your new home," Corwin reminds me as we set off across the icy fields toward his domain. "I could ask Charles and Beth to come over from the palace and make us all one of their fantastic dinners."

My insides are too tangled up for me to enjoy the thought of putting food inside me. I shake my head. "Not right now. I think I just want to be with all of you for a while, without anyone else there, without anything we're supposed to be doing."

The memory rises up of the time when I felt at my most despondent last month, when the answer to the winter curse was eluding me and I seemed to be failing everyone. I brought Corwin into my bed, and just cuddling against him melted some of my anguish.

Everything we did together *after* cuddling didn't hurt either…

I want to have all my lovers—my mates—around me, to be enveloped in their love. To see just how far we've come… even if we won't take our relationship any further after all.

Corwin takes in my emotions wordlessly. When we step over the threshold on the diamond side of the border castle, he sweeps me off my feet as August likes to do and tucks me against him.

As he heads through the halls to the central rooms where crystal and wood merge, my Seelie lovers emerge from their side of the castle to meet us. Sylas takes in our expressions and frowns.

"My colleagues have been especially hard on our mate today," Corwin says, his use of *our* setting off a glow of warmth inside me just like that. "I think the cure she needs is to be wrapped up in as much adoration as possible."

August's expression also turned solemn when he saw

Corwin carrying me, but at that last remark, a grin springs to his face. "I'm all for that."

Whitt arches his eyebrows. "Let's break in that new bedroom of yours, mighty one."

A blush heats my cheeks even though I'm not sure just how thoroughly I want to break in the bedroom right at this moment. "That sounds perfect to me."

As we head up the stairs with their alternating wooden and diamond steps, Sylas draws up beside Corwin and me. "Should we be concerned about your colleagues' current demands, whatever they are?" he asks.

"No," I answer for Corwin. "Mostly they just want me to make a decision before much longer about whether I'm staying here or going back to Jamie. Which I probably should anyway. I've been putting it off, but it's only getting harder to sort out my thoughts, not easier."

A more somber mood settles over our group. Whitt slips his hand around one of my dangling feet and strokes his thumb over the arch. "If there's anything you need to know that would help you get a clearer picture of the situation, come to me without hesitation. And keep in mind that any decision you make now doesn't have to be final. They can't prevent you from changing your mind."

"We'd all fight for your right to return here or there if you wanted something different later on," August adds, the muscles in his shoulders flexing.

Knowing that should comfort me, but instead it only expands the melancholy ache in my chest. They're already preparing to say goodbye to me if that's what I insist on. The sorrow that lances through Corwin at that thought carries through our connection, and I know the other men must be similarly affected. Even considering the possibility of losing any of them hurts me just as much.

I swallow thickly and will down those emotions. Right now I want to be focused on this moment, in case it's the only chance I get to enjoy our shared home with the men I've been so looking forward to sharing it with. My decision can wait for tomorrow.

I haven't seen my fully finished bedroom before. When we step inside, a delighted laugh bubbles out of me. The walls are the same mix of diamond and wood as the other rooms in the middle of the castle, twined together here in delicate swirls. The furniture is a similar mix: a diamond washstand, a wooden wardrobe. The bedposts are wood with diamond spheres glinting at their peaks.

But what most delights me is the size of that bed. They've conjured one that's at least twice the size of those in either of my old bedrooms, more than large enough for all of us to comfortably fit on.

Corwin sets me down gently in the middle of the soft bedspread and then eases back. I can tell from the impressions trickling through our bond that he wants to show the other men he's not staking a greater claim on me, that he's willing to let them come to me first.

August and Whitt pause, studying him. They've never been part of any shared intimacies that involved my newest lover.

Sylas, who initiated our first shared encounter, settles next to me with his shoulders propped against the headboard, his fingers brushing over my hair. Seeing their lord make the first move, the other two climb onto the bed. August sprawls out at the opposite end of the bed and starts massaging my feet. Whitt presses a kiss to my belly and nestles his head against my hip.

Only then does Corwin properly join us, completing the ring of manly warmth around me with his head tucked against my shoulder. I kiss his forehead, run my hand down Sylas's chest, tease my fingers through Whitt's silky hair, and push my sole into August's touch encouragingly.

Just like that, we're all together as one unified collective. The lingering tension that stirred in Corwin at the prospect of navigating this situation fades away into contentment.

It's impossible not to feel like this is exactly where I belong—where we all belong. The love doesn't only pass between me and them but also between the men to each other, even if they share different sorts of affection and respect.

We brought the Seelie and Unseelie together after decades of war. We've challenged both societies' ideas of who could be a proper mate. So much trust and faith has grown between us. How can there be any problem we can't conquer?

But the problem of tomorrow's decision hasn't gone away. When my worries start gnawing at me again, I know just snuggling here in this ring of warmth won't be enough to chase them away. A starker desire ripples through me and collects between my thighs.

I want to know just how well all five of us can come together in every possible way, whether it's only the beginning or a memory I'll be able to hold on to tightly in days to come.

As often, my fae men's keen senses tip them off to the

shift in my mood before I've given any purposeful sign. August's caresses become more provoking, traveling up my calf to the sensitive skin of my inner knee. Whitt traces his fingers across my abdomen, his breath spilling hot enough across my hip for me to feel it through my dress. Sylas slips his fingers under my chin and draws my face up to meet his kiss.

And through it all, my soul-twined mate watches with a weird mix of exhilaration and envy. His instinctive possessiveness hasn't totally left him, but he isn't letting it control him.

I want him to be a full part of this interlude. As I kiss Sylas back, I tug on Corwin's shirt. *I need you too, my soul.*

With the silent impression of a groan, he leans in to nip the curve of my neck. My breath hitches against Sylas's mouth.

No matter what happens, nothing can erase what I'm experiencing right now. Nothing can break the love we all share. That much I'm sure of.

The certainty comes with a joy that's bittersweet but also so potent I can't hold it back. I draw back from Sylas just enough to murmur a true name into the air. "*Sole-un-straw.*"

Light shimmers over us like a shower of tiny shooting stars. Corwin exhales sharply, and then he's guiding my mouth to his.

As he kisses me with more passion than I've ever felt from him before, my Seelie men intensify their attentions too. Sylas cups my breasts and nibbles the lobe of my ear. August and Whitt make a joint venture of guiding my dress up to my waist, kissing their way up my legs in tandem. By the time they reach my upper thighs, I'm squirming and soaking my panties.

August pauses for just an instant as if he's worried Corwin will change his mind if things get too intense. I tug on his hair, and he lowers his head to mouth me through the thin fabric over my sex. The heat of that intimate kiss sends a shudder of delight through me. A mewling sound escapes my throat, and Corwin's tongue delves between my lips at their parting, devouring me even more deeply.

Oh, God. I already feel like I'm on the verge of exploding, and not a single piece of clothing is off any of us.

As if sensing that thought, August yanks my panties right off and kisses me skin to skin. The slick of his tongue over my opening has me arching off the bed with a rush of pleasure. Whitt clasps my bottom and holds me up at an even better angle for his brother's attentions, dappling kisses across my hip bone at the same time. When August delves his tongue right inside me, Corwin has to swallow my cry.

But my soul-twined mate isn't selfish. He worships my mouth for a few moments longer and then releases me with a nod to Sylas. As my Seelie arch-lord reclaims my lips, Corwin opens the fastenings on my dress. As soon as he's gained access to my breasts, he lowers his mouth to them and works them over with just as much enthusiasm as August below.

With bliss burning through me from every direction, it's a miracle I keep enough of my head to know I want a little less clothing on the rest of them too. Picking up on that silent wish, Corwin straightens up to peel off his shirt. A tremor of discomforted modesty travels through our bond, but then he announces to the others, "Our mate would prefer not to be alone in her state of undress."

It's an awfully formal way of saying that I'd like them all naked, but it does the trick. Suddenly there are shirts and slacks being shed all around me. In the middle of it, they manage to completely remove my dress as well. I find myself kneeling between my four lovers with them wearing just their boxers, their erections straining against the fabric.

Another urge takes over me that I don't question. I reach for Corwin first, sliding my hand down his lean chest to the waist of his undergarment. "I want to taste all of you."

His breath stutters as I duck my head. I tug the waistband lower to free his shaft and take it into my mouth.

The salty flavor that mingles with his wintery forest scent is familiar now. I swirl my tongue around the corded length. Every twitch of his member, the desperate tensing of his fingers in my hair, and the echoes of the pleasure I'm offering him make me giddy. There are so many ways in which these men have more power than I do, but when it comes to the bedroom, I'm at least their equal. I don't have any more doubt that they want me just as much as I want them.

I move from Corwin to Whitt, freeing my sly strategist in turn. His eyes turn heavy-lidded as he strokes my cheek. "Taste as much as you like."

The scent that clings to every part of him is almost the

opposite of Corwin, like sunbaked sand, but I relish it just as much. The groan that spills out of Whitt when I suck hard on his rigid length makes my own sex throb.

I'm tempted to stay there and see how long it takes to draw out Whitt's release with just my mouth, but I don't want to leave my other lovers neglected. I lap the head of his shaft and turn toward August.

The warrior's face has flushed, his eyes shining with both affection and lust. "I'm right here for you, Sweetness," he says in a husky voice.

And he is, his thick member nearly filling my hand as I draw it out. I lick around the tip and then take as much as I can into my mouth. His fingers drag over my scalp with just the right mix of tenderness and tension to set off a wave of sparks. I could drink in his sweetly musky flavor all day.

But I still have one more lover I want to include in this impromptu ritual. I give August a quick kiss on the mouth, our flavors mixing on our lips, and ease around to face Sylas.

The Seelie arch-lord watches me with nothing but love and desire in his dark eye. I tip forward so I can kiss a path down the middle of his chest, over several of his true-name tattoos, before I reach his boxers. When I delve inside them, he presses into my grasp as if he can't help himself. His earthy, smoky scent fills my lungs.

I suck him down slowly, tracing my tongue along the rigid shaft to find the spots that make his muscles tighten and his chest hitch. I'm learning how to make this man come undone. All of these men. They're mine, and I'm theirs, and that'll be true no matter how far away I am at any given moment.

As I draw a rough sound from Sylas's throat, one more hunger shivers through me. I've taken each of them one-by-one, but can I make our union completely literal and make love with all four of them at the same time? See us all reach our releases together?

I don't know, but I have to try. I've managed it with my three Seelie lovers before. One more should be possible.

I ease back, glancing around at the four men, my lips tingling from the use I've just put them to. Corwin shouldn't have to speak this desire for me.

"I want all of you… with me, together," I said. "I'm not sure exactly how…"

When I trail off awkwardly, Corwin smiles, his expression full of heat and affection. "I'd imagine we can accommodate that wish as well as the other," he says in a lower tone than he normally takes on. "I know you've already discovered many of the ways we can pleasure you and you us."

A sharper flare of heat surges through me. I think of him touching my other entrance when we made love in the cave, of Whitt penetrating me there weeks ago, and a heady tingling washes through me.

Through communication that's mostly unspoken, the men move around me, pausing to offer kisses and caresses as we navigate my request. I find myself braced over Sylas, my knees by his hips, my hands braced against his chest as he sprawls back on the bed. He holds my waist to steady me, not to control me. In answer to the question in his dark eye, I rock myself against him so the head of his member slides across my opening. It feels so good I quiver with eagerness.

As I sink down onto him, a deeper pleasure flares through my core. A whimper works its way from my throat.

Whitt gives August a lightly playful nudge. "Do you think you can see to our lady's other needs this time, whelp?"

August mock-glowers at him, any trace of rancor dissolved by the broad smile that stretches his mouth at the same time. "It would be my honor."

He kneels behind me, carefully straddling Sylas's legs, and kisses a scorching path from the middle of my back to the nape of my neck. His fingers work me over, spreading my own liquid and an added slickness he conjures with a murmured word to prepare my other opening.

With the blissful sensations swelling all through my core and up into my abdomen, it's hard to focus. I manage to tug Whitt and then Corwin closer on either side of me. I bow down to kiss Sylas hard and lift up again to kiss the men next to me, gasping against Whitt's mouth when August eases into me.

Oh, that sensation of being doubly filled makes me feel as if I'm soaring and burning up at the same time.

Corwin makes a strained noise as my delight passes into him. I curl my fingers around his jutting erection. As I begin to stroke up and down it, I lean the other way to take Whitt into my mouth for the second time. This time I'm going to see him all the way through to the end.

Relishing all of my men at once doesn't go perfectly

smoothly with so many moving parts. Sometimes I become so overwhelmed with the pleasure racing through me that I lose myself in a momentary daze. I have to adjust my position a few times, taking the moment to steal more kisses. But as I sink into the rhythm of the two men thrusting into me, it drives my momentum with the other two until we're swaying together in a rush of heated delight that's swiftly becoming an inferno.

To my surprise, it's Whitt who topples over the edge first, with a hissed curse and a squeeze of my shoulder. After he's flooded my mouth, he pants for a moment and then turns closer attention to every area of my body he can reach to spark more pleasure in me. His thumb swivels over a nipple, both Sylas and August buck into me in unison, and my hand jerks around Corwin's shaft so hard I feel the surge of his impending release. I duck quickly enough to wrap my lips around him just as he reaches his peak.

I rest my hands on Sylas's chest again, sliding them over the sweat that's formed there. He lets out a growl and pumps into me faster. August matches his pace, and all at once I'm hurtling toward my own orgasm at top speed. All I can do is hang on through the tsunami of ecstasy until the final wave crashes over me.

I come apart with a cry that's almost a sob, shaking in my lovers' joint embrace. Sylas groans and August clutches me tighter as they both follow me over the edge.

I end up slumped on the covers in a nest formed by my four mates, their limbs tucked around mine, finding a comfortable space next to each other. When I catch

Corwin's gaze, his eyes glitter with the same thrilled satisfaction that's resonating through our connection.

We are five, and we are one.

And tomorrow I have to decide whether keeping us together is the right thing or an avoidance of my true responsibilities.

CHAPTER FOURTEEN

Talia

We've gotten to the sports field outside Jamie's high school just as the last class of the day is getting out. Students are already streaming across the grass and the sidewalk around it. I pick up my pace, worried that I might have missed him. If he doesn't head to our aunt and uncle's house from here, I won't know where to find him.

August and Kesral have accompanied me for the same reasons as before. In a way, Corwin is following me too, sharply aware of my emotional state through our bond. I can tell he wants to know the second I've made a decision—and to be able to weigh in if I only find myself more confused.

I hurry over to the school building as fast as my limp allows, scanning the teens ambling around us. To my relief, it's only a minute or two before my gaze snags on a familiar head of curly brown hair.

Jamie is meandering around the side of the school, talking with another guy as they look at papers they're both holding. The vibe of their conversation strikes me as more businesslike than friendly—maybe they're supposed to work together on a project or something.

From seeing my brother eating on his own at lunch the other day, I don't get the impression he has much in the way of friends here at school. He must have met his girlfriend and the people they were hanging out with in his photos somewhere else.

There are so many other people around, it's hard to get close enough to him to pick up anything but fragments of what he and the other guy are saying. My fae companions and I have to weave between the dispersing students as we keep pace with the two of them. They head off across the field, where the other teens are starting to gather in clusters, leaving more room for us to maneuver. Would it be too much to ask for Jamie to stop walking and finish his conversation standing still?

A bunch of the teens nearby glance toward Jamie and his partner as they pass. I recognize a couple of the guys who hassled him at lunch the other day. One of them points to Jamie and makes a grossed-out expression for the benefit of the others, who titter with laughter.

Jamie keeps talking to the guy with him, but I can tell he's noticed the attention. His jaw has tightened, his gaze staying studiously on the paper he's motioning to.

I bristle on his behalf, glaring at the bullies, not that they can tell anyone's pissed off with them. Jamie's partner rubs his mouth, looking like he wants to be anywhere but with my brother.

A dog's bark reaches my ears from somewhere behind me. I don't pay much attention to it, too focused on my brother, until the pounding of heavy paws comes after it. A squirrel streaks past us over the grass, making for a tree at the other side of the field—and a big black hound charges after it, leash streaming, right into Jamie's path.

It doesn't look all that much like the massive wolves the Seelie can shift into. Its fur is shorter, its muzzle boxier, its ears floppy. As big as it is, I think the top of its head would only reach the level of Sylas's shoulders when he's in wolf form. But the sudden movement, the flash of bared teeth, and the general canine shape are enough to make my pulse hiccup in the first moment before I recognize what it is, even though I've had a lot of time and practice getting over my fears.

Jamie flinches so hard the papers he was holding and the book he had them propped on thump to the ground. He jerks back a couple of steps, a panicked sound escaping his mouth, a tremor running through his body.

He hugs himself but can't seem to stop shaking. My heart wrenches with the urge to run right to him, throw my arms around him, and tell him he'll be okay.

Before I can, a mocking laugh rings out. The bunch of teens who were giggling over Jamie's appearance are sauntering closer, the two guys from before in the lead.

"Monster boy is afraid of a pet dog?" one sneers, glancing over to where the dog's owner has finally caught up with the hound and grabbed its leash. "Pretty sad getting terrified over something that's a whole lot less terrifying to look at than you."

Now I want to wrap Jamie up in a hug *and* tell August

to rip out that jerk's throat so he'll find out just how much reason my brother has to react like this. I step forward, my hands flexing, the words rising from my chest to ask August to take the magic off me so they can see me.

So what if I seem to come out of nowhere? It couldn't be more obvious that my brother needs me—he needs me right *now*.

"Wait!" Kesral says, probably with instructions not to jeopardize the secrecy of the fae world. He grabs my arm before I can get close enough that they'll feel my presence even if they can't see me.

I turn to tell him off, but my voice catches at Jamie's movement. His shoulders still rigid, he bends to pick up his things from the ground. There's a bit of a stutter to his next couple of breaths, but then it evens out. He's no longer shaking or cringing like I would have been just months ago when shocked into the memories of the past.

But then, I guess Jamie's had a chance to work through some of those fears too. Maybe he hasn't gotten to confront his attackers face to face, but he's had access to things *I* never got, like therapists and years of life outside a cage.

He straightens up and faces his bully. Even his partner is staring at him, having backed away as if to avoid any association with Jamie at all.

"You got a problem with me, McCarty?" the other guy says, folding his arms over his chest and raising his chin like a dare.

Jamie fixes him with a cool but cutting stare that I suspect Whitt would appreciate. "Not really. See, the thing is, I don't care if you think I look terrifying or whatever. Why the hell *should* I care what a dick like you thinks?"

The bully's jaw drops. His friends stay totally silent with varying expressions of shock. It takes a moment before the guy manages to speak, and then it comes out with a sputter. "Who the fuck do you figure you are? *Everyone* thinks you're a deformed loser who belongs in a freak show, you know."

Jamie shrugs. "Then 'everyone' can go fuck themselves. I don't need some stamp of approval from you. I've got a family and a girlfriend and friends who don't think I'm a loser, and they matter to me way more than a bunch of random idiots. And you know what? Because *I'm* not a prick, I hope you never have to go through what I did to end up looking like this."

He makes a swift gesture toward the scars on his face and then turns on his heel to walk away. I'm gaping now too, but with as much admiration as shock.

"Look at the spine on him," Kesral says with an approving chuckle.

August slips his arm around me and nuzzles my hair. "It must run in the family."

Maybe it does. My brother's stronger than I guessed. But I pull away from August to follow Jamie, my heart thumping harder. Was he really so confident in what he just said, or was it a bold front to cover up the pain he didn't want the bullies to see?

I doubt that their comments left him completely unscathed, but they don't appear to have done any major damage even to his mood. As Jamie leaves the schoolyard behind, he pulls out his phone. I manage to peek over and see he's texting the girl from the pictures in his room, who just sent him a selfie and a message asking him to meet up with her after dinner.

Sure, Jamie types back. *I can't wait. But I should warn you, I just told off the second most popular guy at school, so being seen with me is probably bad for your reputation.* He adds a winking emoji at the end and grins as he sends the message off.

His girlfriend replies a moment later with a laughing emoji and the words, *Who needs a reputation? I'd rather have you, thank you very much.*

They banter back and forth a bit more, and by the time Jamie tucks the phone into his pocket and slips into a convenience store to grab a snack, he looks totally relaxed.

He's okay.

The knowledge settles over me with a weirdly bittersweet sense of relief. He handled that situation all on his own, no need for a big sister to come running to his rescue. Maybe the trauma of the attack isn't gone, but he's obviously figuring out his way past that.

What could I do for him that he isn't already doing for himself? If I insisted on staying and pushing my way into his life, would it honestly be for his benefit, or would I only be looking to absolve my own guilt?

I can't completely walk away from him. I don't *want* to. But maybe… Maybe it would be all right for me to go back to the life I've made for myself away from here and just check in on him every now and then.

Something about that idea sends an uncomfortable twinge through my gut. If I only stop by once a month or something like that, a lot could change without me realizing it. If he was in serious trouble, I'd want to know right away.

As we trail after Jamie along the sidewalk, I worry at my lower lip. He heads into a bowling alley next, and ducking inside after him, I see him setting up behind the shoe counter. So he's got a part-time job too.

"The kid seems pretty independent," August remarks.

"Yeah." I grapple with my thoughts as we return to the street. If there's anyone who could help me with this, it'd be August, right?

I touch his arm. "You know a lot of medical and bodily magic, right? Is there some kind of spell you could cast that would sort of connect me to Jamie from a distance—that would alert me somehow if he was in major physical or emotional distress?"

August cocks his head. "I can think of a couple of strategies that might work. But they'd require a sort of token to attach the spell to. Something you'd keep close to you and something he would too."

I glance down at myself, and my gaze falls on the bronze bracelet Sylas gave me. As I trace my fingers over the smooth metal, an image sparks in my mind that brings a smile to my lips.

I don't have to leave my brother completely. I can give him a little piece of our family to hold onto. He might not totally understand it, but from what I've seen, I think there's a good chance he'll keep it nearby.

"You can conjure up some bronze even here, right?" I say. "I want to make him a cuff bracelet that matches mine. We'll use those."

August beams at me. "Whatever you need, Sweetness."

It only takes him a few minutes to construct a bracelet nearly identical to mine, just a little larger and more manly-looking, with a notch in the bottom so Jamie can slide it on if he decides to wear it since he can't magically expand it.

"I'll do the finishing touches," I say with a rush of exhilaration. It really will be a present from me.

Grasping the metal loop in my hands, I focus intently on it. "*Fee-doom-ace-own.*"

With my will and the syllables, I etch four names into the inside of the bracelet: Dad's, Mom's, *Talia*, and *Jamie*. Sweat has broken out on the back of my neck by the time I'm done, but I hand the bracelet to August with a deep sense of satisfaction.

He takes my own bracelet as well and sits down on a patch of lawn to work the more intensive magic I requested. I glance around, realizing there's one more thing I'd like to include.

"Do you have a piece of paper and something to write with?" I ask Kesral, figuring I can pilfer one from somewhere around here if not.

The winter fae man has been watching the proceedings with obvious curiosity. He looks almost pleased now to be brought in on our little mission.

"I can create them for you," he says, and murmurs a few magic-laced syllables of his own. In a matter of moments, he's offering me a slip of fine paper like the stuff in Whitt's books and a narrow stick of charcoal.

I debate the message for a while and finally settle on something short and to the point. *Always with you,* I scrawl on the paper.

By the time August has finished his spellwork, evening is descending on us. We sneak to my aunt and uncle's house, and I slip through the back door to Jamie's bedroom. Folding the note around the bracelet, I set it on his pillow for him to find when he gets back from his date.

I straighten up and look down at it, weighing my decision and the ache in my chest. Am I doing the right thing—for me? For him?

I won't know for sure until more time has passed, but after seeing his strength today, it feels right. I will be with him, just not every moment of every day. The fae *and* the humans back in the fae world need me so much more.

Taking a deep breath, I head back out to meet August and Kesral. "Okay," I say. "Let's go home."

As we head back to the park, a trace of dread creeps into my stomach. I rub my fingers over my bracelet, but my apprehension has nothing to do with Jamie.

The other arch-lords were very eager to see me gone from their world. How are they going to react when they find out they can't get rid of me so easily after all?

CHAPTER FIFTEEN

Corwin

"You're not normally this cheerful when we have to go talk to your colleagues," Talia says in a teasing tone, glancing at me over her shoulder from where she's standing in front of the full-length mirror. She called me into her bedroom to inspect the outfit she's chosen for the meeting. Rather than one of her Seelie friend's elaborate creations, she's gone with a subdued and practical gown completely in the winter fae style—one of my own craftsmen's creations.

"I suppose I don't typically have quite so much to be cheerful about," I reply, a smile tugging at my lips. As much practice as I've had keeping my emotions bottled up, it's hard not to grin like some kind of maniac.

She's staying. There'll be minor compromises to be made to allow her to watch over her brother, of course, but she isn't returning to the human world for any substantial length of time. I get to have my soul-twined mate by my side where she's meant to be.

I doubt my colleagues will be anywhere near as enthusiastic about that fact as I am, but I can't bring myself to care. She's *my* mate. The Heart has willed it. Not even the most arrogant of arch-lords can put up much argument to that fact.

Talia smiles back at me. She does a slow twirl in front of the mirror, careful of her wounded foot in her usual boots, and smooths down the dress's skirt. "I thought if I go looking as much as possible like I belong here, they might be a little more open to my request."

Not just lovely to behold but so keen-minded as well. I nod. "I think that was the right choice. But we still want you to look an arch-lord's lady as well. Perhaps… Wait here a moment."

I duck out of the room and hurry to my own, where I left a jewelry box I meant to offer her when it seemed like a good time. I'm sure she'll appreciate it now when it'll support her goals as well as amplifying her beauty.

The box is cool against my fingers, a mix of ebony wood and silver not so different from the blend of oak and diamond making up this castle, wound together in an intricate pattern. It holds several treasures passed down through my family. When I step into Talia's bedroom with it, I open it up and take out the piece I was thinking of: a silver necklace dappled with tiny, pale blue diamonds that shimmer like sunlight on snow.

"This was my grandmother's," I tell her, going to her to clasp it around her neck. "The first arch-lord to rule from Heart's Cadence."

I adjust the necklace, resisting the urge to let my hands linger against Talia's smooth skin, and step back to take in the whole picture. The dress was only a little on the plain side, and that simple piece elevates her ensemble from professional to honor-worthy.

Talia touches the necklace, awed gratitude carrying through our bond. "Thank you. It looks perfect."

"It is perfect. I dare them to try to say no to you when you look like that."

She shoots me a wry glance. "Somehow I think they'll take that dare. They don't even like me when I'm helping them. They're definitely not going to be happy about me poking around seeing what they might be doing wrong."

She speaks easily enough, but I can sense the worries tangled inside her. She does have an accurate measure of the other arch-lords.

I rest my hands on her shoulders and press a quick kiss to the back of her head. "You have a reasonable request. I'll speak up for your right to make it, and so will Sylas— and perhaps even Neve and that Donovan fellow will support it too. If they resist, they'll only be admitting they have something untoward to hide."

Talia makes a disgruntled sound. "But they might prefer to admit that than to have it outright exposed." She sighs. "I wish we could at least have the meeting here instead of in the Hall."

"Laoni wanted everything to be 'equal,' and since we had the last joint meeting of the arch-lords on the summer side…" I give her an apologetic grimace in the mirror. "After this, it'll be balanced out, and perhaps we can convince them to make use of the border castle for all future collective conferences."

There's a knock on the door, and Whitt's dry voice carries through. "We're due across the way in a few minutes. Is the mite ready to go? Don't keep her all to yourself now."

My instinct is to bristle at the word "mite," but Talia's internal reaction is all warm amusement, so obviously the nickname isn't meant to offend.

"I'm coming," she calls out, giving her dress one last straightening tug, and clasps my hand to draw me with her to the door.

Sylas's strategist has dressed sharply for this meeting as well, although from what I've observed, Whitt is the most clothing-conscious of Talia's Seelie men at any time. His bright brown hair, though, is rumpled as if he hasn't done more than run his fingers through it. I suppose I should be glad it's Sylas who'll be doing any talking out of the bunch.

Whitt looks Talia over with an appreciative gleam in his eyes that raises my hackles all over again even though I approve of it. As I tamp down on the jealousy I've mostly but not entirely conquered, he takes Talia's other hand so we can lead her downstairs together.

"Let's go see what those feather-brained winter arch-lords can find to complain about today," he says breezily.

Talia mock-glowers at him. "It isn't as if all the summer arch-lords have been so welcoming. If you're coming along, you'd better play nice."

Whitt presses his free hand to his chest as if in shock.

"Of all the things I may be called, I'd think you'd know by now that 'nice' isn't one of them."

My mate elbows him teasingly, and he grins. I keep my mouth shut, not sure how to respond to the ribbing banter.

Out of the three Seelie men, Whitt is the one I'm the least at ease with still. Sylas and I have formed a sort of understanding as equals, both dedicated to Talia and the fae folk we represent. August wears his emotions clearly on his face and is generally straightforward in his speaking. Whitt is the type of fae who'll happily weave a story that skirts the very edge of lying and laugh about it later. Which is the sort of temperament I suppose one would want in a spymaster, but that doesn't make me any surer of where anything stands with him.

He adores Talia, though. That much I'm certain of from the interactions I've observed both in person and through her memories. Even now, there's no missing the fondness that brightens his expression in her presence. That's all I really need to know.

Sylas and August are waiting downstairs. "Beautiful as always, my love," Sylas says to Talia, who beams at him, and we head out through the broad doorway on my side of the castle toward the Hall of the Heart.

The other Seelie arch-lords have come across the border from their own domains. We spot Donovan and a couple of his cadre-chosen crossing the icy plain and entering the Hall before we reach it. Halfway there, Zelpha and Verik catch up with us. The discussion today could affect a great deal about how things are run in both realms, and we want our closest associates quickly apprised.

Laoni and Uzziah are already at the table when we arrive, along with Celia and Donovan, who's just getting into his place. Terisse arrives a moment later, and Neve wanders in last, on her own and not appearing at all concerned about that fact. She grants Talia a smile that makes me more hopeful about her taking our side.

Laoni is scowling, her expression even sourer than it's been the last few times we spoke. "I understand your mate has come to a decision about her living situation," she says to me briskly. "Let's hear it."

I can tell from her tone that she's already reasonably certain what that decision is and she isn't pleased about it. My body tenses, but I let Talia speak for herself. The more she shows she can hold her own among them, the harder it'll be for them to dismiss her.

Talia raises her chin, looking impressively regal. "After further observation and reflection, I believe that it's in everyone's best interests, including mine and my brother's, if I stay here in the fae world. My brother has adapted fairly well to the trauma he's been through, and I don't want to risk dredging up the past by coming back into his life out of nowhere. And it'll be much easier for me to continue helping with the curse if I'm here."

Uzziah makes a scoffing sound that sets my teeth on edge.

Celia narrows her eyes. "Are you sure you've made that judgment with all the factors fully considered and not simply following the desires of your heart? I can understand you have many reasons you'd *want* to think it best to remain here."

Sylas stirs. "Neither I nor my cadre nor Arch-Lord Corwin, that I'm aware of, have done anything but support Talia's right to choose where she goes. We haven't swayed her in any direction."

I incline my head in acknowledgment, and Talia sets her hands firmly on the tabletop. "I've thought long and hard about this. I'm completely confident in my decision."

Laoni's lips curl. "And we're supposed to go by a human's reasoning rather than what we fae feel is best for our peoples? Are we the arch-lords here or is she?"

"We are," I say tersely. "And not all of those arch-lords feel she should leave. In fact, I haven't heard any clear explanation for why that is a more practical course of action. Are you sure those of you pushing for my mate to live elsewhere aren't being swayed by *your* emotions rather than reason?"

Laoni's eyes flash with anger as I knew they would, but I don't regret my remark one bit.

Before she can retort, Donovan shifts on his feet with a hint of discomfort. "It will definitely be easier tending to the curse with Talia close by. Especially for the Unseelie when each of the victims requires separate treatment."

"There are other factors to consider," Celia puts in. "This isn't truly her world. Her presence may have other effects that are less desirable."

"Like what?" Sylas asks, fixing her with a level stare. "I've asked before and never had any proof offered: has her relationship with any of us present affected us or anyone else negatively in any way?"

Terisse's jaw works. "We can't be certain that it won't in the future."

"But it hasn't yet," Talia breaks in. "It's because of the close relationship I've formed with fae on both sides of the border that you're able to have meetings like this rather than continuing to *kill* each other in the first place, isn't it? Why make up problems that don't exist yet when I can help so much with the biggest problem you do know about?"

I fight back a smile at her tart remarks. That would only enrage my colleagues who are against her decision even more. But all of them fall silent, obviously not having any real argument to push forward.

"Actually," Talia goes on, gathering confidence, "Arch-Lord Celia brought up a point that leads into the other subject I wanted to discuss today. I may not theoretically belong here, but it was fae who brought me here, and you've brought plenty of other humans into your world as well—humans you've kept for their entire lives."

"What of it?" Uzziah demands.

Talia gazes at him and then the others around the table, not letting her determined stance waver. "I've done a lot to help improve the lives of the fae by fending off the curse. I think I have a duty to step up for *my* people who are living among you too. I'd like to visit more of the domains on both sides of the border with a decree from the arch-lords that the lords and ladies are to allow me free access to talk to their human servants."

Laoni draws in a hiss of breath. "There we have it. Your dust-destined mate is looking for ways to make trouble already. What purpose could that mission serve us?"

"Watch how you speak to my lady," I say, just barely holding back the rancor I want to aim at her. I have to keep my cool in this company, but I can't stand by while they insult my mate either.

Talia turns to Laoni, her voice still even. "It will serve the people you've forced to become citizens of the fae world. When I've seen enough, I expect to have recommendations on improving the treatment they're currently facing. We can debate exactly which you'll agree to then, but I won't stand by quietly while others like me are being drugged and tricked into slavery."

A flare of pride warms my chest. How could anyone doubt that she's meant to stand beside me as my lady?

But naturally Laoni doesn't see it that way. Her shoulders go rigid, her jaw even tighter than before. When she speaks, it's in a tone venomous enough to kill. "It's not your place to question traditions that have been in place for thousands of years longer than you've been alive. Your freak circumstances might have given you the appearance of power, but don't forget that you're still a dung-body underneath."

An emotional wince travels from Talia into me, but my anger has already rushed to the front of my mind. All at once, my reserve seems ridiculous.

Why should I care what these people think any more than Talia does? What good is there in courting the favor of those who deal it out so grudgingly and unfairly? From the very start of this conversation—from the first moment

Talia came among us, really—they've shown nothing but disrespect to her and our bond.

They're never going to change their views until they see some consequences for them.

I wrap my hand around one of Talia's and aim a glare at Laoni. "How you shame the Heart by speaking of the one it's blessed with so much—the one who's given us so much—with such insults. We don't need to stand here and listen to your hostility any longer. My mate has stated her request. Unless you can come up with a logical reason to deny it, not based on the prejudiced assumption that she matters less than the rest of us, I have no interest in hearing anything further spoken against it. We'll proceed whether we have your acceptance or not."

Talia glances at me, startled, but when I draw her away from the table, she walks with me as steadily as she can, her head held high. I catch a muffled chuckle from someone behind us, and then Sylas is striding to catch up. My coterie members and his cadre-chosen follow behind us.

"Corwin!" Uzziah calls, but I don't even look back. They need to do more than that to earn my attention again.

As we step out into the wintry air beyond the building's walls to head back to the border castle, Talia squeezes my hand. The emotions churning within her are a potent mix of amazement, trepidation, and... love. *I can't believe you told them off like that. That you walked right out on them.*

I know it might lead to more difficulties down the road, I start, but she shakes her head.

I was impressed. I don't know if it'll make any difference to how they treat me in the long run… but I appreciated that you'd stand up for me that much anyway.

A lump rises in my throat. *I always will, my soul.*

"Well," August says a little awkwardly, rubbing his hands together. "After that, I think we could all use a good meal to wash away the bad taste left in our mouths. Talia, do you want to join me in making the first epic dinner of your new home?"

A little more of the tension fades from my mate as she smiles at him. "That sounds wonderful."

When we reach the castle, Zelpha and Verik set off to fill the rest of my coterie in, Zelpha giving me a jaunty salute and an approving smile as she turns away. Talia and August make for the kitchen.

Sylas pauses in the winter front hall and studies me. "Should we be prepared for any fallout from that move?"

I manage a strained laugh. "I'm not sure. I've never defied my colleagues that blatantly before. I suppose we'll see. What about your own?"

He shrugs. "Donovan is already friendly to us. I can deal with Celia if she has any further concerns. I have a few things to see to with my pack, but I'll return in time for dinner." The corners of his mouth twitch upward. "Knowing August, it'll be at least a couple of hours before he can see through his full vision of this feast."

He strides off, leaving me in the hall—with Whitt, who's lingered nearby. He's eyeing me too, with a more appraising air than I felt from his lord. My skin prickles uneasily, but then an easy grin stretches across his face.

"You'd pick her over any of them, wouldn't you, Lord Bird?" he says.

The nickname irks me, but not enough that I'd focus on that rather than the important part of his question. "In an instant," I reply automatically.

Not one of my colleagues has earned more loyalty from me than Talia has. I'll do what's best for my people as well… but what's best for my people is having her with us, protected and free.

And loved.

Whitt tips his head to me. For the first time since I met him, I have the sense I'm seeing the real man, not a carefully constructed façade. "I'm glad," he says. "That'll make things easier for all of us. And it's what she deserves."

I allow myself a little smile in return. "I couldn't agree more about that."

He motions to me. "Come on then, you chilly raven. Let's see if we can't move this dinner along a little faster than those two can manage on their own. I could eat a horse already."

I've drawn a firm line with my fellow arch-lords for the first time since I took this position, and no doubt they're fuming about it. But as I walk with Whitt down the hall to the kitchen, a sense of peace settles over me greater than any I've felt before.

CHAPTER SIXTEEN

Talia

I'm woken by a gentle rapping on my door. August stirs next to me on the bed, looping his brawny arm around my waist and nuzzling the back of my neck. I rest my arm over his as I rub my eyes with my other hand. "Yes?"

Zelpha's voice carries through. "I'm sorry to disturb you, but we've got visitors. A woman struck by the curse… and rather a lot of her flock too." Her tone turns a bit dry with that last bit.

I bite back a groan, which really wouldn't be fair of me, and swipe the stray locks back from my face. "All right. I'll be down as soon as I can."

"You don't have to rush too much. Corwin's wrangling them for the moment, and they're pretty pleased just being attended to by an arch-lord."

Sensing our conversation through the bond, my soul-twined mate sends a tendril of confirmation, reassurance, and apology my way. I get the vague impression of him directing the carriages that've shown up over to the stretch of plain by the Heart where I offered my cure last time. I guess that's going to become the standard healing spot.

August hugs me closer and presses a kiss to my shoulder. "Always so busy, Sweetness."

"I'm the only one who can keep them alive." But my busy-ness is only going to get worse as the curse victims who need their cure repeated multiply.

Pushing aside that thought and the sinking sensation in my gut, I roll over to give August a quick kiss on the lips and then push myself upright.

The border castle is going to be my primary home from here on, and all of my mates decided I shouldn't be left alone there, especially when we can't be totally certain of good intentions from every other fae around. At least one of my men will be staying with me every night, and Corwin plans to have a coterie member on hand as much as possible. Both he and Sylas have also assigned a rotation of staff from their packs to see to cleaning and other basic needs... and a couple of guards to monitor the entrances.

No one can pass through those doorways without taking the border oath of non-violence, but we all know that fae are adept at finding loopholes.

I limp over to my wardrobe and grab a dress that'll look reasonably lady-like. Most of my clothes have been moved here already, but the bedroom still feels new, not quite home yet. I've only spent a few nights in it so far.

As I give my face a quick wash and dampen down flyaway hairs at the basin, August ducks out to return to his bedroom in the joint castle. By the time I've pulled on my boots, he's back and dressed, his handsome face ruddy from its own washing. "I'll walk you over," he says.

"I'm sure Zelpha would, if you need to get back to anything in Hearth-by-the-Heart," I say.

He shakes his head. "I'm supposed to run through some training exercises with a bunch of the pack later this morning, but at this time, I expected to still be sleeping." He winks at me to show he isn't at all bothered by the disruption, though. "And I owe you breakfast after you finish your curse-curing work."

"Corwin's kitchen staff have been sending meals over," I remind him.

He claps his hands together with a grin. "I'm sure I can come up with something fitting to accompany their spread. And you should eat a little before you get to work too."

His good cheer puts me in a better mood. He hustles ahead of me to grab some berries he brought from the summer realm, and I pop them into my mouth a few at a time as I make my way to the door, focusing on the tart sweetness and not the task ahead of me.

It isn't as if we're facing that much of an intrusion. I'll go out, see to the curse victim in a matter of minutes, and then there'll be the whole rest of the day ahead of us.

We step outside into the cool wind, and I'm grateful again that the weather is never too intense close to the Heart. A few sparkling flakes of snow tumble around us, the sky hazed with pale clouds overhead.

The crowd gathered around the Heart looks to be about the same size as the last one that arrived, a few dozen fae. Don't they have anything better to do than come all this way just to watch me brush a few tears to someone's cheek?

That thought sends a prick of guilt through my stomach when our guests turn to watch me approach, so many of their faces lit with eager hope. Maybe they're not ready to see all humans as anywhere near their equals, but they've been willing to see me as someone special— someone worthy of gratitude and awe.

Corwin raises his hand in greeting where he's standing right in front of the Heart. The pulsing glow makes the blue tone in his dark curls shift along their curves. He smiles at me with another tingle of apology through our connection.

It's fine, I say. *This is one of the reasons I stayed here.*

The folk must have hurried the cursed woman to us as soon as she showed the first signs of the curse. Her skin is eerily pale but not yet tinged with blue, and she's managing to keep her back fairly straight in the chair someone brought for her, though her shoulders are hunched. She takes in my approach with a weird mix of excitement and fear playing across her features.

I can't imagine what it must be like to be on the other end of the curse. To have to wonder whether the cure might not work this time, or whether the supernatural chill will really ever leave once it's taken hold.

Here I am worrying about how healing them affects *me* when they're the ones with their lives on the line.

Just like that, I'm a little choked up. I walk up to the woman and dip my head in acknowledgment. "I hope your journey here wasn't too long or uncomfortable. I'll do my best to see you back to your normal self as quickly as possible."

She manages a smile that seems to take some effort. "Thank you, my lady. The stories about your generosity are obviously true."

Ignoring the niggling of discomfort that comes with the idea of the fae spreading stories about me, even good ones, I focus on the ache of grief inside me. How must it feel to find yourself suddenly on the brink of death? Imagine all the things I'd be horrified at losing if some horrible illness struck me out of nowhere. There's so much more I want to do with the life I've only just gotten back...

She must have so many people she'll leave behind, so many dreams unfulfilled. And all her hopes of survival rest on me. Even a couple of months ago, she'd have had no hope at all. No choice but to slowly seize up until she was locked inside her own body even more thoroughly than Aerik locked me in that cage...

At the first burn of tears behind my eyes, I turn away. August stands at a careful distance without a word, Corwin silent too as he gives me the space to follow my instincts.

One tear and another slips down my cheeks, the cold air nipping at the wetness. I brush my fingers across my face, suck in a breath, and face the woman again.

Her posture stiffens as I step toward her, as if she's afraid to find out whether it'll actually work. Afraid that if it doesn't, that'll be her death sentence right there. But she holds still as my fingertips graze her cheek and inhales sharply when warmth spreads from the spot where I touched. When her gaze meets mine again, a glint that's almost watery is dancing in her eyes.

"Thank you," she murmurs, her voice gone rough. "You truly are a lady for us all."

"The Heart's lady!" someone calls out amid the crowd. Other voices rise in agreement. The folk of the woman's flock close in around us, checking her over to make sure she's recovering, peering at me with open amazement. I manage to smile back at them, not sure how to respond. What would they expect from me?

Most of them bow, some lower than I've ever seen anyone bow to Corwin or Sylas. Then a strident voice carries from the fringes of the crowd. "All right. The cure is done. You'd best get back to your homes and allow for a full healing."

I glance up to see Laoni has come over with several other fae. The visiting flock gives a few reluctant mutters, but they drift toward their carriages after offering me more praises.

They only make it halfway to the vehicles before someone near the front of the group points into the distance. "There are more coming!"

He's right. A few more large carriages are soaring into view, heading for our plateau around the Heart. Everyone stops to watch their arrival. Laoni frowns, her brow creasing, but she doesn't seem to want to be too forceful in shooing the first set of visitors away. She does still need to keep some good will as arch-lord.

What do you think this is about? I ask Corwin. *Were you expecting them?*

He gives an inward shake of his head. *It can't be*

another curse victim. There's never been two anywhere near this close together.

The curse has been steadily intensifying in both severity and its pace, though. But when the carriages come to a stop and another crowd pours out, I recognize the man being carried over the side by his mate.

It isn't a new curse victim but an old one—the second fae I healed successfully, on the day of my confirmation ceremony. He's been hit a second time just like Fina was.

I suppose it works out that you're already here, Corwin says, but some concern carries through in his voice.

My chest has constricted. It *is* better that I help both victims one after the other rather than being called back hours later. But this is just a preview of what my life will become more and more like as the curse takes greater hold, isn't it? How will I be able to accomplish anything else I want to when they need me so much, so often?

How can I possibly complain when they're the ones freezing to death?

I swallow down my frustrations, not wanting to show my discomfort when both the new arrivals and the original visitors are gazing at me so adoringly... worshipfully. Without even looking at Laoni, I can feel her critical eyes fixed on me too. She doesn't like the standing I've gained among her people at all. Too bad for her she can't do anything about it.

I focus on the man who needs my help, my mouth slanting into a bittersweet smile. "I'm glad you could make it to me before you're too ill, but I'm sorry you needed to come back to me at all."

He manages to shrug with a bit of a hitch to the

movement. "It is what it is. I'm grateful I have you to turn to, my lady."

His mate lowers him to the ground and sits next to him, even though she shivers being so close to his chilly body. The members of his flock who joined him gather around, and the other flock drifts back over to observe this new spectacle.

I think of all the fae who died before I came—of Corwin's father, of his former best friend and the lover who betrayed him, of the hundreds of others who succumbed to the cursed ice with no one to push it back. So many lives lost in such a horrible way.

And what will happen when I'm gone? To the fae, to the humans living here that I haven't even started to properly defend…

The tears return, hotter than before. I go through the same show of hiding them, wiping them away, and then reaching out to the cursed man. As my fingers slide over his cheek, he sighs in relief before the warmth even sparks beneath his skin. As if my touch on its own is enough to tell him everything will be all right.

Except it won't. The curse will come back for him again and again, until my days are full of crying these tears of temporary healing.

An unexpected sense of panic twists around my stomach, as if time is slipping through my fingers with every breath.

The man bows his head and his mate quickly squeezes my forearm in thanks. The two flocks exclaim to each other about what a marvel I am and how wonderful it is that the Heart has blessed me with this power… And my gaze settles on Laoni again.

Her face is stern and what I can hear of her voice is terse as she orders her staff to get the visitors moving toward their carriages. A muscle in her jaw flexes. She *hates* that I'm getting so much recognition, doesn't she?

But I have it all the same. And maybe—maybe I can use this new power in my favor like I have the others I've discovered. I tried to wield my possible influence once, just encouraging that other flock to consider their treatment of humans. What if I could turn the social pressure of their devotion to me into some kind of leverage here?

A flicker of uneasy excitement darts through my chest. The pieces of the idea click together in my head, and I step forward before the visiting flocks move any farther away. Corwin gives me an encouraging nod. I push the words out, not letting myself second-guess my impromptu plan.

"Thank you all for the honor you're offering me even though I'm not fae," I say, pitching my voice to carry. "It means so much to me to have your respect and admiration. I hope to discover how many of the other humans in your realm have talents and skills to offer that you might not have realized. If Arch-Lord Laoni will agree, I'd love to start by speaking with the humans she has seen fit with her keen judgment to bring into her domain."

Laoni's gaze jerks to me, sharpening into a glare for just an instant before a chorus of approval swells through the crowd. "Yes, of course, the blessed human lady should see to the others of her kind," someone near me says.

Another nods, beaming. "Who knows what other good Lady Talia may be able to do for us?"

I don't exactly like that I've had to frame it more about what the humans might be able to do for them than my fellow mortals deserving lives in their own right, but if it gets me to my goal, I'll take it.

I keep my eyes fixed on Laoni, waiting for her response. Corwin steps up beside me and sets his hand on my shoulder, signaling his support for my request. *She's going to be angry, but I have to say I think it'll be worth it.*

Everyone is watching Laoni expectantly now. She glances around, her lips pressing flat, and then forces her mouth into a smile. How can she say no to my request when it's phrased like that? And once she's given her word here before the Heart and so many of her own flock-folk and others, she won't want to shame herself by going back on it.

"An excellent idea," she says with just a slight edge to her tone. "We can certainly make arrangements for that."

Arrangements that might take the rest of my lifetime, she's probably thinking. I put on the sweetest smile I can manage myself. "Perfect. I could come by tomorrow. I wouldn't trouble you at all. You could simply leave instructions with your staff that they should show me to your human servants. I'll have someone from my mate's coterie attend to me."

Laoni manages to keep her expression impassive, but I have the feeling she'd be killing me with her stare right now if she could. "I suppose that would be acceptable," she replies grudgingly.

The gathered flock-folk let out a little cheer. Corwin

dips his head graciously to his colleague. "We appreciate your openness, Arch-Lord Laoni."

I turn back toward my castle with lighter spirits. Even with my duties for the curse, I can still take a stand for the other humans here.

Now I just need to figure out what I'm going to do once I see just how horrible their situation is in Laoni's domain.

CHAPTER SEVENTEEN

Talia

"You're lucky I like you as much as I do, Talia," Zelpha remarks in a wry voice. "Because spending the day hanging out in Heart's Resilience is not my idea of a fun pastime."

"It's not mine either," I say, looking ahead to the glinting fortress of Laoni's castle. The pale metal walls and spires look elegant and intimidating at the same time. The building reminds me of a cage more than I like. "But if we can make a case for changing how the arch-lords are treating the humans in their domains, then we have a much better chance of getting the other lords and ladies on board. I guess Laoni's main strength is metalwork?"

Zelpha nods. "That place was her father's construction, though she's added bits to it here and there. Solid iridium. Not what I'd want to be surrounded by day in and day out, but we all have our own tastes." She makes a face as if to say she finds Laoni's particularly questionable.

We tramp the last short distance across the plain, our boots crunching in the thin layer of newly fallen snow. As we approach the front doors, our wavering reflections move to meet us. *That's* not unsettling at all. I restrain a shiver.

The door opens, and one of Laoni's guards ushers us inside. "We're ready for you, Lady Talia," he says stiffly. He doesn't sound any happier about my visit than his boss was. I hope she didn't take out too much of her frustration over my gambit on her staff.

I offer him a tentative smile. "Wonderful. Where can we speak to the human servants?"

He motions for us to follow him. "A few of them are still busy in the kitchen. The others we've gathered in their repose room to speak to you."

The walls inside the castle are just as reflective as those outside. Skewed echoes of our forms ripple across them on both sides of us as we make our way deeper into the castle. They give the eerie impression that you could never be alone in this place, that there could be people watching your every movement no matter where you go.

A soft light beams down from fixtures on the high, curved ceiling, amplified as it bounces across the metal surfaces. I wouldn't generally associate Laoni with anything soft, but a starker light would be nearly blinding.

It's a long walk with several turns and a trip up a flight of stairs. The dry air tickles my nose. By the time the guard stops outside a doorway, my warped foot has started to ache. I keep my limp as in check as I can when I ease past him into the room.

A woman I recognize from Laoni's coterie is waiting

there, along with more human figures than I was expecting. At our entrance, a dozen of them get up from beds laid out in rows across the room as if on command.

Not just as if. They must have been commanded to do exactly that. One glance at them, and I can tell they're all in the same drugged haze as most of the humans in Petalrise, too spaced out to react that quickly to my arrival otherwise. I doubt they have much room to make any decisions for themselves in their muddled minds.

As I take in the room, my throat tightens. The floor and walls gleam, the beds are small but neatly made with blankets that look brand new. I can't help wondering how much work Laoni put into prettying up this space in anticipation of my arrival.

But there's nothing in the space other than those beds and a single wash basin by the far wall. No shelves, no cupboards, nothing hanging on the walls. No sign of any personal possessions. They don't even have storage for clothes. I suppose they wear the same outfits continuously, and the fae simply bring them replacements as needed.

The clothes they're all wearing now are of the simpler winter-fae style, fitted tunics and trousers in shades of gray. I don't spot any stains or wrinkles, and my suspicion grows that a lot of preparation has gone into making their situation appear as comfortable as possible. The servants can't have done much work in these clothes, which means they were given new outfits specifically for my visit.

From their glazed expressions, they don't have the capacity to care at the moment. The fae treat their *horses* better than the humans they've kidnapped.

"There, you can see them," the coterie woman says,

and glances narrowly at Zelpha. "There's no need for you to remain. I can see to Lady Talia's needs."

A prickle of apprehension runs down my spine. I have ways of defending myself, including the new bronze bracelet with its delicate weight around my wrist, but I know I'm not a match for a fae when it comes to magic or physical strength. What would she do to ensure this visit goes well if I didn't have one of Corwin's people with me?

No doubt Zelpha has similar thoughts. She arches her eyebrows at the other woman. "That's all right. My lord instructed me to accompany Talia the entire time, and I intend to follow his orders."

Leaning on Corwin's authority seems to work. Laoni's coterie woman frowns but doesn't argue further. She sidles closer as I step toward the humans, her gaze fixed on me now. I wonder if she's watching for any excuse to complain about my behavior and kick me out of the castle after all.

I simply won't give her any excuses, then.

I smile at each of the servants, even though they're too out of it to smile back, and offer each a "Hello" and "It's good to meet you." When I hold out my hand to shake each of theirs, just to see how they move, I can't help noticing bruises that look like fingerprints clamped around one man's arm where his sleeve falls back. One slim woman's grasp feels so weak and brittle I'm afraid I'll break her fingers if I squeeze. Another man holds his shoulders awkwardly when he extends his arm, favoring one.

"What happened to your shoulder?" I ask him.

"I didn't finish quickly enough," he says in a dull tone, "and I—"

"It was an accident," the coterie woman breaks in. "A momentary clumsiness. We healed him as well as we could."

They healed him when it happened or only as well as they could *now*, who knows how long after it happened? And was he really just clumsy, or did it happen because of some kind of punishment?

I suspect pushing him to say more will get him in more trouble than it might be worth.

"How much time do they spend in this room?" I ask.

"It's only for sleeping," the fae woman replies.

I look around. "And what about when they have time off?"

Her mouth opens and closes again as she seems to grapple with her words.

"They don't get time off, most likely," Zelpha puts in. "Work them from waking until they're falling asleep on their feet."

"We aren't so hard on them," the other woman protests. "They have plenty of idle moments."

"And what do they do in those moments?" I say. "Just stand there like they are now?"

"That's all they want to do." She turns to the servants. "Are any of you unhappy with your situation here?"

I get a chorus of murmured "No"s in response, but no audible enthusiasm. I hold my tongue against pointing out that they haven't been allowed to feel unhappy. This woman isn't the one making the decisions about what happens here anyway.

I'm obviously not going to get anything more useful out of them while she's overseeing things, but I've seen enough anyway. I turn to her. "What about the kitchen servants? I'd like to see the space they're working in, even if they're not done with their jobs."

The coterie woman wavers and then nods. "Fine. They should be just finishing up as it is."

She stalks out ahead of us, clearly expecting us to follow her. The guard who brought us to the room has vanished.

As we trail behind the coterie woman, I glance at Zelpha, keeping my voice low. "Is there any reason fae would *need* to bring human servants in? I mean, Corwin only has a few. Sylas has managed to do without any for decades. There's nothing they can do that fae couldn't— and more easily, since the fae have magic—is there?"

Zelpha shakes her head. "Not that I can think of— other than giving the fae who wish it a better chance at having more children." She winces just as I cringe inwardly. I know in an instant that some of those fae must outright rape the human servants while they're in that drugged-up daze. There's no way they could really consent in that state. They'd barely understand what they're agreeing to.

"It's tradition, like the arch-lords said at the meeting the other day," Zelpha goes on. "Many think we shouldn't have to handle any sort of drudgework, magically or otherwise, if we can get humans to do it. And I'd bet a great deal of the ones who think that way also enjoy always having someone around they can lord it over, regardless of whether they're lords themselves."

It's not hard for me to believe that.

I exhale slowly, willing down the urge to squirm with

horror. This isn't an insurmountable problem. The fae don't *need* the humans, so they could treat them better, or let them return to the human world, or—so many other possible compromises. I just have to find the compromise they'll agree to. And with so many of the Unseelie seeing me as some kind of blessed savior, hopefully I can manage that just like I managed to get myself invited into Laoni's castle.

We turn down a wider hall with a couple of painted portraits nearly as tall as I am hanging on the gleaming wall. The one we pass first shows Laoni with a slender, knob-chinned man I assume is her soul-twined mate. I've never met the man, but then, I'm not sure I've met any of the arch-lords' mates. They don't typically bring them around to the meetings.

The next painting shows a couple I assume are Laoni's parents. The man looks as stern and brawny, and the woman has a turquoise tint to her hair like Laoni does. They sit straight and formal but with their hands clasped together in a way that seems to show genuine affection.

I pause, taking it in. Corwin said something about Laoni coming into her rule suddenly and early like he did, didn't he?

"These are the previous lord and lady, right?" I say. "What happened to them?"

The coterie woman stops in her tracks and swivels on her heel. "They are no longer with us," she says tersely. "As I don't think it right to remind the arch-lord of, should she happen to pass by."

It's hard to imagine Laoni actually grieving, but losing one's parents early can't be easy for anyone, even her. But why would it affect her that badly to hear someone mention it after all this time? Just what *did* happen to them?

The woman taps her foot at my hesitation. "Come along. Did you want to see the kitchen or not?"

I bite back the questions she obviously won't answer anyway and hurry after her. I'll get a straighter answer from Corwin. I could ask him right now, but I'd rather not divert my attention while I'm in the home of someone I already know wants me out of the picture.

We descend a staircase and walk into a large room even bigger than the kitchen in Corwin's palace. The pale iridium is broken by the darker metals used to form the ovens and countertops.

A few fae staff are setting some trays of pastries in the cold room to sit before baking. The coterie woman lifts her chin toward a man who's just taking a final dish out of the sink of wash water. "There's one you're looking for."

I limp over, and he turns toward me. His face is as vacant as the others upstairs.

"Hi," I say anyway. "I'm Talia. How long have you been working in the kitchen here?"

He sways a little as if to some melody only he can hear. "Oh, it's been... It's been a good long time."

A portly fae man with bushy eyebrows marches over to us. "What's this about, now?"

The coterie woman speaks up before I can. "You should have heard, Serev. Lady Talia has come to check up on our mortal helpers."

I look around. "Where are the others? We were told there were a few in the kitchen."

Serev lets out a huff. "What you'd want with those dust-destined—"

The coterie woman clears her throat, and his mouth snaps shut. He glances at me again, and understanding seems to click in his eyes. I smile back at him tightly. It isn't as if I'm surprised to find more fae with dismissive attitudes toward humans among Laoni's staff.

"They're sorting something out in the storeroom," he says. "I'll get them for you."

He bustles off and returns a minute later with an elderly man and woman. The second I look at their whitened hair and the wrinkles lining their faces, I can't help thinking that back in the world where they belong, they'd be retired by now. Instead, they're still working away day in and day out. The horror inside me clenches tighter.

When I ask them how they feel about their work, the woman blinks at me with confusion. "Always something to do," the man says in an unnervingly dreamy tone. "Keeps us busy."

The woman nods slowly. "It does that."

"What would you do if you weren't working here?" I venture, aware of the coterie woman watching us like a hawk. I'm treading on thin ice.

But the elderly couple aren't aware enough to really complain. "What is there but here?" the woman asks, sounding genuinely bewildered.

Beside me, Zelpha looks like she's biting back a grimace. I step aside and let Serev dismiss the couple, ideas about all the ways I want to help these people whirling in my head. All I know for sure is that things can't go on like this. Not while I'm here, not while I have some kind of leverage with which to stand up for people like me.

As I turn to tell the coterie woman I've seen enough, a few fae in guard uniforms barge into the kitchen. I don't know two of them by name, but the third, coming up behind them, is Kesral.

They go to a shelf where it appears the food is up for grabs. The first two grab hunks of dried meat, but when Kesral tries to push past them to take something for himself, they jostle him back with their shoulders. One lets out a cruel chuckle.

"First pickings for those who don't have dung in their veins," the other sneers.

Kesral's jaw tenses, but he steps back while they look over the offerings and grab a few more treats. "Have at it, son of dung," the first guard tosses over his shoulder as they bump past him on their way out.

My hands ball at my sides on his behalf. My gaze darts to Serev, expecting him to join in the jibes after the way he started to talk about the human servants, but his expression has clouded over.

When Kesral has ducked out, I risk a much more pointed question than I've tried before. "You don't think it's right that the fae who are more human get treated worse?"

Serev's head jerks around. His mouth works. "It isn't the same. He's still fae. Fae is fae. I don't know why our lord allows them to get away with it."

His lord *participates* in the harassment from what I've seen. I knit my brow. "What do you mean?"

He waves his thick hand in the air. "Ah, Kesral started

hanging around the castle helping out where he could when he was a very young thing. He and Arch-Lord Laoni are close in age. They got up to rather a lot of exploits together, from what I saw. Back when they were children, you couldn't tear them apart."

What? I have to stop myself from staring at him. "I guess her opinion of him changed."

"An arch-lord has many responsibilities without worrying about every member of the staff," the coterie woman says tartly.

Serev shrugs. "True enough. They must have grown apart as they grew up. It happens. I just can't imagine her approving of that kind of talk toward him, faithful as he's been."

And yet when I saw them together, she seemed incapable of doing anything but snapping at him. I catch Zelpha's eye, but she makes a puzzled gesture in return.

Well, whatever's gone on between Laoni and her former friend, it doesn't change what I need to do. Maybe helping the humans in the fae world will help the human-leaning fae as well.

CHAPTER EIGHTEEN

Whitt

Sylas studies me for a long moment after I've finished speaking. It's difficult to tell which of his eyes, the dark one or the deadened one, is seeing more.

"You're sure about this," he says finally.

I lean back against the doorframe of his study, listening to re-confirm that no one's nearby in the hall outside. "I've been sure *I* want to since before this whole business with the Unseelie. I only needed to be sure of Corwin. But since it affects the cadre and my service to you as well, I wouldn't go forward without consulting you."

A hint of wryness curls my brother's lips. "And if I said no, would you heed me?"

The wryness stops me from bristling. It's still a new sensation, feeling this at ease with the man I serve. Knowing he's only teasing, that he trusts me and I trust him. A fleeting jab of irritation runs through me that his former mate stole that ease from us for so long, but what's done is done. At least we've ended up in a better place.

"I wouldn't have brought it up otherwise," I reply with a crooked grin. "You are my lord. And you've spent more time with Corwin than I have—it's possible you've seen reasons for concern that I've missed."

Sylas shakes his head. "My assessment is much the same as yours. His loyalty is to Talia above his colleagues, and to the alliance between our peoples over their self-interest. The fact that you've drawn the same conclusions reassures *me*."

He pauses and rubs his hand across his jaw, his gaze going momentarily distant before refocusing on me. "I think what you suggest could benefit us and is unlikely to harm us. I wish I were in a position to offer it myself. If you're confident in the decision, by all means, go ahead. But I would ask that you don't speak of it to anyone else, including August, unless absolutely necessary."

I don't need to ask him why, even though the thought of keeping something from our other brother sends a vague uneasiness through me. August isn't as adept at dissembling and subterfuge as either of us. He'd never let a crucial piece of information slip purposefully, but in an urgent situation where he didn't have much time to think, he could give something away. And the wrong person finding out about this could be disastrous.

I dip my head in acknowledgment. "I completely agree. Thank you."

Sylas gives me a softer smile. "I'm glad you've found a

partner who brings you more peace than most ever achieve. I was starting to think you'd keep your bachelor ways forever."

The warmth of his words leaves me a bit awkward. It's true that I'm not often at ease with any sort of affection, brotherly or romantic. I let out a rough chuckle. "You well know what a spectacular mate she is."

After I leave the study, I gather a few items I wanted to stash in my new rooms in the border castle and then make my way over there at the agreed time. Talia has been with August and then Corwin for most of the day, but this evening and the night belong to me. As the accord between the realms becomes stronger, I expect we'll all spend more of our time working out of that space together, but I can't say I mind getting the mite to myself for a little while.

I speak my vow and go in through our entrance. Before I've made it more than a few steps inside, Talia appears at the other end of the front hall, which is nearly as grand as Hearth-by-the-Heart's. Her cheeks are nearly as ruddy as the pink strands of her windblown hair, suggesting she's just come in from outside in the winter realm. The hue makes her look so wildly alive that my heart skips a beat when she beams at me.

No, I never thought any woman would ever affect me so deeply either. What a marvel she is.

As she limps over and gives me a hug in greeting, Corwin peeks in from the hall. He offers me a nod of welcome and then heads off. The man is a bit of an odd duck, but it's become clear that his stiffness and formality are simply part of his general personality, not any reservations he still holds about our joint relationship— and he's willing to shed them as Talia needs him to. Unlike the rest of his jabbering colleagues.

Now that the moment is upon me, I'm not sure how to begin. But Talia pre-empts me anyway.

"There's something I wanted to ask you about," she says. "If you don't mind getting right into business the second you've gotten here."

I laugh. "If you're scheming something, I definitely want to be a part of that." I hold up the satchel I packed. "I need to bring this to my room—and if you'll join me, we can talk in there with some privacy." I'll want that for the subject I mean to speak about as well.

I grasp her hand, and she follows me upstairs to the bedrooms. As I put my belongings away, she perches on the edge of the bed—only half the size her new one is, but plenty lavish enough for my tastes. I don't plan on sharing this one with anyone other than her.

"This morning I went to see how the human servants in Laoni's castle are treated," she says.

I can't imagine that trip was very inspiring. I glance over my shoulder at her. "And?"

"It went about as well as you'd think, which isn't very well." She makes a face. "I'm going to see if I can check on some other domains on both sides of the border to get the full picture, but I feel like I have a pretty good idea of what's typical already... The hard part is going to be convincing anyone to go against the kinds of things they've been doing for thousands of years. I was hoping you might have some ideas for how to pitch the idea of better treatment for humans to the other fae."

"Me specifically?"

She shrugs with a small but sweet smile. "Strategy is your specialty, right? Who better to strategize with?"

It's a logical explanation, but nevertheless her words provoke a flutter of tenderness in my chest. She has two arch-lords ready to leap to her aid, but there are still things she'd rather turn to me for.

I sit next to her on the bed and slip my arm around her waist. "Let's see. What exactly do you want to convince my brethren to do?"

The way she nestles into my casual embrace so eagerly warms my heart even more.

"In a perfect situation, which I realize I might not get, at least not without a few stepping stones along the way?" she says. "The fae would stop taking any humans from their world at all, unless the humans are agreeing to come with a full understanding of what they're getting into and no trickery to hold them here."

I hum to myself. "That request would definitely meet quite a bit of resistance, but I'll put my mind to it. What of the mortals already among us?"

She tips her head to the side in thought. "For the humans already here, no more drugs should be forced on them. They should be given some time to clear their heads and see their true situation, and then get to choose whether they stay or go home. And if they choose to stay, they need to be respected and given a chance to have lives of their own as much as the fae staff."

I nod slowly. "Even the fae servants aren't always

respected, but they're definitely better off than the humans nearly everywhere. Your biggest challenge is going to be convincing all the lords and ladies to do without their easily controlled workforce."

Talia grimaces. "They don't *need* human servants. Anything the humans are doing, fae could do it too. Probably faster in most cases. We can point to Sylas as an example of a lord who's managed with only fae on staff for, what, about a century now?"

"Having an arch-lord as an exemplar certainly can't hurt. And as our people's respect for *you* grows, I'd imagine it'll become easier to convince them that those like you deserve better as well." I rub my jaw, mulling it over. "We'll definitely want to approach the situation one piece at a time rather than trying to overhaul the system all in one go."

"Where do you think it'd be easiest to start?"

That's the big question. "Perhaps rather than focusing on one element at a time, we'd be best off tackling one domain at a time," I say. "Starting with the arch-lords. Hearth-by-the-Heart already operates without human help, and Corwin's human servants are all fully conscious and accepting of their situation, aren't they? We could go to Donovan next. I think he'd be our best bet for convincing."

Talia's eyes light up. "That makes sense. After him, maybe we could talk to Neve on the winter side. She seems like the most flexible of the other winter arch-lords."

"Perfect. If we have both of them, then half of us would be setting a new standard. Easier to start pressuring the others into following suit. And once the regular lords and ladies see that their arch-lords are making a change, they'll be more inclined to do the same themselves."

She taps her lips. "I should probably see how Donovan's human servants are doing in general before we make any suggestions to him. Do you think you or Sylas could speak to him about me making a visit there?"

"No problem at all." I ruffle her hair. "Is that a solid enough plan for you, at least as a start?"

"Definitely. Thank you." She leans into me again, and I tuck her tighter against me instinctively.

There's so much I want to say to her, so many ways I've imagined this, but now that I'm on the verge, the act feels so momentous it takes me a minute to gather myself. I trace my fingers over Talia's cheek and kiss her temple.

"Talia… A couple of months back I told you there was something I wanted to offer you when I felt I could do so without jeopardizing my other responsibilities. Do you remember that?"

She pulls back, her gaze snapping up to meet mine. I can tell right away that she does.

Her voice comes out quiet. "It's all right. I understand that with the situation with Corwin—accepting him as my soul-twined mate and having that unshakeable connection with him—it isn't totally secure. I never expected you to trust even *me* that much, let alone him as well."

Love swells inside me. I cup her chin, holding her gaze. "That's not why I'm bringing it up. I trusted you enough that I'd have offered you my true name back then if it'd only been about you. And having seen the strength of Corwin's will and his dedication to you… I trust him as well. If *you* don't find it too much of a responsibility to carry."

Talia blinks at me. "You want—you'd give me your true name now?" she says, a little breathless.

I want to wrap her in the tightest of embraces, but I can't do that and look her in the eyes at the same time. "I would. I want you to be able to call on me no matter where you are, no matter what's happening. You have Corwin, of course, but if I should be closer, or he should be incapacitated… From what Sylas heard from the sage, Heart only knows how much more complicated our lives may become in the coming years. And I'll be here for you in every way I can be—as you've been here for me."

Her eyes mist with tears, but her smile eliminates any fear that they're unhappy ones. "You really don't have to. I know what a big deal it is."

I give in to the urge to gather her up in my arms now, breathing in her tartly sweet scent. "I want to. I have no doubt about that. My only concern is whether you want to accept."

"Yes," she says without hesitation. "Yes. If I could have a soul-twined bond with all of you, I'd want it, and this is as close to that as I can get. I'd die before I let anyone use it against you."

My throat constricts. I believe she means that. "I intend to see it never comes to that, mite."

I dip my head so my lips brush the shell of her ear. The syllables I've never spoken to anyone before catch in the back of my mouth. I urge them onto my tongue. "*Wye-con-ell.*"

"*Wye-con-ell,*" Talia repeats in a murmur, and just like

that, a tingle races through the center of my being. She looks up at me. "So if I need you, I just say it—the way I say the other true names—and I'll be able to reach out to you with my thoughts?"

"You can include a request with the name," I say. "Ask me to open my mind to you if you have something to tell me, ask me to answer a question, ask me to come to you— I have to obey. So, use it wisely."

"Of course." Her eyes shine with awe. "How will I know— With the other true names, I couldn't get a handle on them right away."

I was prepared for that question. "I thought we could play a little game of hide-and-seek," I say with a wink. "There's a spot in this castle it wouldn't be easy to get to without special guidance. Give me five minutes to reach it, and then speak my true name and focus on your awareness of me with as much concentration as you can. If you've got it right, you should be able to follow the route straight to me. Ready?"

Talia laughs, though she still looks a bit shy about it. "No time like the present."

"Then come to me as soon as you can." I kiss her once more, on the lips this time, reveling in the knowledge that I belong to this woman in every way that matters to me— that she *wanted* me to belong to her. Then I get up and leave the room.

I'm not sure when I'll have need of the office set aside for my use on the border castle's third floor. I'm reluctant to move my books and other supplies over just yet when I still need to do much of my work in Hearth-by-the-Heart. But it's here nonetheless, and during the construction I added a personal touch: one of my secret passageways.

By pressing the right spot on the built-in shelves, one section slides to the side to reveal a narrow hidden doorway. The spiral staircase beyond leads both down to a disguised exit at the base of the castle and up to a small terrace near the top of one of the turrets.

I head up, lifting my nose to the traces of fresh summer air that seep past the door above. The turret is set forward enough on our side of the castle that it escapes the haze of the border completely. I step out onto the wooden platform with its polished, waist-high railing to a view that encompasses nearly the entire hill around the Heart as well as some of the sprawling terrain beyond it.

Evening is creeping up on us. The shadows of the buildings below stretch long, and pinks and purples that echo Talia's hair glow in the scattered clouds. Even if this wasn't a particularly distinctive occasion, the sight would please me. I look forward to sharing it with my soon-to-be mate.

As I lean against the railing, the warm breeze ruffling over my hair with a faint smell of wildflowers, the same tingling sensation that ran through me before touches me again. Talia is calling on me.

I picture my path through the castle from leaving my bedroom, and the tingles condense inside my skull. I get the faintest impression of Talia from them—her slightly uneven gait, her eagerness to find me, her excitement that she's been able to sense my presence at all.

I linger on the bookshelves trick for the longest, until my ears catch the rasp of the hidden entrance opening from below. Talia's soft footsteps patter up the stairs. As she comes through the upper doorway, I turn to meet her.

Her whole face is glowing now. She throws herself into my arms, squeezing me close. "That was amazing. I just… knew which way to go, and then I could feel you guiding me when I needed it. It isn't like the soul-twined bond at all, but it's still wonderful."

"No matter where you or I go, you'll always be able to reach me," I say.

She tips her head up, seeking my lips. I have no problem at all giving her the kiss she's requesting.

This woman has never been short on passion, but there's a depth of ardor to her embrace now that tops any kiss we've shared before, as if she means to meld right into me. It stirs every nerve in my body to eager alertness.

"Thank you," she says when she draws back. "I know the words aren't really enough, but—thank you. I wish I could give the same thing back to you."

But she doesn't have a true name to give.

I tease my fingers along her jaw. "You've offered me plenty, Talia. In some ways I'd say more than I've yet offered you."

She snorts as if that's impossible. Then her gaze drifts from me to the view, and she sucks in an awed breath. "Wow. I didn't know you'd built a balcony up here."

"It's for my use only. And I suppose yours as well, should you have need of it. As spymaster, I enjoy having a good view over my surroundings." I smirk. "It has a spell around it to hide any sight of it from below, so no one will ever know they're being spied on."

"You think of everything," she says, amused. She

moves to the railing, setting her hands on it and peering out into the distance.

We're so high up here that the fae moving about in the domains below look no larger than mice. Talia studies them and the vivid colors spreading across the darkening sky. When her eyes flick back to me, I catch a hint of slyness in them.

She turns her back to the railing and then boosts herself up with a hitch of her arms to sit on it. My pulse lurches. I lunge for her in the same instant, some part of my mind picturing her tumbling over the edge—but as my hands catch her waist, I can already feel that she was keeping her balance just fine.

"Trying to give me a heart attack there, mite?" I ask, bowing my head over hers.

She smiles sweetly up at me. "Showing that I trust you with my life just as you've trusted me with yours. I can't offer the same openness you did, but there are other ways I can bare myself to you."

Still gripping the railing with one hand, she raises the other to the collar of her dress. In the aftermath of my panic, it takes me a moment to realize she's loosening the ties that run down the center of the bodice. The fabric gapes open, gradually unveiling more and more pale skin over her collarbone and the swells of her breasts.

A jolt of lust shoots straight to my groin, and heat floods my body. I wrench my gaze from her chest to her face. My voice comes out rough. "Talia..."

She reaches lower and gives an extra tug to uncover her breasts completely. Her pert nipples pebble in the breeze.

She watches me, avidly and yet still with a shy flush creeping across her cheeks.

"I want you," she says simply. "I know you won't let me fall."

"Never," I rasp, looping one arm around her to hold her firmly in place. She splays her legs so I can step closer between them, and Heart help me, my cock is already straining against the crotch of my slacks.

I understand the symbolism of this gesture, and I want to allow her it, but I can't possibly pretend I'm doing this all for her benefit. I doubt I've ever desired her more.

I lower my head to reclaim her lips. As our mouths lock together, I caress my fingers over her breasts, teasing one nipple into an even harder point and then doing the same to the other, drinking in the whimpers my touch provokes like fine wine.

Talia squirms close enough that her sex brushes my cock, her fingers interlacing behind my neck. She kisses me like she might never get to again, like she's starving for me, and that only makes me all the hungrier for her.

My patience is fraying fast. I slip my free hand between her legs, hefting up the skirt of her dress, and trace the dampness spreading across her panties. A groan escapes me. Kissing her harder, I delve my tongue between her lips to tangle with hers.

As I stroke her faster, her fingernails prick my neck with perfect nicks of pain. "Whitt," she gasps, arching into me.

I know what she wants now, but I intend to give her the highest pleasure I can before I take my own.

I tuck my fingers right inside her panties to fondle her

skin to skin. My mouth captures every needy sound that slips from her lips. I pump one finger, then two, then three inside her as my thumb dances across her clit.

Talia's head falls back with an outright moan. The wind rises, tossing her hair around her. I sway with her on the railing, my other arm still firm around her back, her trust in me absolute. Her lack of fear brings an ache into my chest that's far more potent than my lust.

I swivel my thumb, increasing the pressure when she pushes into my touch. Her spine arches farther, and then her channel is clenching around my fingers, a tremor of release racing through her body.

Before it's even faded, she grasps my arm. "I want *you*," she says with the determination I admire so much. "All of you, inside me, coming with me."

I nuzzle her cheek. "Then you'll have your wish, mighty one."

She tugs at my slacks, and together we free my cock. I tear the panties right off her rather than carry out the gymnastics of peeling them off intact while I'm this close to her. I'll bring her a dozen replacements next time.

Her fingers close around my throbbing length, and just like that I'm panting against her hair. "You spark the hottest fire in me I've ever felt," I say. "I will never want anyone else but you."

She tugs me forward. "Then have me."

I don't need any further encouragement to plunge right into her wet heat.

Skies above, being joined with her like this is never less than glorious, but tonight tops every time before. She rocks to meet me, heedless of the height and her precarious position, knowing that even in my greatest rush of passion I'll protect her with all I have. The wind whips over us as if urging us on.

The intensity of the moment is too much for me to hold back for very long. I buck into her, and she reaches her second peak with a giddy cry. The bliss written all across her beautiful face brings my own body surging toward ecstasy. I hold her to me and thrust a few more times before all my desire spills inside her in a blaze of release.

We cling to each other there for a few minutes, catching our ragged breaths. Talia makes a pleased sound and nestles her head against my chest. I think her show of faith has been clear enough that I can now heft her off the railing and sit with her on my lap in a position where falling isn't a possibility.

"I think we should do that again sometime," Talia announces.

A laugh tumbles out of me. "I won't argue with that. You call, and I'll be at your side."

She peers up at me, abruptly serious. "I wouldn't ever use that power casually, you know. Only if it was an emergency."

I brush my fingers over her hair. "If it's just to convey a message, speak to me whenever you like. But yes, I'd prefer if you didn't order my immediate arrival unless necessary. If only because it would make it rather hard to keep our arrangement a secret. But I wasn't at all worried that you would."

"Good." She leans into me again, her face turned

toward the view between the bars of the railing. Then, abruptly, she straightens up. "What's *that*?"

I follow her gaze, my spirits sinking at her tone before I've even spotted what she's reacting to.

In the near distance, coming from somewhere near the base of the hill around the Heart, a plume of smoke is rising, glinting bloody red against the darkening sky.

CHAPTER NINETEEN

Talia

By the time we make it to the front entrance, my dress hastily refastened as Whitt and I hurried down the stairs, shouts are carrying up the hill. Even though the eerie smoke I spotted looked far off, the breeze now carries an acrid, metallic scent that makes my nose wrinkle.

The smoke wasn't coming from anywhere near Hearth-by-the-Heart, at least. As far as I could tell, it was rising from some spot at the edge of Donovan's or Celia's domain.

Whitt glances at me, his expression taut with concern, and I brace myself for him to tell me he thinks I should stay back while he investigates. But he must realize I won't want to be left in the dark—and respect the fact that I'd rather risk a little danger than stay shut up in the castle unknowing—because he gives me a curt nod.

"We can get there fastest if I carry you," he says.

Without waiting for my response, he hunches forward, shifting into his tawny wolf form in a matter of seconds. Watching the transformation now is nothing but exhilarating. He crouches low, and I clamber onto his back the way I did once before when he carried me through the woods to one of his favorite groves.

I don't think today's destination is going to be anywhere near as pleasant.

I lean against his muscular back, burying my fingers in the thick ruff of fur around his neck, and he sets off at a lope. The swift, rhythmic pace is easy to adapt to. I tighten my knees against his sides to keep my balance, but I have no more fear of falling than I did perched on the railing of his secret balcony.

He races across the grassy plain around the Bastion and into the forestland that surrounds the other arch-lords' castles. The smoky tang in the air thickens, and the shouts multiply. Other wolfish figures charge through the shadows between the trees around us, heading to the same spot the quickest way the summer fae are capable of.

As we veer along a well-beaten path down the hill, the forest thins into patches here and there. Whitt runs through another dense stretch of trees and bursts out at the edge of a darkened field of wildflowers.

The smoke is rising from a patch of burning vegetation in the middle of that field. I can't see any cause for the ruddy glow that's rippling through the billows all the way up to the sky, but it's hard to make out anything all that clearly in the deepening evening and the flickering light.

It doesn't even look like the actual spot that's burning should be big enough to produce all that smoke. When I squint, I can only make out a dark pile of soot surrounded by that wavering glow, about the size of a campfire pit.

But then, when fae magic is involved, all sorts of unusual things are possible.

Fae have gathered all around the burning spot, more arriving from all directions. None of them has gotten close, though, all hanging back several feet. Some in human form and some still wolves, they prowl around that invisible border, their eyes wary and their mouths curled into frowns.

Why isn't anyone putting it out?

Whitt pushes closer through the crowd and stops in the midst of it. As he lets me slide off his back, I spot a few familiar figures in the crowd: one of Celia's cadre-chosen and a couple of Donovan's. Not all of the fae around us have arrived from the arch-lords' domains, though. Many are hurrying over from farther beyond the hill, from the neighboring domains.

Whitt straightens up next to me, shaking off the transformation. He glances around. "We're right at the border of four different domains here. Whoever's responsible for this, they wanted to catch plenty of attention."

Corwin must catch my uneasy emotions, because his voice breaks through my thoughts. *What's going on over there?*

I'm not sure yet, I reply. *Don't worry—there are plenty of fae here. I'm sure we can deal with whatever it is.*

He accepts that answer with a twinge of concern but no protest.

"What *is* it?" I ask Whitt, peering at the smoking

patch, which doesn't appear to have grown. "How is it making so much smoke—and why doesn't someone just throw some water on it or something?"

"There must be some magic to it that's complicating matters. Something about the scent..." Taking a step forward, Whitt inhales sharply, and his stance goes rigid.

"What?" I demand, catching up with him.

He nods toward the stream of smoke with a sickly grimace. "It's got iron in it. I can feel it prickling in my lungs. We *can't* get close enough to try to douse it, and it'll drain away the power of any spell. How in the lands...?"

His forehead furrows with confusion. I glance around at the other gathered fae again. They all look equally uncomfortable and puzzled, the shouts having dwindled into muttered conversation as they must be discussing how to tackle this strange intrusion.

The obvious answer is right here. "I can put it out," I say. "The iron isn't going to hurt *me*. Get me a bucket of water or whatever you think will do it, and I'll give it a shot."

Whitt hesitates. "We don't know what other effects it might produce, mite. No one could easily get to you to protect you."

"Then I'll be careful about it. We can't leave this thing polluting the air with toxic metals, can we? What else are you going to do?"

His jaw works, but he must know I'm right. If he hadn't brought me along, calling on human servants to deal with the problem would have been the obvious solution anyway. And I can at least think on my feet better than those in a drugged-up daze.

As he debates, I notice the darkened patch of soot creeping wider. More smoke billows up. The hairs on the back of my neck rise. "It's getting larger. If we wait, *I* might not be able to put it out either."

Whitt hisses through his teeth in annoyance, but I know it's not directed at me. "All right. You'll go in there carefully and withdraw as quickly as you can. I'm not sure water will do it on its own, though... Give me a moment."

He raises his voice to reach the other fae around us. "Did anyone see how this started?"

All we get are shaken heads and responses to the negative. One of Donovan's cadre-chosen comes over to us. "I was one of the first to get here. There was no one around except a couple of the fae from Saplight. By all appearances, it started spontaneously."

"That hardly seems likely," Whitt mutters. He narrows his eyes at the burning spot, which has stretched a little farther again in the time he's been talking, and lets out a growl. "I don't like this at all." He touches my shoulder. "Stay right here until I get back."

He moves to the fringes of the growing crowd and must work some conjuring there, because he returns carrying a thick, sodden blanket. He hands it to me gingerly. "This should be enough to smother and dampen the source of the smoke—it's the best I can come up with that doesn't rely on direct magical effects. We can hope it'll at least cut off the smoke for long enough that we fae can step in and handle anything remaining."

At my nod, Whitt ushers me to the edge of the inner ring. His hand twitches against my elbow as the metallic smoky scent deepens. He raises his other arm to catch the attention of the assembled fae. "Lady Talia, our human comrade, is going to attempt to smother the burning. Please keep careful watch for any signs of a threat to her while she takes on this task for us."

Dozens of pairs of eyes fix on me, hopeful murmurs traveling through the crowd.

I limp forward, scanning the area around the burning patch but refusing to hesitate. The spot is still small enough that I should be able to cover the whole thing with one heave of the wet fabric, but it won't stay that small for long.

The smoke stings my eyes and makes my lungs itch. When I'm just a couple of steps away, a cough erupts out of me. I choke it back as well as I can and heft up the blanket to toss it.

Just as I'm about to fling my arms forward, a tiny shape darts around the burning patch. Even as I register the rat-like shape, it's shooting up into that of a burly man —a man who's lunging right at me, needle-like claws jutting from his fingertips.

A yelp jolts from my throat. I drop the blanket, groping for the dagger at my hip, but the Murk fae is already on me. Still ducked down in a rat-like posture, his head slams into my stomach.

We topple over together. His claws rake across my thigh, and pain explodes through my leg. I smack my hands toward him in a reflexive gesture of defense—

—and a sudden burst of light blazes between us.

The fae man topples over and slumps on the ground next to me. I stare at him, my chest heaving for breath, agony searing through my thigh.

He doesn't move. His half-closed eyes look dull. Is he… dead?

What even happened?

Trembling fingers close around my shoulders. Whitt has made it to me, but the effects of the smoke are already sending tremors through his whole body. He coughs weakly and tries to drag me away, but my gaze jerks back to the smoke.

I haven't finished what I came here to do. The Murk man tried to stop me, but he failed—that's all that matters until this is done.

Talia, Corwin says. *Talia, are you all right?* But I can't find the concentration to answer him.

"Wait!" I shout over the tumult of voices around us, and push onto my hands and knees to grab the fallen blanket. Clenching my teeth against the pain in my leg, I yank the sodden fabric off the ground, lurch toward the burning patch, and manage to hurl the blanket right over it.

With a sputtering sound, the smoke vanishes, the last billow drifting off toward the sky. The center of the blanket quivers and goes still. All we're left with is that square of fabric and the dead Murk man in the middle of the ring of Seelie.

Fighting his wheezes, Whitt stumbles to me and manages to scoop me off my feet. As he hauls me farther from the burning spot, we both cough to clear our lungs. Other fae converge on the blanket, on the Murk fae, and on the two of us. My thigh feels as if a fire has caught within it.

I'm okay, I tell Corwin. *It's done.* The words seem to waver as they pass through our bond.

They mustn't be very convincing, because his only response is a surge of protectiveness and a brief declaration. *I'm coming to you.*

A voice rings out from what sounds like far away to my pain-addled mind. "Lady Talia has saved us again! The Heart worked through her to protect us and fend off the Murk."

"She's sacrificed her blood for us once more," someone else declares from a different direction. "The ravens have been calling her blessed. I think they're right about that one thing."

The only word that totally sinks in is *blood.* I stare down at my leg, recognizing the dark red blotch spreading across the whole front of my dress's skirt as just that.

So much blood. And the pain is like those claws are digging deeper into me with every second. Maybe I'm not okay after all.

Whitt tears right through the silky cloth up to just below my hip so he can uncover the wound. A snarl escapes him at the sight of my gouged flesh, but only for an instant before he's murmuring hasty true names.

The pain numbs just a little. There's too much blood already on me for me to tell whether he's been able to stop more from seeping out.

"Who here is skilled at healing?" he calls out, a note of desperation in his voice.

I want to tell him I'll be just fine, that I've been scratched up plenty before with the scars to prove it, but I can't seem to find my voice.

A woman hunches down beside us and hovers her hands over the wound. At her emphatic words, the agony searing through my leg pulls back even more. The claws of pain dwindle into pin-pricks. I glance down, the movement dizzying me, and see the skin sealing into pale pink lines marking my leg from just above my knee to halfway up my thigh.

"Will she be all right?" asks another woman I don't recognize from behind the healer. She sounds surprisingly concerned for a stranger. I realize a whole horde of fae are standing around us, peering down at me with worried eyes.

"She didn't bleed for long enough to put her in severe danger," the healer says. "Thank the Heart." She touches the side of my face. "And thank the Heart for you, coming here and foiling the Murk's plot. The cuts were deep, down to the bone. It'll still hurt for some time as the muscle fully heals. Be gentle with yourself, Lady Talia."

I think that's the first time a regular Seelie outside Sylas's pack has referred to me by my official title. Now... now many of the fae around us are bowing their heads and offering murmurs of consolation and hope with expressions that are oddly familiar.

It's the same kind of awe I've been seeing from the Unseelie after I cure a curse victim.

I don't feel as if I really did all that much just now. I'm not even sure what I *did* do, other than get my leg carved up and throw a blanket on the ground, which are hardly awe-worthy acts.

"I—I just wanted to help you all," I say.

That remark is met with another volley of murmurs—

and some exclamations about "the light!" As Whitt helps me up, I rub my forehead.

Right, there was that flash of light when the Murk man attacked me. It almost seemed like it was the light that killed him. If he *did* die.

My pulse hiccups, and I turn to Whitt. "Is he dead? The Murk?"

Whitt inclines his head, studying me. "They checked him over thoroughly, as you can imagine. The body will be further inspected for any clues to his other intentions or associates and then disposed of. I've never seen you use light like that before."

Because I haven't. I'm not even sure I did use it now.

I bite my lip, aware of the audience all around us. It might not be a bad thing for the Seelie to start to see me as something more than a convenient tonic ingredient. The more they respect me, the more I can demand they respect the other humans here, just like I've started to sway the winter fae. But nothing about this situation sits quite right with me.

I sway on my feet, still a bit dizzy, and Whitt steadies me. "I think I'd better bring Lady Talia home to rest," he says. "If you discover anything notable about this fire or the ones who caused it, send word to Hearth-by-the-Heart at once."

The nearest fae offer their agreement, a few of them brushing their fingers over my arm as we pass them. I can't tell whether they're trying to offer me comfort or take something from my presence.

When we've made it to the edge of the crowd, Whitt scoops me off my feet as August likes to do and sets off up the hill, obviously deciding I'm in no condition to be riding wolves.

"Corwin's coming to us," I say, still a little dazed. I can sense my soul-twined mate hurrying across the border. "He'll meet us up the hill."

Whitt nods. As he tucks my head against his shoulder, he asks under his breath, "What exactly happened back there, mighty one? I would have gotten him off you if you hadn't managed it yourself so abruptly. I'm sorry I didn't get to you soon enough to stop him laying claws on you at all."

"Don't blame yourself," I say, leaning into his embrace. I run through what I can remember of those panicked moments. "I… don't actually know what happened. I didn't say any true names. The light just appeared."

I pause, my uneasiness spreading farther through my chest. "It didn't *feel* like it came from me. I didn't feel anything at all—no energy or power moving through me, the way I do when I've used true names before."

"Hmm." Whitt's mouth slants downward. "You know what's normal for you and what isn't better than I do, mite. I suppose it's possible one of my brethren cast a spell to intervene and then didn't want to distract attention from the heroics you did perform."

I *could* believe that, even though I'm not totally sure I do. I worry at my lip. "I thought you said your magic wouldn't work that close to the iron in the smoke."

"It shouldn't have been able to." He sighs. "I don't like it. Once you're someplace safe, I'll see what else I can find out. At least whatever it was worked in your favor."

That's true. Maybe it's silly to be fretting about the

source of the strange light when it might have even saved my life.

I let my body totally relax against Whitt's, and my gaze wanders over the trees we're passing between. It catches on a fall of pearly-white hair half-dimmed by the deepening evening shadows.

Celia is coming down the hill along a course several paces away. Even as I notice her, her gaze stops on us. Her lips flatten into a stern line that looks disapproving. Then she moves on, leaving me even more unnerved than I was before.

CHAPTER TWENTY

I'd have thought that being in pain would make it easier to produce tears. As the healer warned me might happen, the wound on my thigh still throbs deep in the muscle when I'm moving around much. But even with that pulsing ache spreading through my flesh, I can't start weeping for the curse victim in front of me like flicking a switch.

I look at her, taking in the frail lines of her aged body turned even more brittle in the curse's grip, and think of the children and grandchildren she might be hoping to see grow older, that the curse would steal from her. Of my own grandparents who passed on, never knowing I was still alive, while I was trapped here in the fae realm. It takes a few minutes for the familiar burn to form.

Our audience, gathered in the glow of the Heart's rhythmic light, is nothing but patient. They might even like it when the spectacle takes a little longer, giving time for their anticipation to grow so their relief when I deliver the cure can be that much greater. When I turn away from the cursed woman, with Corwin's hand on my shoulder in case I need steadying, enough breaths draw in to form a collective gasp.

The fae who came to watch the healing are even more reverent than usual today. It might have something to do with the fact that after seeing how my limp was worsening as I moved around the castle, Corwin insisted on carrying me out to the Heart. There's no outward sign of my wound, but he had a few members of his coterie pass on word that people would need to be more patient with me for a little while. When he approached this group with me in his arms, we were met with a lot of widened eyes and murmurs of concern and appreciation.

I guess that makes sense. It's an even bigger generosity to put my time and energy toward healing the fae when I'm not fully healed myself. Still, the awed silence of the crowd feels even stranger than the eager murmurs I've gotten before.

It's a bigger audience than usual too. As before, the curse victim arrived with a large retinue of her flock-folk. But several others have drifted over from both Heart's Cadence and at least a couple of the other arch-lords' domains—and from across the border as well. One of Sylas's staff in the joint castle must have passed on word in the summer realm that I was being called to do a curing, because a dozen or so Seelie slipped through the haze around the Heart around the same time Corwin and I got here.

They've hung back from the Unseelie crowd, watching

curiously from a respectful distance. Apparently yesterday's encounter with the Murk has drawn even more interest from the summer fae than I realized.

I focus harder on the sadness I stirred up, and my tears finally spill over. After a moment, I swipe them away and turn back toward the aged fae woman. When I reach for her cheek, her stiffened face manages to twitch to form a hint of a smile.

I might worry about how demanding my role will become as the curse intensifies, but moments like this are why I can't imagine backing down from it. No matter what fae like Aerik or Laoni think of me, every single one I've healed has been grateful beyond words.

None of them deserve to die, especially not in the curse's cruel way.

This time, when the woman straightens up and shows that the frigid chill has released her, the crowd around us keeps a careful distance from me, respectful of my injury. Many of them still call out words of thanks and of their hopes that my wound heals well and soon. As I nod and smile to them in return, my gaze slips past them to the distant form of Laoni's iridium castle.

After all the chaos last night, Whitt and I never got a chance to reach out to Donovan about a visit to see how his human servants are faring. And I still have so many questions to expand on what I learned about Laoni's past and family.

I don't have any immediate business to attend to after this, if there's something you want to talk about, Corwin says through our bond, raising his hand in farewell to the now-dispersing crowd. I know he's careful not to dig too deeply into thoughts I'm not purposefully sending his way, but he can't help picking up on my mood.

There is, actually, I say, but before we can head back to the border castle, one of his staff comes hurrying over from the palace at Heart's Cadence.

"My lord," the man says when he reaches us, with a low bow. "And lady," he adds hastily before focusing back on Corwin. "A messenger has come calling—she said she needs to pass on some news to you as soon as you're able to hear it."

Corwin frowns, apprehension trickling from him into me to join my own. *I'll come with you,* I say before he can suggest I go back to the border castle on my own. *I'd rather hear whatever it is myself—and maybe it'll be something that involves me.*

He nods and reaches for me to lift me up. I still feel a bit awkward being carried like an invalid, but my leg is hurting enough just from standing on my own for the last ten minutes that I'm not going to complain about it. The man from the palace doesn't appear to think it's odd.

"Did the messenger give any indication of what matter she wants to speak to me about?" Corwin asks him as he strides toward the palace. The melody the wind makes passing around the diamond spires shivers over us. "Or which domain she was sent from?"

The attendant shakes his head. "She said nothing other than what I've already conveyed. I assumed it was a message that required discretion."

"That's fine. I wouldn't want you to press in a situation like that. Thank you for summoning me."

At the entrance hall, the fae man heads off to whatever

other duties he has to attend to. Corwin keeps carrying me all the way to the room next to the terrace where visitors from farther abroad tend to land. The attendant had said the messenger would be waiting for us there, but when we reach the sitting room with its scattered armchairs and tables, there's no one else there.

Frowning, Corwin sets me down and scans the space. I sink onto the nearest chair, puzzled myself.

After a moment, he walks over to the doors leading to the sparkling terrace and plucks a bit of pale bark that's been fixed to the wall there. "It appears she left a note." He studies it, and I catch the gist through our bond before he speaks again. "She apologizes and says she wanted to confirm one detail of the message, but that she should return within the hour."

"I guess that's not too long," I say. It seems a little strange that she'd have left like that, but I'd rather she delivered an accurate message than one she knew might not be factual. "We were going to talk anyway."

"Yes." Corwin tugs another chair closer and sits down next to me, reaching to take my hand. He runs his thumb gently over my knuckles. "How have you been feeling, my soul? You're sure your injury is on the mend?"

"It's already better than it was last night," I say, squeezing his fingers. He found me and Whitt before we'd even reached Hearth-by-the-Heart, flying to us in a panic despite my reassurances, and insisted on having his own healer check the wound over before he could relax. Then he sent out a few more guards from Heart's Cadence to patrol for any signs of the Murk around the Heart on this side of the border. "The healer did say it'd hurt for a while until it's fully healed."

"What's been concerning you, then?"

I look toward the broad windows, though I can't see Laoni's castle from here, only the sprawling icy landscape beyond the Heart's plateau. "I saw a painting of Laoni's parents when I visited her castle yesterday. Her coterie woman seemed uncomfortable when I asked about them. I wondered if you know what happened to them."

Corwin leans back in his chair, his gaze going distant with thought. "I was too young to participate in any direct discussions around their passings, but I did hear some talk of it, mostly from my own parents. Her mother died before I was born, when Laoni was still a young child. I gather they went on a trip to visit a domain that included a magical whirlpool among its striking features, and there was an accident in which her mother fell in and was sucked down too quickly for anyone to save her."

I shudder. "That's horrible."

"Yes. I think there was a lot of talk about it among the lords and ladies afterward, especially because her father hated to speak of it himself. But my parents said he'd always been strict and became even more so afterward. I suppose he was afraid any carelessness might result in someone else he cared about meeting a similar fate."

It's hard to imagine what "strict" or "even stricter" might look like from winter fae who are already so uptight in general. Maybe that explains a few things about how rigid Laoni is on certain subjects.

"Her father was the arch-lord, then?" I say. "So she didn't inherit it until he passed on?"

Corwin inclines his head. "I was still a child then, and she was… around the equivalent of the age you are now, in fae terms. That incident I know more of the details of. A lord from a domain near the fringes thought he'd better his flock's situation by taking over one of the arch-lordships. He picked Laoni's domain to target. Her father was able to fend off the attack and protect her, but in the process he took a wound that proved fatal. There was nothing the healers could do."

That's horrible too. I rub my mouth, not entirely comfortable with the sense of sympathy the story provokes. It doesn't really matter what awful things Laoni has been through if she's being awful herself. All of my men have been through traumatizing experiences themselves, and they've all kept their senses of fairness and compassion despite it.

Neither account explains why she'd have turned her back on her friendship with Kesral either. "Do you have any idea why she's so dismissive of humans—and fae with human heritage?" I ask.

"I'm not aware of any particular reason for it. I hadn't even noticed her being unusually harsh to staff of more dilute blood until the other day." Corwin grimaces. "But then, that might be my own failing. Before you came into my life, I wasn't quite as attentive to my colleagues' treatment of specific sorts of underlings."

His guilt travels through our connection. I twine my fingers with his. "I think that's understandable. It's such an accepted part of fae society." Which is going to make it even harder to challenge that part.

Before the gloomy thought can fully take hold, one of

Corwin's guards bursts into the room. "My lord," she says, jerking into a brief bow, "I think you'd better come. The other arch-lords have marched on the new castle—they're demanding you hear them out."

"What?" Corwin springs to his feet, his forehead furrowing. "If they want to speak to me, they can come to me here—or meet me in the Hall of the Heart if they prefer that."

The guard shakes her head. "I—I don't think that'll be possible, my lord."

Corwin strides toward the doorway, and I hurry after him, gritting my teeth against the ache that wakes up within a few steps. When he stops to help me, I urge him onward silently. *Better they see me standing and walking on my own two feet, considering what they already think of me.*

He insists on scooping me up on the way to the main entrance and only putting me back on my feet there. We walk out side by side and halt just outside the diamond palace.

It isn't all of the arch-lords—I only see Laoni, Uzziah, and Terisse standing across the plain from us—but it isn't *only* them either. I understand now why the guard used the word "marched." Each arch-lord has a squadron of soldiers poised behind them, forming a semi-circle around the winter side of the border castle.

My gut twists. What the hell is going on?

Corwin strides over to them, slowing his pace just enough for me to keep up with my greater limp. I come to a halt right next to him, holding my head high despite the throbbing in my leg.

"What's the meaning of this?" he demands of his colleagues. "You look ready to stage an assault."

Laoni's eyes flash. "Perhaps we are. Consider yourself lucky that we're warning you before we take matters completely into our own hands."

Corwin looks from her to the other two and back again. "What are you talking about?"

Laoni jabs her forefinger in my direction. She pitches her voice loud enough to carry to all the assembled soldiers. "This human woman has been elevated beyond her station for too long already. No matter how 'blessed' she may be, it goes against the laws of the Heart for one who is not a lord or lady by inheritance to rule from a castle of his or her own. And 'Lady' Talia cannot be considered a lady in the same way as one of our own besides, since she isn't even fae. This structure stands in total defiance to the proper order of things."

I stare at her, trying to wrap my head around everything she's saying. Can she really support all those claims? She didn't bring any of that up while we were building the castle.

Maybe it took her this long to dig up some obscure law she felt she could twist to her ends. Or maybe she didn't bother digging until she saw just how avidly her people are starting to respond to me.

Maybe it's my fault for pushing my luck, forcing her hand to get my visit into *her* castle.

As I swallow thickly, Corwin sets a firm hand on my shoulder. "The Heart allowed it to be built. I think that's proof enough that we haven't—"

"You are hardly the sole judge of what is good for the

Heart or for this realm," Laoni interrupts with a sneer. "We're giving you until the end of the day tomorrow to bring down your half of this unnatural building and salvage whatever you would of it. If you've failed to complete the task by then, our people will destroy it for you."

CHAPTER TWENTY-ONE

August

I'm not sure what agonizes me more: the anguish that's been etched on Talia's face since we started this voyage or the guilt she clearly feels over asking me to help her relieve that anguish.

"I'm sorry to be dragging you away from Sylas with everything that's going on," she says, her hands twisting together in her lap where she's sitting on the other side of the small carriage my brother conjured for us.

"I wouldn't be much use to him or the others right now anyway," I remind her. "The three of them can pore over plenty of books and records without any help from me. We'll be back well before tomorrow, when hopefully I *won't* need to be of use stopping those mangy raven arch-lords from carrying out their threat."

She rubs the bronze bangle fitted snugly around her wrist. "I don't actually feel that anything's wrong with Jamie."

"The spell I cast will only kick in if he's in severe distress," I say. "There are ways the arch-lords could have interfered with his life that wouldn't necessarily have caused that yet. After the way they tried to steal him away before, I can't blame you for being worried."

"And he might not even be wearing his bracelet, in which case I wouldn't be alerted even if he was in a horrible situation. I just… I have to know." She exhales slowly, but her expression stays just as pained.

I've been guiding the carriage slowly since we entered the foggy woods at the very edge of the fringelands. When we've finally reached the area where the portals are more numerous, I stop the vehicle and help Talia out. I mean to carry her while I check the nearest passages, but she shakes her head and slips from my arms. "I'll wait here while you check as quickly as you can. I don't want to slow you down. I'm sure I'll be fine."

As I glance around the hazy forest, my fangs itch in my gums. We haven't had the same incursions of fearsome beasts that the winter realm has experienced, probably because our population hasn't dwindled and our curse actually makes us *more* fearsome rather than less when it takes hold. But there are plenty that still lurk around the edges of the Mist.

I can't smell any of them at the moment. I just won't go too far.

Shifting into wolf form so I can travel even faster, I stretch into the new configuration of my muscles and lope to the nearest portal. All it takes is a sniff to determine whether the human lands on the other side hold the exact combination of unusual scents that marked the place where we found Talia's brother. I think I've narrowed down the patch of forest where we'll find it even more than last time, although the doorways to the human world do have a habit of drifting around some.

It only takes three tries to identify it. I sprint back to Talia, throwing myself into the shift before I've even halted, but when I reach for her she simply takes my hand. "I can walk. I'm not going to be a burden."

I let her limp along beside me, wincing inwardly at the much more pronounced unevenness to her steps with her recent wound. Those wretched Murk. I wish I'd been there to tear the one who did this to shreds.

"You haven't been a burden," I say firmly. "Whatever's gotten into the Unseelie arch-lords, it's them being pricks, not anything you've done wrong. They should be celebrating how much you've helped them like the rest of their people, not getting picky about who lives in what castle."

"I think it's a little more complicated than that," Talia mutters, which might be true, but I can't think of any way she's to blame for the current conflict.

At the right portal, I cast the spell to keep us hidden from mortal eyes. Talia finally lets me pick her up for the journey through, which is a bit disorienting even when you're in the best of health. The colors and shapes around us waver and twist, and all at once we're standing in the secluded clearing in the park.

The smells of burnt gasoline and sun-baked tar that trickle through the air mark this place as part of the human world even without anything in view other than trees and grass. With a few steps, the buildings of the city beyond show amid the greenery.

Talia starts to squirm in my arms, but I let out a mild growl of refusal. "You said you wanted to move quickly. I can walk faster carrying you than you can with your leg hurting you."

Talia grimaces, but she relaxes into me. I wish I could feel more triumphant about my victory. I'd rather she wasn't wounded in the first place.

The Unseelie arch-lords are attacking the first home she's had in our world that's been totally *hers*. It isn't a stretch to think they might come after her brother and use him as leverage for whatever it is they want to gain. I hate to think what they might do to Talia herself if they can find a way to justify it to themselves.

I want to believe that we could simply refuse their initial demands and it'll all die down, but few things in the fae world are ever actually simple. Whitt looked worried when we left, even surrounded by all his papers and with several of his associates among our pack-kin at his beck and call. If *he* thinks there's a reason for concern, then the situation has to be bad.

As I carry Talia through the park, avoiding a woman pushing a stroller and a man walking three boisterous dogs that bark in my direction even though they can't see me, I study the angle of the sun. "It's early morning here. I'd say around breakfast time. Your brother should be at home around then, shouldn't he?"

"I think so." Talia peers around us. "I don't even know if it's a school day or the weekend. Or what month it is.

I'm so out of touch." She lets out a little laugh, but it doesn't sound all that amused.

"I can't tell the exact month since we don't follow them," I say, "but it smells and looks like late spring to me. We could check a newspaper for the exact date."

Talia hesitates and then shakes her head. "No. All that's important is making sure Jamie's okay and then getting back to deal with the arch-lords as soon as possible. I shouldn't be worrying about that stuff anyway."

But she is. I can't blame her for that either. This world was meant to be hers before Aerik and his blasted cadre tore her away from it—why shouldn't she wonder about it? Her life would have been so much different if he'd never rampaged into it.

The pang that runs through my chest at the thought speaks of how much the idea of never having met her pains me. But that alternate path would have led to much *less* pain for her.

Even if we check on Jamie now, how can we be sure the Unseelie arch-lords won't target him later? I swallow that question, not wanting to disturb Talia further if she hasn't already thought of the possibility. The only way we could totally protect him is to, well, bring him under our protection, which would throw off his own life in ways I know she doesn't want.

I may not love the stink of human machines, but the neighborhood where Talia's aunt and uncle live isn't wholly unpleasant. Birds chirp in the many trees that loom from the well-tended lawns. I spot a vegetable garden in one front yard that I might have to examine more closely for curiosity's sake on a less urgent future visit. The breeze that washes over us is as pleasantly warm as it is in the summer realm near the Heart.

When we reach the house itself, I prowl around the structure, peeking through the windows and holding Talia so she can see in too. At the kitchen, I stop. She lets out a relieved sigh.

Her brother is sitting at the kitchen table with two younger children I assume are her cousins, all of them eating cereal from bowls. Another prickle of curiosity ripples over me to find out what exactly that tastes like. Cereal isn't really a thing in the fae world, and I've only sampled a few.

But we're not here for that either.

"He's wearing the bracelet," Talia murmurs, a smile crossing her face for the first time since we set off. The bronze band gleams at her brother's wrist.

I tighten my arms around her in a gentle hug. My mind scrambles to think of what else I could offer to reassure her even after we leave here again.

"I could set down a spell around the house to alert us if any fae come near," I say. "Around his school as well. It wouldn't prevent them from coming, and I can't cover everywhere he might go…"

Talia sucks her lower lip under her teeth as she considers. "No. That would take a lot of time that we don't really have right now, and if they did come to take him, they'd probably be sneaky about it anyway. A false sense of security is worse than not having it at all."

She rubs her forehead, her smile gone as quickly as it came. "I don't think there's any way I'd feel totally sure he's okay other than monitoring him every second, which obviously I can't. I'm just glad to know the arch-lords haven't gone that far yet."

Another possibility occurs to me. "I can ask Sylas to post a rotation of sentries in the area on the fringes near the portal. It wouldn't need to require much manpower, and then we'll have someone keeping an eye on things the one place they'd have to pass through to reach him."

Talia tucks her head against my neck. "There, that sounds perfect. Who says you can't be a strategist too? Thank you, August."

"Anything for you, Sweetness."

I'm about to say we should head back now when a sudden realization creeps up over me. Talia said it wasn't possible for her to stay here and watch over her brother… but technically it is. We were willing to let her stay in the human world for as long as she needed to if she'd decided to do just that.

She'd be safer here than in the fae world, where she's become a target of Seelie, Unseelie, and Murk alike. I tried to convince Sylas to send her here months ago, before we even knew her brother was alive, to protect her from the ongoing conflicts. And maybe if the Unseelie have to go without her healing abilities for a few days, their arch-lords will find reasons to respect her more.

She'd never agree to it, though. She felt guilty enough just asking to make this brief trip.

I adjust her in my arms, my gut knotting. Now that I've considered it, I know it would be so easy. Talia wouldn't be able to make the journey back to the fae realm without a guide. If I left her here, she'd have to go in to her aunt and uncle, reconnect with her brother, and stay here in the best sort of peace I can give her...

Talia stirs, glancing up at me. "Is everything okay?"

I open my mouth and close it again. There's a moment when I'm almost tempted. But only almost.

Those months ago, I was willing to send her away without consulting her about it. The way she reacted when she discovered I'd gone behind her back is burned into my memory. *That* hurt her, much more than any suffering she's shown from her wound.

No matter how much I might want to protect her, I can't do it by denying her own free will. I wouldn't be much better than Aerik then.

She decides what risks she can handle, not me.

I close my eyes, wishing for a better solution but knowing there isn't one. At least I can take a little joy in knowing that her choice keeps her close to me. I'll protect her from as much as I can with my claws and my fangs. Let's hope that's enough.

"Not at all, Sweetness," I say. "Let's go home and deal with those feather-brained winter arch-lords."

CHAPTER TWENTY-TWO

Talia

The forest along the fringes of the Mists is so desolate that the last thing I expect is to run into another fae the moment we step through the portal. Holding me, August jerks to a halt. We both stare at Kesral, who's poised as if he was about to walk through the portal we just came through, staring back at us.

"What are you doing here?" I blurt out with a lurch of my heart. Did Laoni send someone to kidnap Jamie after all?

He backs up a couple of steps, raising his hands in a peace-making gesture at August's instinctive flexing of his muscles. "My apologies for surprising you. Arch-Lord Laoni heard that you'd set off for the human world without any Unseelie accompaniment. She asked me to determine what you were doing."

I guess she really didn't have any plans for Jamie if it hadn't even occurred to her why I'd be checking on him.

Is everything all right, Talia? Corwin asks through our bond, having picked up on my initial reaction. I've been keeping a barrier up against our connection so I don't distract him while he's concentrating on finding counterarguments to Laoni's claims, but I was so startled they fell away.

It seems so, I tell him. *I was just surprised. Don't let me disturb you.*

I give him a moment to take stock of my well-being and then imagine the wall of light rising inside me again so I don't intrude on his work. Relaxing in August's arms, I nudge him to set me down.

"I was worried about my brother," I tell Kesral as I straighten out my dress. "I just wanted to look in on him. With tensions being so high right now… it was hard not to be concerned."

His jaw tightens at my reference to the arch-lords' threat. "I had no hand in any of the demands regarding your new castle. I won't speak against my lady, but—I have no wish to oppose you or your mates."

The fact that he's willing to call all my men "mates" even though only one of them officially is at the moment eases any lingering uneasiness I might have had about his presence. "I'm glad to hear that. We were going to be heading back now too. I assume you'll do the same."

He nods. "I'll tell my lady that you were simply taking a little comfort in being near to your family."

That's true enough, and doesn't outright give any ideas about the way Laoni might use my family. I hope I haven't drawn too much of her attention in Jamie's direction by checking up on him.

Kesral's small winter-style carriage sits next to ours. A glimmer around the wooden structure we arrived in suggests it's encased in some kind of spell. Kesral dismisses the magic with an apologetic air and glances at us again. "It'll be best if I escort you to Arch-Lord Laoni myself so she can see that you have returned—and much the same as you were before."

"All right." I don't want to get him in trouble.

"I'm staying with her," August says with a hint of a growl in his voice.

Kesral gives him a slight smile. "That would probably be preferable. She isn't all that trusting of the Seelie still either."

He turns to climb into his carriage, but a question bubbles up inside me—the one that's been stewing ever since I spoke to Laoni's kitchen manager. "Kesral… Is it true that you and Laoni used to be close friends when you were a lot younger, before she became an arch-lord?"

He swivels back around, his shoulders stiffening a bit. "Who did you hear that from?"

I shrug, trying to keep the atmosphere casual. "When I visited her castle to see about the human servants there, Serev in the kitchen mentioned it."

Kesral dips his head awkwardly. "Well, we did spend a lot of time together as children. But of course she had many responsibilities to prepare for and which she then had to take on far earlier than she should have needed to. She's had to face a great deal, mostly on her own… It's been my honor to continue supporting her however I can."

However much she even lets him these days. But clear

affection rings through his voice, so unmistakeable it jars against my memories of the way *she* speaks to him.

I grapple with my next question and finally just spit it out. "She seems to be the opposite of friendly with you these days. She's always been cold and sometimes even harsh when I've heard her talking to you. And a couple of the other guards were hassling you about the human part of your heritage—she obviously doesn't intervene to speak up for you with your colleagues."

Kesral is silent for a long moment, his expression somber enough that my gut starts to twist. "I'm sorry," I add. "This is probably an uncomfortable subject. I shouldn't have pried."

"I suppose it's fair," he says with a rough chuckle. "Here I am chasing you down on your private business. All you're doing is asking questions." He runs his hand back over his hair, which is in its usual short ponytail. "I can't speak for her, of course. And I promise you she wasn't always so strict with me. When she could be more carefree, she was a good friend. But circumstances change…"

I wait patiently as he seems to consider his next words. He inhales slowly and continues. "I'm not sure how much you know about her family's history, but after my lady's mother died, her father who was arch-lord at the time became much more hostile toward humans and anyone associated with them. They'd brought a few human servants along on the trip where she died, and I think somehow he blamed them for not trying to save her, even though they would inevitably have drowned."

Yes, if the whirlpool Corwin mentioned was so strong

a true-blooded fae could be overwhelmed by it in seconds, a human wouldn't stand a chance. And having seen the state of most human servants in this world, I'm not sure it'd even occur to them to spring to anyone's rescue, they're so dazed with the drugs the fae feed them.

But grief can warp people's minds in unfair ways. Look at what it's done to Corwin's mother, who's practically insane with it.

"And Laoni picked up the same attitude?" I venture.

"Not all at once, but over time, especially as her training intensified, she started keeping her distance and becoming more critical of my failings." Kesral makes a dismissive gesture. "I can't complain. It was unlikely we'd continue as we were once we grew up anyway."

His gaze flicks away from me for a second, and I get the sense he's suppressing more sadness than he's letting himself show. "I'm sorry," I say. "It's still got to be hard."

He meets my eyes again, something softening in his expression. "I consider myself lucky to have had her companionship as much as I did for as long as I did. I can still remember—" A gentle smile touches his lips. "I was there with her when she mastered her first true name, for silver. She was so pleased, and her first thought was that she wanted to help me master it too..."

He pauses and inclines his head. "I know she hasn't been the easiest on you either, but there's a good heart underneath. I'm sure that hasn't changed. And I'll be here for her as long as she needs me in whatever capacity."

As he speaks, a different impression takes a hold of me. Kesral isn't just talking fondly about a friendship of the past. He sounds like he's... in love with her.

A sharp pang shoots through my heart on his behalf. That's so much worse than facing insults from an old friend. Does Laoni have any idea how much she's hurting him, how devoted to her he is despite her harshness?

I don't want to bring Kesral any more pain by harping on the subject. "That's very admirable," I say after a brief fumble for words. "Thank you for putting up with my curiosity."

He gives me a small bow. "I serve my lady, but I can recognize that you've done impressive things for our people—including her and the rest of my flock—as well."

August rests his hand on my head. "*My* lady is hoping to get back to her pack and her flock quickly. I hope you won't mind if we make the trip back a speedy one."

"Not at all," Kesral says. "Let us be off."

I nestle myself on a couple of cushions in the base of our carriage to escape the wind generated by our swift flight. With the warbling of the rushing air passing over us and the wavering shapes of leaves and clouds whipping past overhead, the whole world seems to have gone into fast-forward.

The rocking of the carriage starts to lull me. I didn't sleep all that well last night with my wound aching and my head full of worries about the Murk and the humans living among the fae. Even with all the new worries added to that heap, at some point I drift off with August watching over me.

I wake up at the slowing of the carriage and a sudden shift in temperature. The chilly breeze that touches my cheek tells me we've passed into the winter realm. I sit up in time to see Laoni's iridium castle looming closer.

August stops outside it next to Kesral's vehicle. "Let's make this quick."

The Unseelie guard nods and beckons for us to follow him.

Laoni must have been alerted to our approach, because she strides into the entrance room just as we enter. "Well?" she says imperiously, looking at Kesral.

He bobs low with more respect than I think he really owes her. "There was no cause for concern. Lady Talia and her mate were simply making a routine check on her brother. They were in the human realm for less than an hour, and they readily agreed to present themselves to you to confirm it."

Her gaze darts over us, and her mouth pinches. "In the past, we've agreed to an Unseelie escort accompanying you on such trips. Why did you shirk that agreement this time?"

"I thought that condition was only for while we were still deciding what was going to happen with Jamie," I say. "Nothing important was happening today. And frankly, I didn't think your flock or either of the other arch-lords you trust would want to be bothered with the trip."

Laoni bristles. "I'll decide what's a bother and what's not. It's this sort of impertinence that makes trust difficult to come by."

"Talia's simply answering your question," August breaks in.

"It's the tone of her answer I object to."

Oh, she's one to talk about tone.

But before I can say as much, Kesral speaks up again in a more tender voice than I've heard from him before.

Maybe our conversation has stirred up so many memories of the past that they've clouded his perception of the present. "My lady, from what I've seen of Lady Talia and her companions, they have no ill intentions toward us. I understand your leaning toward caution, and it's as commendable as always, but in this case—"

Laoni spins toward him, cutting him off with a snap. "It's not for you to commend me or not. I haven't asked for your opinion, and you should know better than to offer it as if it's wanted."

Kesral can't quite restrain a flinch. My hackles rise, but in the same moment, Laoni's face twitches, as if she's controlling some further reaction she didn't want to let out. As I pause, studying her, she raises her chin haughtily.

Kesral dips into an even lower bow this time. "I apologize for overstepping, my lady." He makes a movement toward her and halts when Laoni jerks a step backward, away from him. You'd think he had the plague from the way she recoiled. His mouth slants downward. "I'll take my leave."

As he slips away, his spine rigid but his shoulders just slightly slumped, Laoni's gaze follows him for a second. Her jaw flexes, and in that instant, I could swear I catch a hint of pain... or maybe regret.

The trace of emotion smooths away an instant later. I might have thought I'd imagined it if her hand didn't rise just then to the side of her neck.

To the true-name mark etched against her tan skin, the one I know from Corwin's teachings is for silver. The first one she earned, with Kesral by her side.

A lump rises in my throat. She obviously hasn't

forgotten their past together either. Why in the world does she treat him so awfully if it hurts her to do it just like it hurts him?

My frustration with everything she's done to and around me over the past several weeks boils over. "How can you be so hard on him when he cares so much about supporting you?"

Laoni whirls on me. "What would you know about any of it?"

I glare right back at her. "I know that no matter what your father told you, you seem to be smart enough to have figured out that human beings aren't horrible just because a few didn't drown themselves trying to save your mother. And he isn't even human—he's just got a little more mixed in with the fae part than you do. But maybe you just like being a bully more than anything else."

"Talia," August says quietly, grasping my shoulder, but I'm done anyway.

Laoni gapes at me, her face turning splotchy with anger and maybe shock. "You—you have no idea about anything," she retorts in a rough undertone. "Not everything that happens has to do with how human or not someone is. And not everyone gets to have whatever they want regardless of who the Heart ties them to. We do our best with the duties we're given."

At the end of that tirade, she snaps her mouth shut, looking almost sick. "Never mind," she goes on brusquely. "Get out of my castle and see to yours."

My mind is still working over what she said, trying to fit it together with what I already knew and what I witnessed during this confrontation. Does she think I've gotten whatever I want—while she's here demanding my men tear down the home they made for me? What has *she* ever wanted that she didn't—

Regardless of who the Heart ties to them.

Understanding smacks into me like an ocean wave, the pieces colliding. Kesral's account of their history together. Laoni pushing him away and yet seeming to regret it. And that remark...

I'm not sure I'm right, but the suspicion swells in my chest too forcefully to be ignored. Is there any chance she'd admit it?

The more of an audience she has, the less likely.

"August," I say carefully, "would you let me speak to Laoni alone for a minute? I'll meet you outside."

August tenses beside me. He eyes the arch-lord warily. "Are you sure, Talia?"

"I don't think Arch-Lord Laoni wants to damage the woman who's curing her people." She might want to ruin my happiness, but she's accomplishing that by striking out at everyone and everything around me. Having me alone won't help her.

"I have nothing to say to you," Laoni sneers as August reluctantly heads for the door.

"But I have something to say to you," I reply. "And I respect *you* enough, in spite of everything, to do it privately."

She frowns, her hands balling at her sides, but she doesn't send me away. Looking into her eyes, I don't think she has any idea what I want to talk about, which may be the only reason she's listening.

The door thumps shut behind August. I glance around

to confirm there are no other fae nearby. Then I fold my arms over my chest. "You wanted him to be your mate. Kesral. But it couldn't happen because he isn't true-blooded."

"What?" Laoni sputters, but she can't contain the panic that flashes across her expression, and I know I've hit the mark.

"It actually makes a lot more sense than you browbeating him just because he's got a human parent," I say, keeping my tone even. "You can use that as an excuse to be awful to him, and maybe you even believe it a little after whatever ideas your father passed on about humans, and that way there isn't much chance of anyone figuring out the truth. And you can keep him at a distance, so *you're* not as bothered by the truth."

Laoni draws her brawny frame tall, her eyes flashing. "You are the last person who should be talking to anyone about picking mates."

"Why, because I picked four?" *Not everyone gets to have whatever they want*, she said before. Another suspicion prickles up through my chest. "Is that why you're so awful to *me*? Because I'm getting to have all the men I love instead of only my soul-twined mate? Who says you couldn't too? Be with him if you want. Work it out with your mate. You could let yourself be happy instead of trying to make sure I can't be."

Laoni has completely hardened, though. Now I can't spot a trace of the concern that showed through in those brief moments around Kesral. "This is exactly why humans are better kept drugged into oblivion. Making up crazy stories to justify all the rules you're flouting—you're as insane as Corwin's mother. Get out of here before I have you locked up the way he's had to her."

I wince at the viciousness of her remark. "Arch-Lord Laoni, you know it doesn't have to be like—"

"Get *out!*" She jabs her finger toward the door. There's so much fury in her stance that I'm not completely sure she *wouldn't* hurt me if I refused.

I retreat, my chest constricting around my heart as I step out into the cold air outside.

There's still so much I don't understand. Other arch-lords have taken more than one lover. Is it that she feels it'd be shameful to have one who's half-human? Or one I'm guessing she's fallen for in a way she hasn't her actual soul-twined mate?

Does she believe, like Sylas did, in being faithful to her soul-twined mate no matter who they are or what happens?

But the answers to those questions don't really matter in the end. What matters is that regardless of the reasons for her resentment of me and my relationship with my mates, she's holding onto that resentment just as tightly as before.

I swallow hard. In fact, after what I just said to her, she might be even more eager to see our joint castle fall.

CHAPTER TWENTY-THREE

Sylas

No one has made a move toward the border castle yet, but a few soldiers from the Unseelie arch-lords' domains have taken up stations nearby, simply monitoring our activity. Or lack of activity, I suppose, given that we haven't taken down the smallest piece of the structure so far.

I study them from a high window in the winter side of the castle. Corwin added warming spells to these rooms, but being surrounded by all this cool diamond with that icy expanse outside still sends a chill over my skin. It's going to take some time getting used to the less familiar elements of our newly shared existence.

If I'm allowed the chance to get used to them. The winter arch-lords clearly aren't backing down. It's only late afternoon on the same day they made their announcement, the sun still blazing somewhere behind me, and in theory Corwin has until tomorrow to meet their demands, but they're already preparing for battle.

In theory, they've only asked for him to dismantle what part of the castle extends into winter territory—but the halves of the building are so entwined, that would require a complete restructuring regardless. And there's little point to having it if it doesn't allow Talia access to both realms the way Corwin planned.

A heaviness settles over my heart. I turn and stride back through the castle to my own side of the border.

I don't bother to call an official meeting in the Bastion. Donovan's already informed me that if I have the law behind me, he'll back me up against the Unseelie challenge. So in the interests of time and making a more personal appeal, I go straight to Celia's castle.

The fae man who greets me at the door hustles off to inform her of my arrival. She can't have been too deeply occupied, because he returns a minute later to escort me to one of the sitting rooms, and she's already inside when I enter.

Celia makes a vague gesture toward the chairs scattered along the edges of the room, but she remains standing by the elegant fireplace, its frame as sleek and dark as her own form. She sweeps her luminescent hair back over her shoulders and fixes me with a pensive gaze. "I hear there's trouble with the ravens regarding your new castle, Lord Sylas."

Her formality doesn't bode well for my mission. I incline my head. "Three of the winter arch-lords have demanded that Arch-Lord Corwin tear the winter side of the structure down. They claim that it's primarily Talia's home, and that being neither a lady by birth nor fae, giving her a castle of her own goes against the will of the Heart."

"It is unusual."

"So is Talia," I have to say. "As is her situation. My strategist and I—and Corwin as well—have been going through what records we can find on related matters, and I don't believe they have true justification. There have been occasional eccentrics among the faded fae who've built grand homes for themselves, and while they were viewed with some derision, they were never forced to dismantle them. There was no sign of magical backlash from the Heart either. And as soul-twined mate to a true-blooded arch-lord, I think we have reasonable grounds to say Talia has been granted her title in every way she could need it by the Heart itself."

Celia folds her arms over her chest. "It sounds as if you have the matter well in hand then."

I restrain a grimace. "I'm not sure deflecting the claim will be as easy as presenting those arguments. Those arch-lords, Laoni in particular, have had a vendetta against Talia and her union with Corwin since the soul-twined bond first took effect. You've seen how they've spoken and behaved during our past negotiations. Whatever their motivations, they want to destabilize her position among the fae. No matter what we say about it, I suspect they'll force the subject."

"They have definitely proved to be difficult allies at times," Celia allows. "I should hope they aren't in such a hurry to return to a state of war, though."

"I wouldn't think they are, but I wouldn't have expected this move from them either."

"I can understand your concern. However, this seems to be a matter between the Unseelie arch-lords and those of you with a direct stake in the border castle. Why exactly have you called on me?"

The fact that she's making me spell it out is even less reassuring. I square my shoulders. "I would like the Seelie arch-lords to present a united front when the Unseelie come to carry out their demands tomorrow. Donovan has already agreed. If we stand together in defense of the border castle remaining whole, with Corwin on our side as well, we represent half of the Heart's chosen representatives. I believe that may be enough to dissuade them."

Celia hums to herself. "Perhaps. But for how long, if they carry as much animosity as you suggest?"

"I can't be certain, of course. I wouldn't be surprised if they attempt another gambit before too long. But the more times we stand firm against them, the shakier their position becomes."

"And you don't think it's unwise to intrude on the political decisions of the winter realm when they don't directly affect us?"

"They affect *me*," I say. "They affect the woman I mean to take as my mate, who holds back the curse for all of the Seelie. The border castle was meant to represent the cooperation between the realms. So we're already involved, even if Corwin's colleagues are putting on a show of focusing only on him. Giving in to their demands now will only open the door to more problems as they push their advantage, not fewer."

Celia steps away from me, pacing to one end of the room and back again with measured steps. She slides her fingers along the edge of her jaw in thought. "It is also possible that their animosity isn't entirely unreasonable. Talia has risen to a position of great prominence in a matter of months. I can understand some wariness."

I can't stop myself from bristling. "Talia has never done anything but give of herself to help the rest of us in every way she can. To suggest that there might be any maliciousness to her situation is an insult to both one who's saved us from so much suffering and me and my cadre as well."

"I didn't mean that she's intentionally out to harm us," Celia replies dryly. "Obviously not. But there's so much we don't understand about her origins or her connection to the Heart. Every few weeks some new unexpected aspect to her powers emerges. Where does it end?"

"What does it matter?" I ask. "She's only ever used those powers to help us."

"So far. Again, Sylas, I'm not saying she has any ill intentions, only that even *she* isn't fully in control of what role she plays here. And we have no way of knowing how that role may shift in the future."

I frown at her, uneasiness coiling in my gut. Celia is making her points sound perfectly logical, but I have to wonder how much she's guided by her own discomfort with Talia's "prominence," as she put it. Is she truly worried that Talia's presence will end up harming us in some way, or does she simply feel her own authority is threatened by our people's growing fondness for my mate-to-be?

"We will see what comes," I say. "We can only make our decisions now based on what's already true."

"Perhaps." Celia pauses. "But I think I will stay out of your present conflict rather than take a side. What the Heart wants will come to pass one way or another. Let what is right be decided between those of you so concerned. And while I can't prevent you and Donovan from supporting Arch-Lord Corwin's cause while you carry the majority, I do hope you won't bring the conflict back into the summer realm when we've finally gotten some semblance of peace."

She turns away. A protest rises in my throat, but I can see there's no swaying her. If I badger her about it, I'll only be making myself look oafish.

"I'm disappointed by your decision, but I accept it," I say with all the politeness I can muster, and stalk out of the room.

The uneasiness stays with me as I make my way out into the warm afternoon air. The shadows have stretched longer in the time while I was speaking with Celia. I wander between them, too restless to fix on a destination. My wolf stirs beneath my skin, itching to be released.

There's nothing more I can do here other than wait for tomorrow and see how we fare. We have all the evidence we *should* need to confirm our right to keep the border castle. Whitt and Corwin are still gathering more.

And Celia's words niggle at me. *There's so much we still don't understand about her...*

It's true. None of our investigations have explained

how Talia ended up so tied to the fae and our curse. If I knew more about *that*, perhaps it would persuade Celia to support our cause—or even alleviate whatever worries are gripping the winter arch-lords.

I can't think of any avenue I haven't pursued that could tell me more about those origins, though.

No, that isn't strictly true. I stop in a patch of sunlight, inhaling deeply, a cedar scent flooding my lungs. There is one course I haven't taken yet, both out of a suspicion it wouldn't prove useful anyway and a reluctance to ask anything of those involved. Also a small bit of concern that I might end up saying or doing something I'd regret when faced with those villains, discussing the horror they carried out.

But I have nothing else. If there's even a slight chance reaching out will tip the balance in Talia's favor, I should take that chance.

Without waiting for trepidation to set in, I veer toward the grove of juniper trees where I usually conjure my carriages. It's too long a journey to take it at a wolfish run, as much as I'd enjoy letting out some of the tension wound through me by stretching my legs that way.

I send a brief note of explanation to Whitt and set off at the swiftest course I can urge the vehicle to. As I speed over the landscape, I consider the exact questions I want to ask and how to phrase them.

It seems as though barely any time at all has passed before the bone-white walls of Aerik's fortress come into view up ahead.

My muscles tense automatically. Memories trickle through my mind of the night months ago when my cadre and I slunk inside that building and discovered Talia starving and grimy in her cramped cage, with nothing but a dirty blanket to cover her. My fangs prick at my gums.

Aerik has never fully paid for what he did to my love, and perhaps having freed her from his clutches and brought her all due happiness is the best victory we can claim. But I can't help hoping that someday he gives me an excuse to deliver a bloodier consequence.

Today, though, I can't be on the attack. I need his cooperation.

As I draw the carriage to a halt, a few fae emerge from the castle. By the time I've leapt out onto the tall grass, the lord of the domain himself has come out to meet me.

The dwindling sunlight catches in Aerik's vividly yellow hair, which he rakes his fingers through before walking right up to me. Tension tugs at the corners of his mouth. "Arch-Lord Sylas. To what do I owe the pleasure?"

We both know there's no joy in this meeting for either of us. I offer a thin smile. "There's a matter I'd like to speak to you about, if you have a moment. It shouldn't take much of your time."

Aerik's gaze flicks over me, and I suspect he'd put me off if he were bolder. But this is a man who enjoys bullying beings far less powerful than himself, not standing up to those who rule over him. He dips his head. "I can spare you that. Why don't you come inside?"

I like stepping into that bone-white building even less than standing outside it. As Aerik leads me to a small sitting room, my skin crawls. I keep my expression impassive, taking the chair he motions to and waiting until he's settled into one across from me.

Neither of us will want this conversation drawn out. I get straight to the point. "I'd like to hear your full account of the night you found Talia."

Aerik blinks at me. Whatever he might have imagined this visit was about, it clearly wasn't that. "I beg your pardon?" he says cautiously.

I set my elbows on the arms of the chair and fold my hands together in my lap. "The night of the full moon, when you stumbled into the human world with your cadre and came upon Talia. When you discovered the curse-breaking effect of her blood." And mauled her brother and slaughtered her parents. I hold in those accusations. "I want to know everything you can remember about that incident. How did you end up so far from home when the curse took you? Did you see anything else of note after you came out of it?"

Aerik is silent for a long moment, braced as if he thinks this might be a trick, that I'm setting him up for some kind of punishment right now. When I simply wait patiently, he swipes his hand across his mouth. "There was nothing of note about the situation in which we found her or our collecting of her. As soon as I tasted her blood and snapped out of the curse, I realized the effect she had and how valuable that made her. My cadre had already torn through her family—I didn't order their murders, if you were thinking I had."

It had occurred to me that he might have to ensure no one remained who'd search for Talia, but whether he incited his cadre or not makes little difference to the outcome. "I assume you arranged for them to sample her blood and wake up as well."

He nodded. "We healed her wounds so that she'd survive the journey back to our world and set off straight for the nearest portal. It was a small town, quiet. I believe we saw a couple of cars passing on the roads as we made our way, but no one else on foot. Nothing stands out in my memory. Although it would have needed to be rather impressive to have distracted me from the discovery we'd just made."

I can only imagine the whirlwind of his thoughts in that moment. For him, it would have been not just the thought of how she could benefit all Seelie-kind but how he could use her to improve his own standing among us.

My claws twitch behind my fingertips, but I hold them in. "All right. But how did you end up in that small town to begin with? It's a long way from here to the fringes. Surely you didn't normally wander so far on the night of the curse?"

"No," Aerik says shortly, and then knits his brow as if he's having trouble recalling the events. "A distant niece of mine called in a favor that day. Her domain is close to the fringelands. We meant to return before sundown. But..." The furrow in his brow deepens. "Something caught our attention. We tracked it into the woods along the fringe..."

As he focuses on dredging up the memory, an after-image wavers up over his face before my deadened eye. For a few seconds, I'm seeing both the man in front of me and another version of him, scanning his surroundings with a predatory gleam in his eyes and his fangs bared. Whatever he was searching for back then, he meant to rip it apart.

Aerik snaps his fingers, and the ghostly image vanishes

with the blink of my eyes. He taps the arm of his chair. "A rat," he says. "We were chasing down a rat we were sure we'd scented. Those stinking Murk."

"A rat," I repeat. A clammy sensation squeezes around my gut.

Aerik nods. "We didn't want to let the thing get away. I think we suspected it'd caused the mischief my niece called us in over. We must have figured it didn't matter if the moon rose, we'd deal with the vermin just as easily wild as sane."

And in the process they'd ended up rampaging through a portal onto Talia's doorstep.

"That's all you remember?" I ask, even though I'm sure of the answer. None of us holds memories of our savagery in the grip of the curse. That's part of the horror of it—not even being sure what violence you've carried out.

"That's all of it." Aerik considers me. "Did my answers meet your satisfaction?"

"I appreciate your humoring my curiosity," I say, getting up. I'm not going to tell him my real reasons for asking. I *can't* tell him what I've discerned from his answers, since I'm not even sure myself yet.

A rat in the woods by the portals years ago, drawing Aerik and his cadre on a chase. A rat blasting down the homes in the Unseelie summer settlement last month. A rat springing at Talia just yesterday by an iron-laced fire.

I don't know what it means, but the one thing I am certain of is that I don't like it at all.

CHAPTER TWENTY-FOUR

Talia

Laoni said Corwin had until the end of the day after she made her demand, but she doesn't wait quite that long. The sun hasn't yet dipped out of view when many more soldiers from her, Terisse's, and Uzziah's domains begin assembling around the border castle. The arch-lords themselves take positions at the front of their troops, standing tall and stern.

I wonder what Neve makes of all this. But then, Neve doesn't seem to be all that aware of what's going on right in front of her much of the time, so she may not even realize her colleagues have made this challenge. Corwin didn't want to force her into the conflict when it's doubtful she could turn the tide anyway.

As I watch from one of the winter-side windows, our own soldiers gather in a tighter ring around the Unseelie side of the castle. Being the ones most familiar with this realm, Corwin's flock stands at the front, swords at their hips, heads high. A large part of Sylas's pack fills out the area behind them, with some support from Donovan's domain as well.

Our force looks so much smaller than the one opposing us. My fingers tighten where I'm gripping the diamond window frame, and Corwin comes up behind me, setting his hands on my shoulders.

"I should go out there now. Sylas and I will speak to my colleagues and see what we can make of this."

I drag in a shaky breath. "Do you think there's any chance they'll listen to you at this point?"

His mouth tenses. "A peaceful approach is always worth trying."

I can tell from the turmoil of emotions that seeps through our bond that he isn't hopeful at all.

"Well, I'd better get ready for my part then," I say, stepping back.

A pang of concern splits through all the other uneasiness I sense from Corwin. "Are you sure about this? I don't think they'd do you any major harm, but if they succeed in striking at the castle, it could be rather frightening being in the middle of it."

I fold my arms over my chest. "I think they need to see who they're striking at when they try to destroy the home we built. It's more than just a castle. And I'm more than just some random, powerless woman."

He sighs but kisses my temple. "You are indeed. Let's go, then."

He walks with me to the sitting room that leads out onto a small terrace overlooking the winter realm on the castle's second floor. As I step outside, the cold breeze gusts over me, tossing my hair. Several of the heads among the arch-lords' troops twitch upward, noticing my arrival.

I'll do whatever I can to see that no particle of this structure is touched, Corwin says silently as he heads downstairs.

And so will I, I reply.

I stand right at the railing, resting my hands on it and giving those below a clear view of me. A lot of the fae in the throng know me. They've watched me heal their people. Maybe they've never talked to me, but they have to realize what I can do for them is more important than the arch-lords' petty complaints.

The question is whether that knowledge will override their loyalty to their lords.

I pick out Kesral in the crowd, standing a few paces back from where Laoni is poised. When my gaze catches his across the distance, I think his mouth curls into a brief grimace, but he holds his ground. He doesn't want to be there, but he won't let her down.

I don't know if I'll ever understand how awful she's been to him when all he wants to do is support her.

Sylas is already outside, standing among his pack-kin with his cadre flanking him. When Corwin appears below, Zelpha, Verik, and Olander join him. The two groups move through the guards together to the front of the ring. The three Unseelie arch-lords take a step forward to meet them, though still keeping a clear distance.

Corwin speaks loudly enough for his voice to reach my high perch. "Comrades, we have spoken on this matter, and I will put forward my case again. We have found numerous accounts of beings less honored than my mate who have dwelled in structures similar to this one without resistance from the Heart. Since our joint castle has been built, there's been no sign that the Heart or any other natural powers of our world objects to it. Talia has earned the right to a real home of her own that encompasses all her responsibilities."

"Is it her responsibilities she's concerned about or more private matters between the four of you?" Uzziah asks with a sneer, his gaze flicking up to me for an instant.

"I hardly think you can doubt her dedication to her duties after how much of her time she's already devoted to healing your people," Sylas replies. "As to how she chooses to spend what time she has to herself, and in what company, that is indeed a private matter that doesn't affect you at all."

I don't think the other arch-lords agree with his assessment, but they don't pursue that line of argument any further, maybe balking at airing their personal prejudices about my relationships in front of their people so openly. Terisse stirs on her feet, but it's Laoni who speaks next.

"We gave our orders. We disapprove of the shape this venture of yours has taken, the pedestal on which you have placed your mate above all others when she isn't even fae. The majority carries the rule. The summer fae can do as they wish, but we will see any part of this structure that intrudes on our lands fall."

"Our authority as arch-lords can't be thrown about on a whim but must remain subject to the laws and principles already established," Corwin protests.

Laoni has already backed up to rejoin her people. She

motions to her soldiers. They and the other troops move in near-unison, a vast murmuring of voices rising up as true names and other words of magic fill the air.

But our side was prepared for a magical assault. The fae protecting the castle lift their own voices, and a tingling rushes over my skin. The air in front of me shimmers with the barrier they've conjured.

Not a second too soon. The shimmering surface quakes an instant later with the warbling impact of a surge of energy. My fingers curl around the railing as if I need to hold onto it to stay upright, even though I haven't felt more than a tremor in the atmosphere yet.

I know Corwin's right—the arch-lords wouldn't want to hurt the woman who's curing their people. Their soldiers will have been instructed to catch me with their magic and move me to safety as they dismantle the diamond section of the castle. I'm just hoping it doesn't come to that.

The barrier shudders again, but it holds against the onslaught, even when the opposing fae call out their spells louder. Are we that much stronger than them? They've got at least twice as much manpower—I don't see how—

But then I do. As I peer through the quivering air, I spot many fae standing in the winter arch-lords' troops who aren't speaking at all. They're standing silently, their hands by their sides, their expressions somberly stoic. A couple give me the slightest nod when they notice my attention on them.

They're refusing to follow their lords' commands. Have the arch-lords noticed that so many of their underlings are rebelling?

So many of the arch-lords' own people are willing to stand against their rulers on my behalf. A strange shiver runs through me, a sense of power that's unlike anything I've felt before. Somehow I've earned that much devotion, enough to turn flock-folk against their lords.

Maybe the arch-lords aren't wrong to be worried about how I could undermine their authority. I already am. How much more could I accomplish, given the chance and the time for more loyalties to shift toward me?

I'm not sure the fae's dedication to me will be enough to win the day for us now, though. Someone must have sent word back to the arch-lords' castles, because more fae are swooping down in raven form to join the flocks. They add their voices to the chanting.

The barrier wavers. A lick of magic breaks through, streaking across the diamond surface next to me and opening a crack in the wall.

My throat constricts. "Stop it!" I call out. "Think about what you're doing! This castle represents the unity between the summer and winter fae, between our realms —that we can work together to conquer the curse. Isn't that what you want? What else is going to be ruined if you ruin this?"

I think I see a few more of the opposing fae falter. The arch-lords motion to their troops, rousing the others to greater efforts. The forces below me recite more magical words, but a raggedness is already coming into their voices.

It's taking all their energy just to fend off our attackers for another minute or two. How long can their strength last?

As my spirits start to sink, an abrupt motion draws my gaze to Laoni. She's still standing at the front line of her flock-folk, but her hands that were raised a moment ago have snapped to her belly. A strange expression has crossed her face, as if something has startled her, but I can't see anything around that would have caused her reaction.

She turns to one of the guards near her and mutters something. He nods, and in a blink, she leaps off the ground into the form of a raven. With a few swift flaps of her wings, listing slightly to one side, she soars off toward her domain.

What's that about? Has she gone to demand more help in person?

I can't dwell on the puzzle for very long. More ravens are flying toward us, dark specks against the gray sky expanding into clearly winged shapes.

But they don't drop down among the winter arch-lords' troops. They land alongside Sylas and Corwin. Several make quick gestures of respect toward me before they open their mouths to add their voices to the protective spell.

Folk from other flocks must have heard what was happening—and they've decided to stand with me too.

A swell of warmth fills my chest with another of those strange shivers. I don't know if I can live up to the blessed figure they see me as, but I'm glad to see they're showing their support not just with words but actual action. I've helped them, and now they've come to my aid in turn, regardless of my humanity.

Uzziah and Terisse glance at each other and at the vacant spot Laoni left. Uzziah's jaw clenches. He beckons to some of his soldiers, and they march up alongside him. The fae on our side rest their hands on the hilts of their swords or bring their arms up defensively. My fleeting happiness vanishes.

Is it really going to come to this—to the arch-lords ordering their flocks to outright attack the people they're supposed to be representing? How long will our allies stay with us against a direct offensive?

I don't want violence to break out, Corwin says, picking up on my anxiety. *There has to be another way we can settle this.*

He speaks out loud to his colleagues. "Please, can't you see this is going too far? Our own people refuse to watch Talia and her home harmed. Listen to them even if you won't listen to me."

"The blessed one should have everything she asks for," one of the newcomers shouts. "She's going to save us all— we should do everything we can to reward her!"

Another lifts her voice. "By attacking her, you're attacking our hope of a cure. You're traitors to your own people."

An increasingly angry murmur ripples through our side of the crowd. I suppress the urge to hug myself. They're not just willing to defend me—they'd go to war for me against their own arch-lords if it came to that.

The realization is both exhilarating and terrifying. Do I really want that much responsibility on top of all the rest?

Can I afford to turn it away when there's so much I could accomplish with these people on my side?

Terisse glares at our forces, though her expression

looks more pained than defiant. "Who is a traitor isn't for you to decide. We've proven ourselves before the Heart and earned the right to guide the realm in the directions we feel are best for all our people. To doubt our judgment is to betray us."

"Lady Talia has done more to conquer the curse in the past month than you all have in decades," someone snaps back.

I catch a glint of metal as a few of the figures below draw their swords. My stomach balls tighter. "Please," I say, leaning over the railing. "I don't want to see anyone's blood spilled—here or anywhere else. This castle isn't hurting anyone. Why do we have to fight over it?"

I can't tell how well my appeal hit the troops who've continued to follow their lords' commands. A few of the folk-flock have unfurled their wings as if preparing to soar into battle. A snarl carries up from one of the Seelie below me.

All these fae might be willing to fight for me, but that doesn't mean I want to see them do it—not here, not like this. This confrontation could wreck not just the home my mates built for me, but the peace we worked so hard to construct between the realms as well.

But what if the alternative is letting the winter arch-lords win?

Before the conflict actually comes to blows, one more raven speeds into view. Flying toward us from the direction of Laoni's domain, it moves so swiftly it's little more than a dark streak against the sky. It dives down into the strip of empty terrain between the opposing factions, straightening into the form of a man at the same time.

I don't recognize him, but Corwin clearly does. The man makes a signal for truce, and Corwin motions him over begrudgingly. He raises his inner barriers so I don't hear exactly what the man says to him, probably worried it'll be some new threat or insult.

I prod him impatiently. Whatever's going on, I need to know.

When our connection comes back into full focus, the first things I sense from Corwin are shock and distress. *What?* I demand.

He looks up at me, his eyes even darker than usual. *Laoni requests that you attend to her at her castle, with full discretion and an oath from her that you'll be allowed safe passage back. Her coterie man will escort you. It appears… she's been struck by the curse.*

What? A wave of my own shock crashes through me. For a few seconds, I don't know what to do with myself.

If it's true—I have to go to her, don't I? It may even be a chance to settle this conflict. But I'm not risking all the people who'd stood by me to attend to her.

Tell him I'll come as long as her troops and the others stand down first, I say to Corwin. *No magic or blows should be exchanged while I'm gone. Otherwise I stay here.*

Corwin answers with a tendril of approval. He conveys my conditions to the coterie man, whose expression tenses before he nods. He goes to speak with Terisse and Uzziah. After a few minutes, the arch-lords' soldiers back up several paces, lowering their weapons and retracting their wings.

They've given their word, Corwin says. *I can come with you.*

His offer reverberates with worry. I shake my head. *No. You need to be here in case they find a way to go back on their word. Your people need you.*

And it seems Laoni, as much as she must hate the fact, needs me.

CHAPTER TWENTY-FIVE

Talia

As I limp alongside him across the icy plain, Laoni's coterie man lets out little huffs of breath that sound almost like grumbles, as if he's annoyed by my limited speed. As it is, my leg is already throbbing from the pace I've pushed myself to. I'm tempted to snap at him that this would go a lot faster if Laoni would come out to meet me or if he'd arrange a carriage, but my innards are tangled so tight I'm not sure I could form words anyway.

Laoni doesn't want to come out to meet me because apparently she doesn't want anyone to know she's come down with the cursed sickness. I'm not sure what to make of that. Does she not want the flocks to see me healing her, making me even more a hero in their eyes? Or is she not really sick at all, only carrying out some new scheme?

She gave an oath, one her coterie man was able to convey to Corwin. One Corwin trusts. He wouldn't let me go alone if he wasn't sure she has no ill intentions.

The fae don't lie. I can take some comfort in that, even if I have seen them talk their way around the truth plenty of times.

What could Laoni intend to accomplish with this gambit if it is a gambit anyway? It's the castle she wants destroyed, not me. Or at least, she's not so selfish that she'd let any desire she has to destroy me overwhelm what she knows is best for her people.

At the shining iridium castle, the coterie man ushers me in and leads me upstairs. I'm surprised by the thought that Laoni might be willing to let me into a space as private as her bedroom, but the room he directs me into is a small lounge. My reflection wavers on the smooth walls around me, looking paler and frailer on those not-quite-mirrors. A faint scent like dried flowers reaches my nose.

Laoni is sitting stiffly on an ivory settee at the far end of the room, her chin raised and her hands clasped on her lap. There are a couple of matching chairs near her, a side table and a bookcase and a picture window that offers a view over the nearby cliff. It's Spartan and uncluttered, which doesn't surprise me from what I've seen of Laoni's personality.

The air is cold against my skin. Even though the curse's chill must be seeping through her, she hasn't conjured a fire or any warming magic. I guess she's realized it wouldn't really help.

"You may leave us," Laoni says tightly. Her coterie man bobs his head and slips away, shutting the door behind him.

A prickling sensation runs over my skin. Other than yesterday in her front hall with August just outside, this is the first time I've been alone in a room with the most hostile of the Unseelie arch-lords.

I'm right here with you, Corwin says, softly but firmly through our bond. And I know that I could call on Whitt in a similar way if I really needed to. But Laoni is watching me as if she expects *me* to lash out at her somehow, even though it's always been the opposite.

I wet my lips, not sure what to do with myself, and sink gingerly onto one of the chairs. "Your coterie man said you're ill. Are you sure it's the curse?"

Laoni's jaw flexes. "I'd hardly call on you like this if I wasn't." She seems to catch herself and smooths the sharpness from her tone before she continues. "I felt some tightness in my limbs and a bit of a chill developing earlier this afternoon, but I dismissed it as mere tension. Over the past few hours, it's become increasingly impossible to ignore. I—"

She glances down at her hands and lifts one of them, the fingers curled toward her palm. "I can no longer straighten my fingers. My skin is turning cold even against fabric that holds a warming spell. I know what the signs are."

When I look at her closely, I can see the hints of it in her skin, a bluish tinge that's starting to creep into the usual tan hue. And is that the beginnings of a frost pattern touching the edge of her dark irises?

But that could be an illusion, couldn't it? I swallow thickly and can't help pointing out, "You've claimed an arch-lord was cursed before, and it turned out to be a trick."

"I have no wish to play games at the moment," Laoni

snaps, the edge coming back into her voice. "I want this ailment gone before it interferes with my work. If I'm *not* sick, your cure certainly won't do anything for me, so there'd be nothing to gain in tricking you. Just heal me."

Even now, she doesn't offer me so much as the basic respect of asking rather than demanding. I study her for a long moment, my stomach knotting.

A shiver Laoni tries to restrain passes through her frame. Her gaze darts away as if she's ashamed to have let even that much weakness show. Her fingers twitch and clench tighter.

I don't think she's faking it. She's right that there's no obvious reason for her to do so anyway. With no audience, this is between only her and me.

I still feel a little sick myself, a queasiness winding through my gut. Because this woman is asking me to cure her so that she can go back out there and get right back to trying to destroy one of the few good things I've gotten in this world—something that was for my benefit too, not just that of the fae.

"What happens after?" I ask quietly. "After you're cured—because of the power that as far as we know only I can wield. Are you going to go back to my new home and keep claiming that I don't deserve any special considerations, that there's something wrong with the love I share with my mates?"

Laoni narrows her eyes at me. "Are you trying to bargain for the cure? Not the selfless savior anymore when you have a personal vendetta?"

A laugh sputters out of me. "The only one here with a vendetta has been you. I don't care what you do with your castles or the men you love, whether you wish you didn't or not. I've never once acted against you except in my own defense."

And I could do that again now, couldn't I? If I *didn't* cure her, if I let the curse take her… would that be murder or merely self-defense?

The thought sends a shiver of my own through me, even stronger and more unnerving than what I felt watching the fae stand against their arch-lords, ready to draw blood on my behalf if need be. I don't fully understand this power, and I don't have any clue at all why I have it, but it's greater than anything Laoni can wield in this moment, when her life depends on the choices I make next. I'm her only hope of survival.

The possibilities slip through my mind as we stare each other down. I could refuse to heal her until she and her allies swear an oath to take no further action against me and my mates. That request would be justified by her actions, wouldn't it?

Or even better, since I'm not sure I trust her not to weasel out of any oath she takes eventually, I could pretend that I've tried to heal her but failed. Eventually she won't be able to hide her illness any longer. If I make a more public attempt and she dies anyway, I don't think the fae will blame me. They'll assume it's the Heart's punishment for Laoni's attacks on me.

Even as those ideas pass through my head, nausea twists around my gut. To barter over her life, over sparing her all the agony the curse will bring—let alone to abandon her to that agony completely… If I left her to die for my gain, would I be any better than she is?

I have more power right now than I ever recognized behind my eyes and in the tips of my fingers. The power to shape the rulership of the entire Unseelie realm. What's really *right* in this situation?

What kind of woman will I become as I dispense that power?

"I want to know what I can expect after we're done here," I say, pressing my earlier question.

Laoni manages to raise her chin at a haughty angle even now. "Why would you think this will change anything?"

At her sneer, a large part of me wants to spring to my feet and march straight out of the room. I even get some satisfaction out of imagining her hope snuffing out as I vanish out the door. Then my stomach lurches, and I feel even queasier.

Talia? Corwin says softly. All at once, I choke up.

I know what kind of woman he sees in me. That all four of my lovers see. I know what the fae who've raised me up as a savior expect of their blessed human.

That's the woman I want to be. Not a tyrant, not a murderer. I was given this power to heal, not to destroy. There's so much pain and death in this world already. I will *not* add any more to it.

My heart thumps hard, but I hold Laoni's gaze as steadily as I can, letting the certainty I'm slowly building drive the words up my throat. "Maybe it shouldn't change anything. I don't know why you're so set on tearing down the things I've built. But if you'll do just one thing for me, maybe you can set aside all that resentment for just a second and recognize who I actually am."

"And what's that?" Laoni demands.

"Someone who's just trying to make things better for your people, not to hurt them. Someone who'll heal even you, despite all the ways you've tried to hurt me and may continue to after I've done this."

"You expect me to be ever so grateful that you're serving the Heart's purpose for you?"

My spine stiffens, but I'm not going to let her insults change *me*. "I'd like you to see that I have a will of my own beyond the gifts the Heart has given me. I know I could refuse to heal you, or claim that I did and my powers failed me. How many of your people would still stand by you if it looks like the Heart itself has turned its back on you?"

Laoni's expression turns even more sour. "If you claim you're not going to do either of those things, why even bring them up?"

I lean forward in my chair. I'm a little afraid she's going to be provoked into quite literally attacking me, but I can't stop until I've done everything I can to make her understand.

"I need *you* to know that I know all that, but I'm choosing to help you anyway. My life would probably be so much easier if the curse took you, but I'm not and never will be the kind of person who'd make that trade. It doesn't matter how many ways you've insulted me or how horribly so many other fae have treated me—I'm helping you anyway. That's who you've decided is your enemy. That's who you've decided to fight when there are so many actual villains out there. If you can know that, and keep trying to knock me down however you can…"

What can I say after that? I spread my hands. "It's up to you. I just hope that when you go back out to your troops and decide what to do against me and my mates, you remember that I held your life in my hands and chose to do everything I could to save it. I don't worship the Heart of the Mists the same way you do, but I'm pretty sure I can tell which course of action it'd approve of more."

Laoni just stares at me, her eyes smoldering with restrained emotion, her expression increasingly tensed. I've made all the appeal I can to whatever goodness there is inside her. I shouldn't leave her in the curse's grip any longer, or it'll look like I really am out to torment her after all.

"Let's begin then," I say, and stand up.

Looking at the fae woman who's put so much effort into upending my hard-won happiness, it's hard to summon much sympathy. For a second, I wonder if I'll fail after all simply because I can't work up tears on her behalf in the first place.

But then I think instead of the people who'd suffer from her death. I don't know how much she cares for her soul-twined mate, but he might love her a great deal. Kesral definitely does. All those soldiers on the plain outside the border castle look to her for guidance and protection.

What turmoil would it throw the whole winter realm into if Laoni succumbed to the curse without an heir? How many more people might die in the scramble to claim this castle? What would become of her flock when they're ousted from their domain?

Imagining all those figures cast adrift without a home is what finally hits the mark. Heat wells up behind my eyes. I turn around, sure I need to go through the motions of hiding my sadness even when there's no one else here to see, and urge the tears to spill out.

One and then another trickles over my skin. That has to be enough. I wipe them away, inhale slowly, and return my attention to Laoni.

She holds perfectly still as I graze my fingertips over her cheek. I can't read the emotion in her eyes, and her face is too rigid to give a valid impression. Then she takes a sharp breath just as I feel the warmth racing away from my hand over her flesh.

She looks up at me, and just for that instant, I think I catch a glimmer of awe in her gaze.

Then it's gone. Laoni stretches her arms, working her fingers that she can now uncurl, and nods curtly to me. "You've done your duty. You may go."

The words aren't quite as brusque as I might have expected, but they aren't exactly friendly either. I've said all I need to, so I head out the door in silence.

The coterie man is waiting farther down the hall. He hurries over to me and guides me toward the stairs. "She's well again?" he asks, unable to disguise his urgency.

I nod. "I healed her. I'd imagine she'll be out here giving orders again very soon." My nausea wraps tighter around my gut at the thought of what those orders might be.

We step outside into the brisk air to find a carriage waiting for us, Zelpha at the helm.

"Corwin thought you might appreciate a smoother

journey back," she says, giving Laoni's coterie man a cool glance. "I assume you don't mind me taking over her escort from here, now that she's attended to your lady."

"I—by all means, go ahead," the fae man says, awkward enough that I find myself forgiving him for his previous oversight. He must have been panicked over Laoni's situation.

Zelpha helps me into the carriage, and I slump onto one of the benches, feeling as if I've just run for miles. The short walk through the castle has reawakened the pain in my thigh. I rub the spot and look at Zelpha as she directs the carriage back toward the border castle. "Has anything changed since I left?"

"Other than Corwin just about pacing a ditch in the ground?" Zelpha asks, the corners of her lips quirking up. "Not really. They've all just stood around waiting. Uzziah and Terisse talked some. I think they were wondering what's going on with Laoni, since she dragged the two of them into this mess and then abandoned them."

I've been fine, Corwin says through our bond, obviously overhearing her remark about him through my ears. His concern rings through his inner voice all the same. *Do you think your words to Laoni made any difference?*

I don't know. She didn't seem very happy with me even after I healed her.

If it didn't, there's no moving her. You were incredible.

A blush warms my cheeks. He must have had some sense of the inner turmoil I was grappling with, but he thinks that anyway.

All I did was speak from my heart, and I don't think

Laoni cares very much what my heart wants. But I guess we'll have to wait and see.

The assembled fae on both sides of the stand-off watch with open curiosity as Zelpha brings the carriage to my high terrace. I take my former position, catching the eyes of Corwin and then my Seelie mates below, taking reassurance from seeing them still standing firm and the castle unmarked other than the one crack. Uzziah and Terisse are standing close in consultation again. One and then the other glances toward Laoni's domain.

Several more minutes pass in the same holding pattern. The troops shuffle on their feet, trying to tamp down on a growing restlessness that's rippling through the air. I tamp down on the growing urge to vomit.

Finally, a raven with a turquoise sheen to its dark feathers flaps into view. Laoni lands a few paces from where her colleagues are standing in the space between the fae forces, shifting as soon as she touches the ground. She strides over to Uzziah and Terisse and joins their conversation.

Their voices are so low I can't make anything out from my perch or through Corwin's ears. At one point, Uzziah lets out a rough, wordless exclamation that sounds like a protest. Terisse rubs her mouth, her forehead furrowed. I have no idea what any of it means.

I know I made the right choice for my conscience, but was it the wrong one in every other way? Could I have saved more bloodshed if I'd let Laoni die?

But then she turns away from the other arch-lords, summoning a pedestal of ice with a quick word and a motion of her hand. She leaps onto it so everyone in the crowd around her can see her easily. There's still a hint of stiffness to her motions, but I don't think anyone who wasn't already aware of what she's been through would notice it.

"My people," she says in a commanding voice. "And those of the summer realm who've seen fit to be here today. I have meditated long with the pulse of the Heart, and I have come to the conclusion… that I was misguided here today."

My pulse hiccups, and a murmur spreads through the watching fae. Is she saying what I want to think she is?

Laoni clears her throat and goes on. "We don't yet know who our greatest enemies are, but I'm sure they're not among us at this moment. We'll be better if we stand together, prepared to meet them and see the final end of this curse than if we're at each other's throats. The castle may stand as long as the Seelie keep their peace with us and Lady Talia continues to gift us with her healing powers."

She tips her head in just the slightest nod toward me.

My heart fills with so much light I almost think I'll float away. A matching joy resonates through Corwin. August glances up at me and grins wide. I grip the railing, so dizzy with relief I need it to steady me.

I don't think this is the last battle I'll face with the winter arch-lords… but it may be the worst. And now it's behind us.

Talia

I've never seen so many fae gathered together in one place, not even for Sylas's coronation festivities.

We're holding tonight's ceremony in the same place—in the sprawling field around the Heart on the summer side of the border—and that entire space is filled with figures turned toward me with eager eyes. More are standing amid the trees along the edges of the field. There are even ravens perched in the branches and circling overhead to watch the proceedings from where they can get a better view.

It's a little startling to see how many of the Unseelie have crossed the border to witness the ceremony. They're not mingling with the Seelie all that much yet, mostly keeping to one section of the field, but I haven't noticed any hostile glances or words exchanged.

Tonight is about the unity between summer and

winter symbolized in me, and everything about the event so far speaks of the healing divide between the realms.

At this point, there hasn't been much to see except me where I'm perched on a chair on the platform built for the ceremony, right in front of the Heart. Its rhythmic energy washes over me, and its glow casts a golden light over the darkening forest. Beaming orbs shine along the edges of the field and float over the crowd. The breeze, pleasantly warm, tickles over me with a soft scent of clover. I couldn't have asked for a more peaceful atmosphere for this moment.

Harper darts up onto the platform next to me and runs her fingers over the lacy sleeve of the dress she designed for this occasion. It doesn't cover the scars on my shoulder so much as turn them into part of the intricate pattern—into something almost beautiful. I think it's the most amazing gown she's crafted yet.

"Seeing you in this light, I can't help thinking I should have added a little more sheen to the skirt," she mutters, never totally satisfied with her own work.

I laugh. "It's a little late for adjustments, isn't it? It's already spectacular. I'll be surprised if you don't have a hundred orders by the end of the night."

Her cheeks flush, and she ducks her head bashfully. "I've actually already gotten a few."

Knowing her typical modesty, that means she's had at least a dozen requests. I squeeze her hand. "That's wonderful. I talked to Corwin about some of that fabric you were hoping to experiment with—the weavers from the domain that specializes in it should have a shipment to us in the next week."

"Oh, perfect." She claps her hands together with so much excitement I have to grin. Then she shakes herself. "But never mind about me. This evening is about *you*." Her gaze darts to our audience. "I shouldn't even be up here."

"It's fine. My arch-lords had some special arrangements they needed to finish up." I have no idea what Corwin and Sylas were up to, only that it required some intense discussions with the other arch-lords this morning. "Is the man you have your eye on here tonight? You should at least ask him to dance."

Harper's flush deepens. "No, I—I couldn't. It's silly." Her hands twitch over her own dress. It has a sleeker skirt and fewer embellishments than mine but still an eye-catching design that brings to mind a rushing waterfall.

I make a dismissive sound. "It wouldn't hurt to try, would it? I want to see everyone else happy tonight too."

She gives me a bright smile. "I will be happy because you are. Everything else—it'll happen as it's meant to be in time, I'm sure."

I wish I had that same sense of faith. But at least today, it does feel as if everything is coming together as it ought to be.

As Harper slips back into the crowd, I spot Corwin's colleagues in a tight cluster near the other end of the platform. Besides Neve, who's wearing her usual vague expression, none of the arch-lords look exactly *pleased*, but they don't appear to be as sour about the event as I was worried they'd be. I might even see a flicker of a smile cross Terisse's face at one point.

My gaze catches Laoni's for just a second, and she

offers me the slightest nod like she did a week ago outside the border castle, her expression staying impassive. Since that day when I healed her and she called back the assault on my castle, she hasn't been anywhere near warm. But she seems to have accepted that I'm here to stay in the fae world and that it isn't a bad thing.

She even told Corwin that he should encourage the Seelie to get on with this ceremony—that if we're going to insist on doing things in such a strange way, we should hurry up and make it official. The corners of my mouth twitch upward at the memory of her exasperated tone.

Donovan and Celia are standing near them, looking more relaxed. Donovan is chatting animatedly with one of his cadre-chosen, his bright hair dancing like a flame in the undulating glow of the Heart.

Tomorrow I can get started on the work I want to do here for myself and those like me. Donovan has agreed to make a public announcement that he'll be offering many more freedoms to the humans in his domain, and I'm going to help determine what would be best for each of his servants.

If we can convince Celia and Neve to follow suit after that, tackling the other three arch-lords might not be so difficult. Maybe they'll *want* to stop relying on human servitude now that they've seen how much frustration just one human can cause them. Who knows what chaos might be brought by the next human who ends up here?

My amused thoughts fall to the wayside at the movement of four striking figures through the crowd.

My lovers have dressed up in as much finery as I have for this occasion. Sylas's gold-embroidered jacket and slacks are a deep burgundy that brings out the purple in his dark hair. Whitt has gone with a sapphire-blue that makes his eyes gleam even more brightly. August looks a bit uncomfortable in the formal clothes, but the supple maroon fabric shows off his muscular form to great effect. And Corwin, my wintry raven, is perfectly elegant among them in pale blue and silver.

My heart thumps faster, but it's more excitement than anxiety. Nothing else can go wrong in the little time that's left before the ceremony begins, can it? This is actually happening.

I don't know what my life will be like a month from now, let alone years, and the curse still casts its shadow over both realms. But no matter what else happens, I'll have my four men as my mates.

From what Whitt told me, regular mating ceremonies where there's no soul-twined bond aren't usually this elaborate or public. Still, he and my other Seelie men felt that it was important to make a clear statement about their commitment to me in front of their subjects and whoever of the winter realm would join us. I definitely won't mind if the public declaration makes it less likely that more fae ladies will make passes at them hoping to catch the new arch-lord's or one of his cadre-chosen's eye.

As they step onto the platform, I stand up. The ache in my thigh from the Murk man's claws has faded nearly completely now. Thanks to my warped foot, I can't completely erase my limp as I walk to the center of the stage, but I'm not so self-conscious of it now. Most of the fae watching have seen it before. They know who I am and the damage I carry.

But they still honor what I offer them. And tonight they're going to honor the love I've found here—celebrate it, even.

The chatter of the crowd dims to a murmur as I reach the center of the stage. Sylas, Whitt, and August meet me there, standing in a loose line facing me. Corwin positions himself between us, placing one hand on my shoulder. He's holding something in his other hand wrapped in a bundle of dark fabric.

He clears his throat, and the crowd falls completely silent.

"Tonight," he says, "I recognize the bonds of love my soul-twined mate has formed with these three men, who are just as deserving of her affections as I am. I welcome them as her mates into our lives, and I ask that you all do the same. Lady Talia has proven how much kindness and generosity she can offer all of us, and she should have just as much in return."

He steps back, stopping at the back of the platform.

August reaches for my hand first. He clasps it, smiling at me so brilliantly that I feel as if my heart is flying.

In a way, August *has* taught me to fly: showing me how to use my shaky magical powers, giving me control over light and air. I never feel quite so safe as when he's standing by me or so nurtured as when we're building a meal together.

Lifting my hand so the audience can see our entwined fingers, he holds my gaze but raises his voice so all of the assembled fae can hear him.

"Before the Heart, I declare my intent to take Talia of Hearth-by-the-Heart and Heart's Cadence as my mate. I swear to cherish and protect her with all my being."

A magical thrum carries through his words. I can't offer the same sort of vow in return, but I put all the emotion I can into my answering statement. "Before the Heart, I declare my intent to take August of Hearth-by-the-Heart as my mate. I swear to cherish and protect him with all my being."

August squeezes my hand, and a tingle of energy passes from his palm into mine. Our souls might not be tied together like mine is to Corwin's, but the depth of his devotion shines in his eyes. He leans in, and I bob up on my toes to kiss him.

A murmur of what sounds like approval ripples through our audience. I brace myself for a shout of protest, but it seems even the Unseelie have settled into the idea of one of their arch-lords openly sharing his soul-twined mate with the wolfish summer fae.

When August eases back, it's Sylas who steps forward next. He's the one who suggested we take the vows from youngest to oldest rather than political authority. I think he wanted to avoid implying that his claim overshadowed that of his cadre-chosen.

He takes my hand as August did, both of his mismatched eyes fixed on me. I wonder if his ghostly one is catching glimpses of our future together. If he sees anything that worries him, he gives no sign of it.

His lips curve into the gentle smile he reserves for me, and I find myself remembering the first day when I woke up in his keep in Oakmeet after he'd rescued me from Aerik's cage. How he came into my room and spoke to me so kindly, earning my trust rather than demanding it.

We've come so far since then. Through a lot of pain and struggle, but without fail, he's given me the space to take control over my own life. And every one of the painful moments was worth it to make it here tonight.

"Before the Heart, I declare my intent to take Talia of Hearth-by-the-Heart and Heart's Cadence as my mate," he says in his resonant voice. "I swear to cherish and protect her with all my being."

I smile back at him, lit up with a glow of happiness that could rival the Heart itself. "Before the Heart, I declare my intent to take Sylas of Hearth-by-the-Heart as my mate. I swear to cherish and protect him with all my being."

He cups my jaw as he kisses me, holding me steady with his commanding strength. Then he draws back to make room for Whitt.

The last of my Seelie mates, both now and when we started, shoots me one of his crooked grins, but there's nothing but fondness in it. Staring into his ocean-blue eyes brings me back to that moment not long ago when he told me he trusted me with his own true name. Of the impression of his presence those syllables summoned even at a distance, all wryness and hidden passion, leading me straight to him when I called out with my mind.

Of the passion he brought me to balanced on the edge of his secret terrace, his hold never wavering.

Whitt was once afraid that he'd ruin me somehow. I hope by now he's seen how much he's strengthened my will and my confidence instead.

His voice holds its usual hint of dryness, but there's no mistaking the genuine promise in his words. "Before the Heart, I declare my intent to take Talia of Hearth-by-the-Heart and Heart's Cadence as my mate. I swear to cherish and protect her with all my being."

My last vow spills out of me so fast I almost lose my breath. "Before the Heart, I declare my intent to take Whitt of Hearth-by-the-Heart as my mate. I swear to cherish and protect him with all my being."

He claims my mouth with a subtle flick of his tongue that makes me gasp. When he releases me, his smile a little more wicked now, Corwin raises his hands toward the crowd.

"Lady Talia will live between our realms, serving both and served by both. She has brought peace to our world, soothed old hurts, and healed current maladies. As mate to arch-lords of both seasons and our champion against our curse, all four of us bestow on her this marker of her esteemed place among the fae."

I have no idea what he's talking about. None of my men mentioned anything like this.

Then Corwin unfurls the cloth bundle and holds out a thin, glinting crown. The strands of silver and gold curl together like twined vines, gripping five small gems that I understand instinctively stand for me and the four men who stand with me. As he sets it on my head, my breath catches.

It's only a symbol, no extra authority granted with it, he says through our bond with a trace of apology. *But we felt it was appropriate all the same.*

Thank you, I say, too overwhelmed with emotion to

manage more than that. I look to each of my Seelie men with the same gratitude, and from the way they beam back at me, I can tell I don't need to say it out loud.

The graceful weight of the crown settles into my hair. Corwin lowers his arms—and a flare of brighter light streams over us with the next pulse of the Heart. Its glow and its warmth flood the field, tingling like a melody across my skin. For a second, it seems to enfold me in an embrace.

A rush of giddiness fills my chest. As the light contracts to its usual softer glow, gasps and awed exclamations fill the clearing. Even the winter arch-lords are looking around in wonder.

I don't know if the Heart's power actually carried out some magical effect or whether it was merely a symbol of approval, but I'm not sure it matters. If there were any doubts about whether the Heart agreed with this union— and the collaboration between summer and winter— they've been laid to rest now.

"Let the celebration begin!" Sylas announces.

Along the fringes of the field, musicians begin to play. Fae bustle off to grab the food and drinks already prepared for the occasion. August scoops me off my feet and carries me off the platform to claim the first dance.

My body is humming with so much relief and joy that the next couple of hours pass in a blur. I whirl and sway with each of my lovers in turn, reveling in the ecstatic air that's flowing all around us. Sweet juice, tender morsels of meat, and buttery pastries pass over my lips. The hundreds of fae around us frolic, drink, and make merry as only fae can, many of them pausing when they pass near me to bow in respect and congratulate me on my new union.

After a time, even with so much happiness gripping me, I can't ignore the growing ache in my warped foot. I perch on the edge of the platform to watch the festivities go on. Astrid dances with Verik, and Donovan takes a spin with Zelpha before she returns to a slender, doe-eyed woman I've gathered is her mate. I catch glimpses of Harper's pale dress and hair amid the revelers, though I can't see if she's found a partner. It all just feels so *right*.

My mates have stuck close to me throughout the night, but I shoo them off briefly so they can get some food. I'm supposed to be looking out for them as much as they look out for me, after all.

It's just after that when an elderly fae who has a vague expression that reminds me of Neve approaches me from the crowd. It takes me a moment to recognize her—she's from Donovan's pack, one of the attendants who work in his castle. I spoke to her briefly when I came to his domain to meet with his human servants.

She looked more alert then, but who knows what faerie delights she's been eating and drinking tonight with their various special effects.

"Lady Talia," she says in an upbeat if slightly creaky voice. "If I could do you the honor—I have a gift I'd like to offer you. Would you let me show it to you?"

"Of course." I slip off the platform and follow her through the crowd to the surrounding forest.

I suspect Astrid and at least one of Corwin's coterie members will follow to keep an eye on me, but I wouldn't feel particularly worried regardless. Donovan's pack has always been friendly with ours, and it isn't as if the woman could lie so close to the Heart about why she wants me to come with her anyway.

Fae are still meandering between the trees as they take a break from the dancing, joyful voices echoing through the air. The woman walks just a little farther, toward the pack village in Donovan's domain. Maybe she's left her gift in her home there.

But after several more steps, she turns and gives me a little bow. I see nothing in this spot except the dim silhouettes of the trees and the underbrush around them.

"I don't understand," I say tentatively, not wanting to offend her.

The words have barely left my lips when an unfamiliar man steps from the shadows. His smooth, flaxen hair falls to the tips of his faintly pointed ears, and his heavy-lidded eyes gaze down at me from a height that matches August's.

His hand descends to my forehead. Before I can move or even send out a panicked alarm to Corwin, blackness sweeps through my mind.

Just as the darkness swallows me, the stranger's voice reaches me, low and slightly hoarse. "Hello, Talia. It's time you met the one who made you."

ABOUT THE AUTHOR

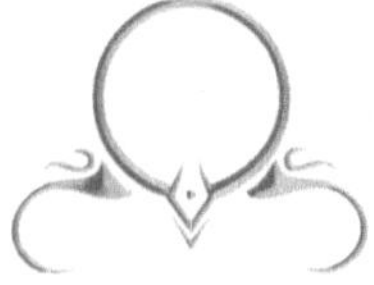

Eva Chase lives in Canada with her family. She loves stories both swoony and supernatural, and strong women and the men who appreciate them. Along with the Bound to the Fae series, she is the author of the Flirting with Monsters series, the Cursed Studies trilogy, the Royals of Villain Academy series, the Moriarty's Men series, the Looking Glass Curse trilogy, the Their Dark Valkyrie series, the Witch's Consorts series, the Dragon Shifter's Mates series, the Demons of Fame Romance series, the Legends Reborn trilogy, and the Alpha Project Psychic Romance series.

Connect with Eva online:
www.evachase.com
eva@evachase.com

9 781990 338120